# *Ripple* EFFECTS

## L.J. GREENE

ISBN: 978-0-692-47771-7 (print)
ISBN: 978-0-692-47460-0 (ebook)

# Other Titles by L.J. Greene

*Effects Series:*
*Ripple Effects*
*Sound Effects*
*Aftereffects*
*Side Effects*

*Standalone:*
*A Fall of Light*

Check out a preview of *Sound Effects* at the conclusion of this novel. All of the *Effects* novels are standalones, but connected. For more information on the series, visit my website at www.ljgreenebooks.com.

To Bug and Bean, the reasons I do everything. And to Mr. Greene, I couldn't do any of it without you.

# Chapter 1

## Sarah

Like ground zero for nerd chic, Charlie's Bar & Grill on University Avenue stood as a mecca—a funky kind of place, equally favored by the hoodie-clad Silicon Valley professionals as by their similarly dressed student counterparts. It was Friday night happy hour on the last day of Stanford's spring semester finals and the place was packed.

"Here, take this." Selene tossed back her long, dark hair, and handed me a very pink, very sweet cosmopolitan. "For the next three months, we have nothing to do but relax. And we're going to start that *tonight*." She raised her drink in a toast, took a large sip, and melted into cranberry bliss.

In truth, neither of us was without responsibility for the next three months, but I understood what she meant. Selene Georgiou and I had been roommates for the past four years, and were heading into our final semesters of undergraduate study in the fall. After that, we'd be going our separate ways—she likely moving to San Francisco for a graphic design job and, me, hopefully continuing on at Stanford for my master's degree in education. This was our last summer together and neither of us was ready to face up to that reality just yet.

So despite the onset of a ham-like state of post-finals exhaustion, I agreed to come out for a drink, and even let her dress me up in an outfit she insisted was very flattering to my figure.

Selene was tall, like me, but lithe to my curvy athleticism, which explained why her floral print blouse felt a little sexier than I had intended. I pulled at the front of it for the millionth time.

"Wow, that is strong." I winced, swallowing another sip of the lethal concoction she'd handed me. Even the sugared rim couldn't disguise the heavy alcohol content. "Who'd you flash to get this?"

Selene rolled her eyes—not exactly a denial. "I'm going to the restroom. I'll be right back."

I took another small sip of my drink and glanced around the bar. I grew up in the Silicon Valley, but in truth, I was still in awe of it. Nowhere else in the world was quite like it. With its frenetic pace of life and vibrant cultural diversity, you couldn't help but feel like people here were always inventing, always trying to solve problems in an out-of-the-box, disruptive kind of way. And it's true that many of the companies founded here had literally changed the world—Fairchild Semiconductor, Cisco Systems, Genentech, Google, Facebook. As a result, the collective wealth in the Bay Area was absolutely staggering.

Of course, that made me a bit of an outlier. Though my childhood home was only miles from the Stanford campus, it was a great distance in terms of economics. But growing up, I was never discouraged by that. The Silicon Valley was rich with lore of seemingly crazy ideas that took shape in a garage and went on to become Apple or Hewlett Packard. It had always given me the feeling that if you worked hard enough, you could do anything—even get into Stanford on a full academic scholarship.

I still counted my blessings for that one, and often looked around myself with a deep sense of gratitude. Tonight was one of those nights. And apparently I was in good company; everyone here seemed to celebrating something.

Charlie's was known for its big open spaces that never felt claustrophobic, no matter how crowded it was. Plus, the used brick interior and cement flooring gave it a chic warehouse vibe that perfectly suited Charlie's passion for showcasing the eclectic artwork of local artists—everything from paintings to sculptures to scrap metal creations.

Today's artist was a photographer, and the restaurant's pin lighting accentuated many sweeping landscapes of the Bay Area, as well as interesting close-ups of local flora and fauna. They were incredibly beautiful, and it was a full minute before I realized I actually recognized a few of the photographs—one in particular. It was an image of the Golden Gate Bridge, with the bridge sitting almost eerily behind a ghostlike band of fog, and the rich, brown sand and rolling waves of Baker Beach in the foreground. The original focal point, whatever it was, appeared to have been cropped out, giving the image a soft, dreamy quality.

It was so distinctive I was nearly certain it was the one I remembered from many years ago, and glancing at the placard beside it, I discovered I was right. *Daniel Moore.*

Wow.

That name brought back more than a few memories—memories from a time in my life I would hardly call a high point. Most of the time I purposely avoided them. Every so often they found me anyway. Like now, when the small-world theory decided to prove itself once again. The photographer in question was standing just a foot away, scrolling through messages on his phone.

"Mr. Moore?"

Penetrating green eyes lifted to absorb me blankly. But I could see he was fighting to place me in his own memory. After a long, awkward beat, we both said my name at once. Though for him, it was definitely more of a question.

Daniel R. Moore was one of three biology teachers at McKinley High

School. He couldn't have been more than a few of years into his career when I last knew him, and always strictly reserved with students. But he was definitely passionate about teaching. His lectures famously prompted some pretty memorable discussions on scientific advancements, and ethics, and conservation. When he was in full flow, he was absolutely captivating.

"Yes, of course, Sarah." He shook his head in apology and slid his phone into his pocket. "And, please, call me Dan."

His expression unexpectedly developed into a large, good-natured grin that was *far* from any recollection I had of him.

"I was just admiring your photographs."

"Ah. Charlie's a friend of mine. I blame him for all this." He looked around at the impressive display and his smile became more self-deprecating.

"No, they're really good.

"You're generous to say so."

We both stood silently for a moment as the pause turned awkward. What do you say to someone you haven't seen in more than five years and never really knew to begin with? Plus, I was now highly conscious of the fact that my blouse felt far too small, which was not ideal for a reunion of this kind. I found myself discreetly tugging at it *again*. To Moore's credit, his eyes remained on my face—a bit of professionalism that did ring true to what I remembered of him.

"Are you still teaching?"

"Yes, but not at McKinley. I'm at Taft now. Seventh grade life science."

"Oh. Nice."

For me, it was almost surreal to see him in this completely different setting and to be talking with him as an adult; I'd been a student the last time we'd spoken. I wondered if he found it strange too. If he did, he didn't let on, but he was a hard one to read. I'd always thought so. Maybe it was a teacher thing.

After a beat, his eyes flickered down to my drink and it dawned on me what was very likely going through his head.

"Don't worry, I'm twenty-two," I reassured him, gesturing with the glass. "Oh, I . . ."

He looked confused. Like maybe he didn't believe me? Did I look underage? I couldn't explain the ridiculous impulse behind it, but I pushed my hand into the pocket of my jeans and pulled out my driver's license and student ID, thrusting them in his direction.

Dan took the license and ID card from my hand and laughed uncomfortably, as though he wasn't quite sure what to do.

"Well, I . . . okay. I wasn't actually . . . Here, you can keep these," he said, handing the cards back. "So, you're graduating soon?"

I took another sip of the cosmo, definitely not looking like I needed the fortification. "Actually, I've still got one more year to go on my bachelor's. I'm doing an internship at Stanford Medical Center so I haven't been able to take a full load. Thus, the five-year plan."

"The medical center?"

"Working with kids with autism."

He narrowed his eyes as if digging even deeper in his memory. "Your brother."

"Yes. Well, Asperger's Syndrome in his case—but that's where the interest comes from."

"That's really great."

He was examining me even closer now, tilting his head slightly as if this was a revelation—like he was suddenly seeing me for the very first time. Evidently, I'd managed to progress in his mind from underage drinker to semirespectable societal contributor. I smiled, pleased with myself, and put the IDs back in my pocket.

But that's when I realized nothing else was *in* my pocket and the happy feeling quickly evaporated. I looked down to find that my neatly folded cash and house key were on the ground next to my foot, apparently dislodged when I took out the cards. And to my unmitigated horror, the tampon from my pocket was *also* on the ground, lying conspicuously close to his shoe.

Adrenaline shot through my veins. Oblivious to what was happening, Dan shifted casually in his stance and his foot came down on top of the tampon, crushing it.

His eyes went wide when he realized what it was, and worse *whose* it was. He looked back at me. "I'm sorry. Did I . . . ah . . . disable it?"

*Disable it?* Like a tampon bomb?

"No, no I'm sure it's fine," I insisted in high-pitched distress.

I sank to my knees, mortification gripping my body like a vise, and scrambled around at his feet to retrieve the items. Dan seemed to be of the opinion that keeping the conversation going while I did this was the best way for us to pretend he didn't just step on my tampon. But I couldn't focus at all on what he was saying. There was something about his completing a PhD in education at Stanford, which I wouldn't have thought was necessary for a middle school teaching position.

With one hand, I was able to stuff the tampon and the rest of my things back into my pocket. Unfortunately, I did it with enough gusto that the cosmo in my other hand sloshed over the edge of its delicate glass and all over his pristine leather loafer.

"Oh my god, I'm so sorry!" I was mortified. I tried brushing at it vigorously with my hand, but to little effect. The leather was soaked and the sticky sweet liquid was now running over the top of his foot and into his shoe.

"Sarah, stop. Please. It's not a big deal."

He gently grasped my arm and began tugging me back up before I had the chance to humiliate myself any further. But even that was not to be—another wave of liquid shot from the mouth of the glass as I rose, this time soaking the leg of his pants, just inches from his crotch. He let out a little grunt and released me.

We were both gaping at the wet spot now and it was clear there was no hope of a dignified recovery for either of us.

"Okay. . . well . . . uh . . .," he started.

But the only thing I had handy to help him dry himself was a tampon and believe me *no one* wanted to see that again. And no one wanted my hand anywhere near his crotch.

Suddenly I found myself on the verge of tears. Real tears. The big ugly kind that required a nose blow and usually ended up in hiccups. I looked up at his face, my eyes wide, fully expecting to see the return of the stern Mr. Moore I remembered from five years earlier—the one who seemed to compensate for his youth and stunning good looks with somber formality.

Instead, his expression was . . . well, it was shockingly patient. Maybe even a little amused. I hardly knew what to make of that.

"It's okay," he said kindly. "This won't be the first time I've left a bar wearing a cosmopolitan. Though it's been a while," he added.

Then he made a playful show of squishing the liquid in his shoe and I had to laugh, in spite of my absolute horror. I wondered if it was always this way for insanely attractive men—women doing bat-shit crazy things in their presence. He seemed to know just how to handle it.

I took in a deep breath and let it out, making the best effort I could to gather myself.

"I'm so embarrassed."

"Please don't be." He waved a hand dismissively. He was being much nicer than he needed to be, given that he was going to spend the rest of the evening looking like he'd urinated himself, courtesy of me.

"And I'm really sorry—I missed what you said. Did you tell me your PhD is on education reform?"

"I did, yes."

"That's so funny—I'm writing my grad school fellowship essay on the same topic."

"Really?" he said with interest.

"Yes." I lifted my glass in a toast. "And here's to hoping yours is going much better than mine."

Education reform was turning out to be an especially broad and complex topic and I was hopelessly stuck on how to deal with it properly. It was a major source of stress for me because my fellowship depended on getting it right.

But I didn't want to think about that now. The room was warm, and I was still radiating with the heat of humiliation from my scalp to my toes. Oddly the skin between my breasts felt cool. And something about that registered in my brain, distracting me from our conversation. I turned to see if there was a breeze coming in from an open door.

"I think mine's coming along pretty well, actually," he told me.

"Good, maybe I'll just copy it and save myself some trouble."

It's fair to say that *thoughtless* adequately described how I was keeping up my side of the exchange. Glancing around the bar, I couldn't see any open door, or any reason there should be a breeze where we were standing. Tiny alarm bells began to go off in my head, which was probably why it was a second or two before I realized what I'd just done: I'd proposed plagiarism to a teacher. My former teacher. And then it dawned.

My attention snapped back to the tall, athletic man standing in front of me and he had the strangest expression on his face. He seemed to be searching politely for some appropriate thing to say—which, god knows what in the world that might be.

"No, I didn't mean I would *actually* want to plagiarize your PhD. I never do that sort of thing. *Ever.*"

He laughed again, but there was something definitely uncomfortable beneath it. "No, I didn't think . . ."

Rubbing the back of his neck, he looked away briefly. Then, he turned again in my direction. But he wasn't really looking at *me*; he was looking pointedly at my forehead. Something wasn't right here. His eyes darted around the room again, as if searching the place for any kind of help he could find. At last, he refocused his attention precisely on my face.

Clearing his throat, he continued in a businesslike manner: "What I was going to say was, it's definitely an ambitious topic for a short essay. You'll have to narrow your focus considerably or your work will come off as superficial." The intensity returned to those devastating green eyes. "If you want, I'd be glad to review your outline and give you a few ideas."

I was flooded with relief that we seemed to have returned to more stable ground. Okay, see, *this* was how a normal conversation was conducted. He was just a regular person, after all—no more or less than I.

"You forget that I've had a pretty intimidating experience with your infamous red pen," I teased, then watched his reaction.

Mr. Moore was not known for his sense of humor, and in light of his surprisingly personable manner tonight, I was suddenly curious to know how he'd respond to mine.

Before my eyes, his gaze turned from intense to almost sparkling. He was still oddly rigid, but he cocked his head to the side and adjusted his stance.

"What are you implying?" That disorienting smile was back, and something about his demeanor eased my concern.

"I'm not *implying* anything," I said, relieved to feel like myself again for the first time since he uttered my name. "Our papers always looked like they'd been victims of a violent crime."

He blinked for a moment, and then threw his head back and laughed. Actually laughed. It was a hearty, masculine sound with a bit of a rasp around the edges, and it washed over me with unexpected warmth.

"Some of them definitely were a crime. A crime against science—and against my intelligence, for that matter."

I'd never heard him laugh.

Years ago, I wouldn't have thought he was capable of it. This whole exchange showed a side of him I could not have imagined back then. He had an actual sense of humor.

And an incredibly sexy laugh.

It was an altogether pleasurable discovery. Unfortunately, it was followed by a rather cataclysmic one: The three middle buttons on my blouse had popped clean off. And now my shirt was hanging open—*wide* open. And it had likely been this way for many minutes!

My eyes shot to Dan's face. I frantically groped at my blouse with my one free hand, hoping he hadn't noticed the malfunction. But *of course* he had; his ears were now the same shade of pink as my cosmopolitan. He quickly looked away, avoiding my conspicuous attempts to pull the two sides of my shirt back together, but there was no mistaking the fact that I was failing miserably. Finally, he reached back across his shoulder and tugged the light gray sweatshirt over his head. His thick, wavy strawberry-blond hair was sent into wild abandon, which he mostly righted with a quick shake of his head.

"Here—in case you're . . . cold."

He handed me the sweatshirt with one hand, and took the sticky drink from my shaking fist with the other. Then he stepped away to set it down on the bar.

*"Run!"* my brain shouted, helpfully. *"Or cry!"* That was much less helpful. Dan must've already thought I was a barely legal flasher—crying would just make him think I was an *unstable* barely legal flasher.

How did this night become such a complete disaster?

I gratefully pulled the sweatshirt on, still warm from his body and roomy enough to accommodate his size. With truly heroic effort, I forced myself back to some semblance of control. Or the best version of it I could fake under the circumstances.

"I'll send this back to you," I offered when he returned. He waved that off and scribbled something on a napkin.

"Here's my email. Send me your outline. I'd like to help." He looked at me earnestly, as though rightly sensing some hesitation on my part.

Honestly, I wanted to cry. My whole composure was in disarray. I nodded, looking down at the napkin, and fought to hold myself together.

"I mean it, Sarah," he added gently.

"You're very kind. Thank you." Finally, I lifted my gaze to his.

He was being so incredibly nice that I scolded myself for every bad thing I'd ever thought about him, and in doing so tried to reconcile my memories of that humorless teacher with the man standing before me. I simply couldn't.

Selene walked up to my left, smiled pleasantly at Dan, and then turned to me. "Are you ready to go?"

"Yes." *God yes!* I could not have been more ready to go. "It was really good to see you again . . . Dan. And thank you for—" I gestured to the sweatshirt.

"It was good to see you too. Glad to hear you're doing well."

The sincerity in his face was oddly comforting. It was impossible to think I'd conveyed anything remotely resembling my best self, but his genuine kindness made the calamity of the last half hour feel, maybe, slightly less calamitous. If only for a moment . . .

§

Leaving Charlie's, Selene and I walked along University Avenue. Neither of us said a word for long minutes.

"He was my high school biology teacher," I finally whispered as the indignity seeped back into my consciousness.

"*That* guy is a science teacher?" She was definitely taken aback by this little nugget of information, and gave herself a moment to process. "He's not like any science teacher I've ever had."

That was probably true for most people, but it didn't help my humiliation in the least to dwell on it.

"That was *horrifying*."

"Yeah, it pretty much was." Selene never pulled punches. It was actually one of the things I liked best about her. Although every once in a while, I wouldn't have minded being lied to, just a little bit. "Someone needed to step in there before you reprised the Celtic dance you did at Sheryl's twenty-first birthday. You were definitely heading in that direction."

"Was it that bad?"

"So to recap: You dropped your tampon at his feet; bent to pick it up, thus, spilling your drink on his shoes and pants; and carried on a full conversation while exposing your breasts. Did I leave anything out?"

"I told him I wanted to plagiarize his PhD."

"Oh, nicely done!" She said this as if it were an achievement. "Well, look at it this way—you probably won't ever have to see him again."

I took a deep breath. *That's true*, I told myself in a consoling manner. Although . . .

"He offered to help me with my fellowship essay."

Selene turned to me, eyebrows raised. "Was that before or after you popped your blouse open?"

"Oh my god." A fresh wave of nausea rippled through my stomach.

"You should definitely take him up on it, though."

"There is no *way* I could do that now. I just gave him a peep show!"

"So what. They're just boobs. He's a biology teacher, after all."

*Right.*

"What was up with you, anyway? He's ridiculously hot, but that was . . ." She shook her head as if she was at a loss to commit an innocent adjective to that particular scene.

"I really don't know what that was. I think I'm just tired."

Truthfully, it was probably more than that. It's a funny thing to see someone after many years, and to find him so different from what you remember. Maybe he seemed different to me because *I* was different, but I would never have described him as friendly or warm.

Although to be fair, I couldn't imagine I'd weather much better in his memory. I could only guess how I would've come across at that tumultuous time in my life: introverted, sullen, obsessively focused on my college resume. I stopped short before allowing myself to consider how I might have come across tonight.

When we finally reached our apartment, I went quickly to my room and collapsed on the bed. For a long time I just stared up at the sparkling popcorn ceiling. It was astonishing how running into someone you knew years ago threw you back immediately to who you were when you knew him. I felt the need to mentally shake off that person I once was. But it was also a good reminder of what had changed in the time between—how far I'd come in many ways, and what was still in front of me to do.

On an impulse, I dialed my friend Marcus.

"I need to ask you a favor . . ."

# Chapter 2

**Danny**

"Just marry me. We don't even have to have sex," I announced to Mel, as I walked into the Callahan's spacious kitchen on Sunday night. "Unless of course you want to."

She was facing the eight-burner stainless cooktop, and slicing up lasagna so good, it could make a grown man cry. I grabbed her by the hips, and planted a kiss on the top of her straight, shoulder-length brown hair.

"You're about eleven years too late on the marriage proposal, but I'll consider the sex," she told me. "I hear you're adequate in bed."

"Fine. As long as our relations can involve your cooking."

Mel Callahan was my second-best friend in the world, only narrowly trailing her husband, Jamie, who'd been like a brother to me since we were nine years old.

"Are you offering your body again in exchange for dinner, mate?" Jamie cracked, as he strode in.

"No, this time I offered to marry her too."

"And here I thought I'd never see the day."

"You're a dick," I said grinning. It was good to see him again.

Jamie was the frontman and guitarist of Cadence, an alternative rock band whose global fame had risen considerably over the past decade. He'd spent the last few weeks on tour in the Southern states to promote the new album, which was already getting great reviews.

"How'd it go in the Bible Belt?"

"Pretty damn well for a bunch of sinners, I suppose." He laughed, tossing me a beer from the fridge, and then casually leaned against the counter. "The new material went off well; crowds were friendly."

It was still a surreal experience for me to watch his success and fortunes grow so high because in my head, he would always just be Jamie—a scrawny Irish kid with a funny accent and auburn hair. A tough guy with a big mouth and a huge heart. Now he was a superstar. Everywhere except in his own house, that is. Here, he was still just Jamie. And, proudly, he was also now dad.

As we were catching up, Mel came over and tapped him on the hip so he'd step to the side of the silverware drawer.

"Need some help?" I offered.

"Nope, we're good," she said, gathering up a collection of forks and knives. She handed the mass of utensils to Jamie. "Grab some water for the boys, as well?"

She capped off the request by pushing up on her toes to plant a swift kiss on his jaw, which he answered by wrapping his arm around her waist and going in for a much more thorough one.

I was used to the affection between them, especially when Jamie was fresh back from touring, so I pulled the phone from my pocket and checked my email. Almost instantly, my inbox refreshed, and a message appeared from Sarah Kyle.

It had been almost two months since I gave her my email, and I was surprised to hear from her. I figured she'd either lost it or she didn't want my help.

"What is it?" Jamie asked.

"Nothing. Just a work thing."

He continued to stare expectantly. Nosy bastard.

"It's from a former student of mine I ran into at Charlie's a while back. I told her I'd help her with an outline she's working on for a fellowship essay."

Jamie headed over to the large farmer's table and began haphazardly dropping silverware and paper napkins at each place setting. While he did, I quickly glanced through the attached outline. It was a good start, which didn't surprise me. I remembered Sarah being very bright and hard working. But some of these ideas could use development, and I knew I could help her choose the ones she'd be able to land most effectively.

I was glad to do it, honestly. The other thing I remembered about Sarah was that we shared a similar fate. From what I'd heard, Sarah's father died suddenly of a heart attack when she was fifteen, and when I knew her a couple years later, she still seemed sad to me. I understood it. I lost my parents to a car accident at twenty-three, and I knew all too well how devastating something like that can be. It was an experience I wouldn't wish on anyone.

I wanted to help her, and I was also glad for the chance to pay forward some of the generosity others had shown me in my own career.

"So, what have you got, there?" Jamie interrupted my thoughts, nodding his chin at the box of supplies I'd left on the island. "Tell me you're not going to blow anything up in my backyard."

I laughed. Because here's the thing: My godsons, Patrick and Shane, loved science. I'd made it my mission in life to enhance their education by bringing over a science experiment for us to conduct almost every time I came over. We made slime, determined the necessary components of combustion, dissected things, checked out our body parts in a microscope, whatever was interesting. The boys and I never limited ourselves to any one scientific discipline—pretty much everything was fair game. And the messier the better, in their eyes. They loved to get dirty. Mel might not have loved it quite as much, but she was a good sport.

This particular experiment was a rather dramatic example of a chemical reaction—a real fan favorite among kids, assuming, of course, you took the proper safety precautions. For that reason, I'd brought test tubes, goggles, and protective clothing, which in turn formed the basis of Jamie's suspicions. We were going to demonstrate an exothermic reaction by dropping Gummi Bears into heated potassium chlorate. The effect promised to be a spectacular conflagration of total Gummi Bear annihilation.

Awesome.

"I think *blow up* is a little strong." I said it with a straight face, pretending not to feel the full weight of Mel's gimlet eye behind me. "This is just a friendly little experiment involving the oxidation of sugar."

"A friendly experiment?"

"Very."

"Requiring safety gear and a fire extinguisher?" Jamie crossed his arms over his chest and leaned back against the table.

"All overkill, really. I'm a professional. And the kids will be observing from a safe distance."

He laughed. "Curiously enough, it actually wasn't the kids I was worried about. But I'd rather not have the neighbors going bats, thinking I'm getting ready to torch the place."

"The amount of potassium chlorate we're using requires only a very small flame. Tiny, really. Smaller than the one on your barbecue."

Jamie looked to Mel for back up. "It's like arguing with Bill Nye."

I grinned. "It's all in the name of *science*."

He shook his head, finishing his task by tossing the small forks in the general vicinity of where Paddy and Shane would be sitting. Then he turned to me, his dimples fighting their way onto his face.

"Mark my words, mate. When you have kids someday, I'm buying them a drum kit."

# Chapter 3

**Sarah**

Even if I lived in some alternate universe, I never would have predicted the email I received back from Dan on Monday night.

> *Sarah,*
>
> *You've got some great ideas here but, as I expressed to you, I'm concerned about your trying to tackle too expansive a topic. Attached is your outline with my suggestions. Be warned: There's a lot of red, although no crime was committed, I assure you. ☺ If the notes don't make sense, I'd be glad to talk through them with you, either live or by phone.*
>
> *Dan*

Attached to the email was my outline, as promised, with a voluminous amount of commentary, articles for reference, and various political and educational organizations that were doing work in this area. In short, he must have put hours of time into this. And he wasn't kidding—there was a lot of red. My head was spinning as I scrolled through his notes and suggestions, trying to make sense of the flow and content.

Wow. I had no idea what to think.

I'd debated for weeks whether to reach out to him as he'd suggested. I drafted an outline—actually, I drafted seven of them—but he was right, they all felt like a superficial treatment of the subject. And I knew I couldn't jeopardize my fellowship for the sake of vanity—well, utter humiliation was probably more accurate. The essay was literally worth tens of thousands of dollars in funding. I wanted the help—god knows I needed it—I just didn't know him well enough to know if his offer was genuine. Apparently, it was.

Selene walked in to our kitchen as I was looking through the material. "What's wrong?"

"Nothing. I just heard back from Dan Moore. He sent me enough suggestions to fill a novel."

She moved around to see the screen, and whistled at the maze of comments, uttering something expressive in Greek.

"He offered to walk me through this. Would that be too weird to do in person?"

"No. Why would that be weird? You can keep your top on, right?"

"Oh, very funny."

Selene never missed an opportunity to tease me about that night, and I often wanted to strangle her for it. But the truth was, I trusted her judgment. She'd been my best friend since freshman orientation, and I knew for a fact she'd never let me do anything stupid.

So emboldened by her confidence, I responded to Dan's message that, indeed, talking through his comments would be very helpful. And after some back and forth, (and *much* consideration on my part over my clothing selection) we exchanged cell numbers and agreed to meet at five o'clock on Wednesday afternoon at Starbucks near campus.

§

I arrived right on time but Dan was already there, seated at a small round table in the corner, his laptop in front of him. He looked just like the teacher I remembered, dressed professionally in a lavender-striped button-down shirt that set off his coloring nicely.

Over the course of the next hour, I took him through my original idea. He listened carefully, taking notes and asking questions. Then he walked me through his comments, pointing out areas in which the research wouldn't support my thesis, and helping me to focus my area of interest to a more manageable scope.

As our final concept was coming together, we were sitting close, both of us focused on the computer. I was typing and he was leaning in, watching the screen to make sure I captured the idea in its entirety. I was so close to him I could smell the light, fresh scent of his soap. Whatever it was, it was good on him. In fact, I was secretly pledging my eternal brand loyalty to it as I typed.

"That's perfect." He smiled, turning to me and nodding his head slightly. "You're just missing a hyphen right there," he said, pointing casually to the screen.

Now, fun fact about Sarah: I was a bit of an enthusiast when it came to grammar and punctuation.

Dan was, in fact, one of the smartest people I'd ever met. But in this particular instance, I knew he was incorrect. So, I ignored his comment.

Annoyingly, he reiterated.

I inhaled a deep breath. "Actually, it doesn't need a hyphen," I said carefully.

"I think it actually does," he countered, squinting one eye, and making kind of a pirate face as though he was embarrassed to be pointing out my ignorance.

And that was exactly what kicking the hornet's nest looked like. I pursed my lips and counted silently to ten. Oh Lord, I was dying to tease him. *Dying.* If I were a stronger person, I'd have been able to resist. I knew I should resist.

But I just couldn't.

"*Doesn't*," I enunciated.

Dan was initially taken aback. I could see this was an issue for him—his intelligence at war with his strong, diplomatic instincts. His eyes were moving rapidly back and forth across mine like he was desperately searching for the answer to a monumentally important question that was somehow written right there.

Then, patiently, as if it explained everything, he drawled, "I'm a teacher."

Equally as patient, I replied, "A *science* teacher."

"I'm a doctoral candidate," he responded in dismay.

"In *education*," I said slowly.

He blinked several times. He had the most incredulous look on his face. It wasn't anger; it was more like shock and awe, like no one had ever challenged his authority before and he wasn't sure quite how to handle it.

In that moment, there was no breath between us, no movement, whatsoever. You could've heard a pin drop in China with all the stone-cold quiet. We were having this crazy-ass standoff over a hyphen, the world's most innocuous of all punctuation marks. And yet, here we were.

"I'm just saying," I prodded him casually. "Being a teacher doesn't make you an expert in *everything*." Then I raised my eyebrows for dramatic effect.

Dan barked out a laugh and placed his hands on the table, palms down. A smile spread across his stunning face, as he looked me over from head to toe. His posture was pure challenge; the smile was pure glee, mischievous glee—100 megawatts of perfect white teeth and supermodel confidence. It was the kind of smile that could knock a girl a little off balance if she were prone to that sort of thing.

"A bet, then." His sparkling eyes never left mine.

"Fine," I replied, matching his confidence.

He glanced down at his watch and then back to me. "Dinner. Tonight. Winner pays."

But I saw right through his game. He thought he was going to win the bet, *and* enjoy the upper hand by paying for dinner. The problem with his smug plan was that I *knew* he was wrong about the hyphen. It's not that I cared, but now he'd thrown the gauntlet and, quite frankly, I was enjoying myself too.

"Deal. I owe you dinner anyway. I'm going to use the restroom. You look it up on any site you trust and show me what you find when I come back."

That's when his confidence faltered for just a moment, revealing a flash of uncertainty I never thought I would see. I took that opportunity to get up and leave the table, laughing to myself at the image I had in my head of him bent over the computer, furiously scouring the internet for his answer.

Sure enough, when I returned he was leaning back in his chair, arms crossed over his chest, looking both bewildered and amused. We stared at each other for a long moment and, at last, he lowered his eyes, smiling, shaking his head slowly, and muttered a curse under his breath.

He was adorable.

I burst out laughing. Teasing Dan was officially my new favorite thing.

§

## Danny

"So why does a middle school science teacher need a PhD?" Sarah asked me. "Are you planning a career change?"

We were seated at a causal little Italian place up the street, and I leaned back in my chair, crossing my arms over my chest. I got this question a lot, actually, and my answer was well practiced, even if wasn't entirely true.

"No, mostly it's a personal goal. Although with some of the consulting work I do on the side, it's definitely useful."

"So, you still love teaching?"

"Yeah, it's sort of my thing," I said with a grin. That part was true. Teaching was the best job in the world.

She nodded as if she understood, but not quite like I'd satisfied her question. And now I was curious to know what was such a puzzle in her mind.

"What? You can say it."

A warm flush rose in her cheeks and brightened her pale blue eyes.

"Okay—don't take this the wrong way," she started. I laughed inwardly because when wasn't that opening used to soften something you couldn't help but take the wrong way? And just because she seemed fun to mess with, I had an urge to feign great offense, and give her loads of shit for whatever it was that came out of her mouth next. But I didn't know her well enough for that. Instead, I opted for professionalism, schooling my features into a look of pleasant curiosity.

"What made you decide to move to middle school?"

It was funny she thought that question would offend me. I'd had far more contentious conversations with people over the years about teaching—mostly about budget cuts or tenure or global competitiveness.

"I actually think the middle school years are the best years to teach. Kids are primed for huge leaps in learning if you can get them engaged. And what's more engaging than science?"

"That's true," she said, but she was looking at me like she knew there was more to it than that.

"I guess what I like best," I added, "is that they're old enough to be able to handle more complex instructions and concepts while at the same time, they're too young to decide they don't have an aptitude for science. Or that it's not cool to get excited about learning. Seventh graders are just wide open. And I feel like if I do my job well, I can make a difference for them."

"You do make a difference. You did for me."

Her expression was so warm and sincere that I found I couldn't stop looking at her and I struggled for something to say. *Thank you* was what I might have said, but the Italian waiter arrived just then to take our orders.

I was still looking at her as he went on and on, highlighting the specials and explaining in fine detail the process by which the rabbit was prepared. And I laughed to myself at the expression of barely concealed horror on Sarah's face as he repeatedly referred to the animal as a *bunny*. I knew for a fact she wasn't ordering that. And I wouldn't have confidently bet against her storming the kitchen for survivors, either.

But throughout dinner, the conversation was surprisingly easy. Listening to her talk about her career plans only deepened my respect for her—she was genuine and substantive. Anyone could see it took a special person to have the career she was working hard to achieve, and from the way she spoke of it, it was a very personal thing for her.

"Anyway," she finished, when it seemed like she didn't want to talk about herself any longer, "I just want to thank you again for helping me today. I really need this fellowship to come through."

The slip in her confidence was just barely perceptible but it reminded me of something. McKinley High School drew from both wealthy and very middle-class areas of town, and I didn't recall ever having the impression that Sarah came from the wealthy part. My guess was that this fellowship was the difference between her getting an advanced degree and not getting one—at least not from Stanford.

"It's my pleasure. I enjoyed it too."

I honestly did—I wouldn't have expected to enjoy it as much as I did.

Taking another sip of wine, I felt myself relax and settle into the pleasure of just being here in the moment. It had been such a surprising evening in many respects, and yet, truthfully, it was one of the nicest I could remember.

"You'll get a kick out of this, Sarah. I actually sold two photographs from that exhibition at Charlie's. One of them was that picture you might remember of the Golden Gate Bridge."

She smiled. "I remember it well. It's a beautiful shot."

She toyed with the tiny necklace at the base of her throat, and I didn't realize I was watching her fingers until she spoke and I looked up.

"I have this hike I love to do up in Wunderlich Park," she said. "As a photographer, you'd love it. The trick is to leave by about five o'clock in the morning so you can make it up to the crest by sunrise. You can get shots of the most incredible early morning landscapes from that vantage point. If you haven't been there, you definitely should."

I did a lot of hiking. In fact, it was always a major point of incompatibility with my ex-girlfriend, Carolyn, because hiking was not her thing. Early in our relationship, she'd go with me. But over time, her interest in spending a portion of her weekend on a trail diminished substantially, until hiking became something I did without her. And often.

It surprised me that I hadn't been on the particular trail Sarah was referring to. But something else struck me even more—the part about her hiking in the dark, which is so dangerous on many levels.

"I hope you don't go alone."

The words came out sounding far sharper than I had intended. I realized a little belatedly that the expression on my face was probably no better. I consciously adjusted it back to something more neutral, but whatever pleasantness I might have been feeling from the wine was definitely gone now—replaced by an odd sense of . . . what? Uneasiness?

"Yeah, it's stupid, I know. But I don't get many takers at five o'clock in the morning. Don't worry. I always carry mace." She lifted one shoulder, her mouth pulling up slightly at the edges.

"Christ, Sarah. Please don't do that again. I will gladly go with you any time you want to hike."

Truthfully, I'm not sure which of the two of us was more shocked by my offer. We both just let it sink in for several seconds. My heart began pounding as I tried to decide whether the proper thing to do here was to soften the comment or deflect from it somehow. But I couldn't quite bring myself to do that. Something similar seemed to pass over her face at exactly the same time.

She said nothing for a long minute, and finally she nodded. "That would be great. Let me know when you're free."

I let out a long, nervous breath and then: "This weekend?"

§

Sarah's phone rang in her purse, and when she saw it was her roommate, she held up a finger and stepped away from the table. I heard her say she was fine, and that she'd be coming home soon.

While she was gone, I flagged down the waiter, and quickly paid the check. I certainly remembered what my budget was like as a student, and there was no way I was letting her pay for dinner. She'd be mad at me since I was the one who lost the bet but, truthfully, I almost looked forward to seeing what she'd do when she found out. She was a riot.

Predictably, she was pissed.

I forced back a smile as I listened to her berate me for several long minutes about welching on a bet. She told me she could think of a few choice words to describe me and, coincidentally, two of them were hyphenated.

This girl—this woman, actually—was unreal.

When we finally made it back to our cars at the end of the evening, we said our goodbyes. But I couldn't help noticing the smile on my face lingered for a long time after she was gone.

# Chapter 4

**Danny**

It was dark when I pulled into the lot on Sunday morning and I was impressed to see Sarah's ancient burgundy Camry already parked at the trailhead. She was taking a daypack from her trunk when my headlights caught her attention, and she gave me a small wave.

I stepped out of my truck with two cups of coffee.

"How'd you manage that? Starbucks doesn't open until five o'clock."

"They can be very accommodating."

"I don't even want to know." She shook her head and took the cup I offered her. "But I suppose having a charmer for a friend has its benefits."

I laughed at her expression. Inwardly though, I was more than surprised to find that her use of the word *friend* twisted slightly in my gut. Plus, I didn't really like the impression she seemed to have about how I managed to get the coffee before Starbucks opened. The truth was pretty innocent—Mel's nephew ran the place. But it didn't seem like a good idea to pursue either of these things, so I let them go.

We started up the trail with flashlights, and it was so dark around us that it felt a little like the opening scene of the Blair Witch Project.

27

There were oak trees thickly lining both sides of the narrow dirt path, throwing eerie shadows from the moonlight on the ground. We saw what looked like birds flying above us but, given the darkness, they were more likely bats. And there was an almost unnatural quiet that felt intimate and adventurous.

"So what's your mom doing these days?"

I asked the question more to make conversation than anything else, figuring it was pretty safe territory. I remembered meeting Carol many years ago at a parent-teacher conference, and sympathizing with her situation of being widowed so unexpectedly.

But Sarah was quiet for a moment, which made me wish I could have seen her better to understand it. "She moved to Auburn a few years ago. She works part time as a bookkeeper."

The sun wasn't up, and there was only enough early morning light to cast shadows on her face, yet I had this odd sense that I'd stumbled onto something sensitive.

I hesitated. "Do you miss having her local?"

"She and I have some issues. She's an alcoholic."

Christ. That was not at all what I was expecting. Flashing back to my meeting with Carol, I recalled her telling me about Sarah's father, but I didn't have any other distinct impressions of her—and certainly not that.

"I'm sorry—I didn't know."

"It's okay. She's been sober for a while now, but her relapses are hard to predict. Sometimes it's a relief not to have her close by."

I recognized the bravery in Sarah's answer; the price of honesty showed plainly on her face. I knew it was a brutal reality that probably every child of an alcoholic eventually came to recognize: There comes a point when you have to take care of yourself first.

"Was it always that way when you were growing up?" I asked, and then quickly added, "Or if I'm intruding . . ."

Sarah shook her head. "No, it's okay. When I was young, she was a really good mom . . . to both my brother and me. She was tireless, really. It wasn't until my dad died that she started drinking. She couldn't cope with his death. And she couldn't handle my brother's needs so, more and more, she left that to me."

"But I thought you were only fifteen when he died?"

"Yeah." Her voice was soft, distant.

"Oh. Sarah, I'm so sorry." I knew this was wholly inadequate. "Where's your brother now?"

"CalTech. Computing and mathematical sciences."

"Really? That's impressive."

"Yeah." She smiled proudly.

It really was impressive, and we walked along for a few minutes in a lighter form of silence. I found there was so much I wanted to say to her now that the pieces were beginning to fall into place. The sad, reticent girl I remembered was a product of the compounded loss of not just one parent, but, in effect, two. And it was all right there in her posture, the weight of the burden she must have carried for years. I ached for her, and I had an urge to console her, or offer some sort of comfort. But I also knew from experience that sympathy was not what she wanted.

Instead, without much thought, I began telling her things I hadn't told anyone in a very long time.

"When my folks died, I kind of went off the rails. I couldn't seem to get a handle on my grief; I had no perspective on it. I ended up getting kicked out of my apartment, and blowing off most of my friends. I nearly got thrown out of the master's program at Stanford. Honestly, I was a mess."

Her light blue eyes locked on to mine. She seemed to understand this was a difficult subject for me too.

"That's hard to imagine. How did you pull yourself out of that?"

"I didn't. I couldn't. But one day I was in a bar, not so much

29

drinking as just hiding from my life, and Dr. Frick walked in and literally yanked me out by the collar of my shirt. He sat me down on the curb and handed me a letter of expulsion."

"Dr. Frick, as in our department head?"

"The very same one. I didn't know him well—we'd spoken a few times, I guess. But when I started missing my student teaching, they notified him. He got a hold of my sister, Casey, in New York, and she put him in touch with my friend, Jamie, who I was crashing with at the time. Jamie helped him find me.

"When he came to the bar, he told me I needed to make a choice right then and there, and he'd either tear up the letter or make it official. Did I want to finish my program and get my credential, or did I want to piss away the opportunity the university had given me? He said life can deal some devastating blows but, in the end, it's always our own poor choices we regret the most."

"Jesus."

"Yeah," I nodded, remembering that day. "The thing is, I was so lost. I was at sea with nothing to hold on to, so I just grabbed on to him. He made me come to his office every day after classes, and most Saturdays to make up for the coursework I'd missed. I think I actually did far more than anyone else in my program because he knew I needed the distraction—I needed something to apply myself to. But it worked. I graduated with the rest of my class, with honors even. Frick was the one who referred me for the teaching position at McKinley. And later, he made a special exception to oversee my PhD."

"I had no idea." Her eyes were wide and she looked at me with the recognition of someone who shared a similar history.

I raised my shoulders and let them drop. "I'm just telling you because we both know grief is a terrible thing. And lots of people lose their way trying to deal with it. I was really fortunate to have people who were able to step up for me when I couldn't do it for myself. Your mom was alone with two kids. I'm sure she never meant for things to end up the way they did."

Sarah didn't respond, just nodded slightly and continued to walk up the trail, now totally lost in her head.

§

When we reached the top, the sun was just beginning to peak above the horizon. Sarah was right about the views. It was a photographer's heaven. From the crest of the mountain we hiked, you could see a 360-degree view of the valley, covered in old oak trees and blanketed in a light veil of mist. The soft pinks and silver blue of the clouds in the sky didn't look real. No artist can ever replicate the colors in nature.

I pulled out my camera and began to adjust it for the lighting and conditions, snapping a few test shots to make sure I had it just right.

Sarah took out her camera too, but she still seemed deep in thought and I knew from experience that being trapped in your head wasn't usually a good thing. Sometimes a distraction helped.

"I think you just took a picture of my ass," I told her with my camera to my face.

She looked up, surprised, and it was like her brain was trying to decide if she'd actually heard what she thought she just heard. "I definitely did not take a picture of your ass!"

"I think you did."

"You're high," she said laughing.

And just as she began to turn her face away from me, I took her picture. It was a close-up of her profile, with the tall grass blurred in the background. A few pieces of her long, blonde hair had come loose from her braid and were drifting lightly across her shoulder. Her gaze was soft and unfocused and she looked relaxed. She looked happy.

And absolutely fucking beautiful.

Not just beautiful. Ethereal. It was as if my camera was trying to show me something that my brain had been too slow or too reluctant to acknowledge. This woman was special. Remarkable, really.

For several beats, I just stared at the shot in my viewer. I was almost breathless by the perfection of the subject. Maybe Sarah was right; maybe somewhere along this unexpected road we'd found ourselves on, a friendship *had* begun between us. But perhaps I needed to admit to myself that there was a kernel of something else there, too—something just a little bit more.

"You'll like this one," I said hoarsely, the words catching in my throat.

She took the camera from my hands and looked at the photo wordlessly for a stretch. Then turning to meet my eyes, she gave me back the camera. But she held my gaze for several long moments while the breeze toyed with her hair.

"Thank you," she replied softly, though I didn't think it was actually the picture we were talking about.

§

The hike back down the mountain was much faster than the trip up. Mostly, we avoided all heavy topics of conversation, keeping the mood light and easy. Sarah told me she was playing in a beach volleyball tournament hosted by Stanford in Half Moon Bay next Friday. She wondered if I was planning to go. I wasn't—actually, this was the first I'd heard of it. At this point in my PhD program, I wasn't on campus much.

"You should come watch if you have time. It should be fun."

Normally something like that would be an automatic *no* for me; I didn't attend many Stanford events. But her involvement kind of made me more interested in going, though I knew I probably shouldn't.

*What are you doing?* my better judgment asked.

*Getting to know someone nice,* some other voice answered. And I guess that's the one I listened to.

"Yeah, maybe I will."

But Sarah misread my hesitation, and her expression quickly turned to embarrassment.

"I didn't mean to pressure you," she quickly added. "I know I've monopolized so much of your time already and you probably have plans with friends, or a girlfriend or whatever. Honestly, don't worry about it. I wasn't trying to suggest you should come for me."

*Whoa.* What?

First of all, if I went, it would *only* be for her. That was the problem. Second, a girlfriend?

I hadn't even thought about the fact that *my* relationship status would ever be remotely concerning to her. But did she really think I was the kind of man who would ask her to do something alone with me at five o'clock in the morning if I had a girlfriend? Friends or not, that kind of thing wasn't appropriate.

"I don't have a girlfriend. We broke up—not too long ago."

A dozen things seemed to cross her face as she digested this. "I'm sorry, Dan. Are you okay about it?"

I shrugged. "Both of us knew it was coming for a while."

She nodded, continuing to hold my gaze. "How long were you together?"

"Five years. It probably should have ended sooner but that was my fault."

She didn't respond, just walked carefully down the path, seemingly considering this. I had a flash of worry that maybe my *not* having a girlfriend was actually more of problem for her than if I had had one. Maybe she worried how this might look to someone in her own life. Maybe she worried it would look like a date.

I broke the silence with the question that felt like it was hanging heavily between us.

"How about you? Are you seeing someone?"

I tried my best to make it sound like a casual inquiry, but I was objective enough to know I couldn't entirely claim indifference to her response. I wondered if she could hear it in my voice.

After what felt like an eternity: "No, we broke up in November. We were living together, but it didn't work out."

My entire body relaxed, releasing tension I hadn't realized I held. I took in a deep breath, removed my Giants cap, and ran a hand through my hair.

"It sounds like it was serious," I said, replacing the hat.

"I thought it was until I came home and found him in our bed with someone else."

"He *cheated* on you?"

"Oh, spectacularly."

This, I could hardly believe. Seriously. Who on God's earth would have a woman like this, and think there could possibly be something better out there than her? On the one hand, I instantly despised the guy, whoever he was. On the other hand, I considered the fact that stupidity may very well turn out to be his greatest virtue—for me, at least.

I immediately reprimanded myself for that entire line of thinking.

"That guy is a douchebag and an asshole and a fucking idiot," I told her, and really, I was just getting warmed up.

Sarah sniffed out a laugh. "I think you left out cocksucker."

"I was getting there, believe me."

She smacked me playfully on the arm, but in the next moment, the humor disappeared. "It wasn't all his fault."

"Uh, I seriously beg to differ."

"No, I mean the cheating was all his fault, of course, but the relationship was far from perfect. It was superficial in the ways that count. I don't know if he would have wanted anything more, but I'm not great in that department."

I could see in her face the magnitude of that admission. And I recognized something entirely similar in my own life. Since my parents' deaths, I'd struggled to build close relationships of any kind. I had a wealth of casual friendships—I wasn't reclusive or isolated—but I often found myself not allowing relationships to go deeper than a certain level. Even with Carolyn, maybe especially with her, I was never quite able to open up and it was a big part of our problems as a couple.

Sudden loss will do that. It's a stark reminder of just how easy it is to lose something you value and depend on. Life can turn on a dime, and the relationships that give you the greatest joy can easily become those that break you most decisively. It's no way to live, I know, but self-protection is a powerful and instinctual thing.

It's a hard habit to break.

We walked along the trail in meaningful silence. But I didn't want to end the hike on that note; truthfully, I didn't really want to end it at all.

"You know what would be perfect right now?" I finally said, and she turned to me. "Pancakes."

§

## Sarah

We settled on one of my favorite breakfast places called Buck's. It's kind of an icon in the Silicon Valley, known for being the place where a lot of finance-types and entrepreneurs met through the years to launch the Next Big Thing. It's a classic diner—not the kind with red booths and sparkling chrome finishes—but the kind with kitschy artifacts on the walls and a long bar, crowded with regulars having coffee and reading the paper. If you don't get in early, you can never get a table.

Luckily, early wasn't a problem for us. It wasn't even eight o'clock in the morning and, after the hike we had, both of us were so starving we didn't even glance at the menu. When the waitress came by, Dan ordered us both pancakes; he also wanted a side of sausage.

"Do you have turkey bacon?" I asked her.

"Hmm?" she responded. She didn't seem to be able to take her eyes off him.

"Turkey bacon," he repeated. "For my guest."

Admittedly, it was hard to fault her interest. You could probably walk through a thousand shopping malls and airports and never see anyone as half as handsome. But it was nice that he wasn't one of those guys who encouraged it.

The contrast, in that way, between Dan and my ex was stark. John would've had a completely different response to the attention. He would have milked it for all it was worth—an extra muffin, a free orange juice, a phone number discreetly written on a napkin. He loved that sort of thing—loved it even more when I was present to witness it. If I wasn't, he loved to tell me about it later.

"Turkey bacon is not bacon, by the way," Dan said as soon as she left the table. He looked warmly incensed with my breakfast order, and was shaking his head for emphasis.

"Of course it is. And it's a lot healthier than sausage."

"But it's *fake*."

"It's not fake. It's bacon. They wouldn't call it turkey *bacon* if it weren't bacon."

"Bacon should come from a pig. Not a turkey. Turkey bacon isn't any more bacon than root beer is beer."

I stared at him for several beats. Then, with a huff of exasperation and a dramatic eye roll for good measure, I replied, "I find you exhausting."

To my delight, he erupted in a deep, gravelly belly laugh that warmed me to my core. It may have been the best sound I'd ever heard.

§

Sitting across from Dan at the table while we ate, I finally had a chance to just look at him. He didn't really look real—more like something out of a magazine. It's not that I'd never noticed this before, but somehow it felt different to be able to appreciate his looks in something other than a professional setting.

Today I noticed that his angular jaw was set off by a defined Adam's apple I never thought could be so attractive. It seemed to announce that this was a man, not a boy, not a guy. He'd removed his hat, and his hair was a sexy, wild mess. He always wore it a little longer, so you could see the waves and the many subtle colors running through it. It was decadent, that hair. And it looked so soft that the temptation to run my fingers through it was almost unbearable.

I reminded myself again that this one was off limits.

Dan had left his sweatshirt in the car, and the white T-shirt he was wearing fit snugly across his lean, muscular chest and arms. He was a basketball player in college, I recalled suddenly. He had the height for it; he was well over six feet tall.

As he plowed through his pancakes, I couldn't help but watch his throat move with every swallow. I was so distracted by this I wasn't paying attention to the question he asked between bites.

That's when he looked at me oddly and I realized he'd probably been waiting too long for me to answer. I blushed. "I'm sorry—what?"

Something flashed across his face momentarily and then disappeared.

"I asked if you played volleyball growing up."

"Oh. Yeah. Among other things."

"Does that mean your father was into sports? I mean," he added quickly so as not to cause offense, "most women I know who grew up playing sports had fathers that were into sports. Or maybe that comes from your mom? I was just wondering who you took after."

The funny thing was, I'd thought about this frequently through the years—about which of my parents I was most like—mostly because I didn't want to believe I was much like the mother that my mom became after my father died. But truthfully, I did get certain things from her, and they weren't all bad.

"I look like my mom, and I probably get pig-headed stubbornness from her but I think overall, my personality favors my dad. He was into sports and music, and he had a pretty sarcastic sense of humor that not everyone appreciated."

I smiled because I knew for a fact that Dan not only got, but also seemed to enjoy, my inherited sense of humor.

"I can see that." He nodded, eyeing me closely like he did.

Sometimes the directness of his gaze made me feel the need to deflect it. He had the intensity of an academic.

"How about you?"

He leaned back in his chair and dragged the nails of his left hand back and forth across his head, leaving his already tousled hair even more disorderly. The fact that he seemed unconcerned about that to the point of obliviousness was charming.

"I like to think I'm more similar to my mom. We were close. I don't look like her, but she was warm and funny, and she never took herself too seriously. She just had this zeal for life that was contagious. I hope I'm that way."

"And what about your dad?"

"What about him?" Something in his voice made me falter.

"Are you like him at all?" I realized as I asked the question that I couldn't recall his ever mentioning his dad in more than a passing way.

"We're all a product of both parents, I suppose." There was something in his tone I couldn't place. "My dad was a really honorable man, the smartest person I've ever known, and a really hard worker. He was all about education. I definitely got that from him."

*But?* I was waiting for him to finish the thought because his tone and his words didn't match. He didn't continue.

"It's getting pretty busy in here," he said, instead. "I guess we should probably give up the table?"

"Oh. Yes, I guess we should."

He started to reach for the check, but I was faster.

"Don't even try." I pointed a finger in his direction and gave him an arched look for emphasis. He'd already bought me dinner and I'd be damned if I was going to let him pay for this too.

I patently ignored his grumbling something about this being his idea to begin with, but he let it go, albeit reluctantly. With that, I grabbed my wallet from my backpack and left enough cash to cover the check and tip.

"Thank you for treating me to breakfast," he said, though he looked like I just force-fed him snails.

"I know you can handle it."

# Chapter 5

**Danny**

Mel and the boys were building a Star Wars Lego set at the kitchen table when I walked in.

"Uncle Danny!" Shane shouted, and wrapped himself around me. "Come look at our Millennium Falcon."

The kid was a hugger. I kissed him on the top of his auburn hair and moved around to give a similar kiss to his eight-year-old brother.

"What did you bring for us?" Paddy asked me, eyeing the bag of supplies and equipment I was holding.

"I'll show you in a minute, but you have to go change into some old clothes first so your mom doesn't make her mad face at me." I made a greatly exaggerated mad face and the boys giggled. Mel rolled her eyes. As they piled out of the kitchen to change, I gave her a wink. She looked tired.

"You staying for dinner?" she asked.

"What are you making?"

"Does it matter?"

Hell no, I was in. She knew me well. Jamie and Mel got together when Jamie and I were about twenty-two, so I'd known her a long time. She was a lawyer by trade, but her full-time job, aside from raising two rowdy boys, was managing the band. She was very good at it. She was tough, and a killer negotiator—petite, but a real powerhouse. She had this no-bullshit vibe I'd always respected. Plus, being a woman and a mom, I liked that I always got a different perspective from her than I would from a guy.

"Where's the band tonight?" I asked, lifting a lid off a pot on the stove.

"Detroit. They go to Kansas City tomorrow. Home next week."

I tried to check in on her and the boys as often as I could when Jamie was on the road. They'd been married a long time, and they were happy by all accounts. But I'd always felt Mel carried a lot of the weight of the choices they'd made. It was a lonely life for both of them in many ways.

The difference was that for Jamie, this was what he'd wanted to do from the time we were kids; he never had a Plan B. He was an artist. It's just who he was, and there was no way to separate the man from his profession. But for Mel it was a decision. Though she loved their life together, I knew it was hard on her sometimes.

"What'd you do today?" she asked me as she began scooping Legos back into the box.

"Went hiking with a friend."

I grabbed a beer out of the fridge and sat down on one of the leather barstools.

"Tom, you mean?"

Hesitating for a moment, I answered. "No, just that girl I'm helping with the fellowship application."

"Oh, Sarah?"

Hearing Sarah's name come out of Mel's mouth was strange. It felt startlingly nice if I was being honest, and equally unsettling at the same time. So much so that I didn't immediately respond.

"Was this a date sort of thing? I didn't realize you two were doing things outside of the project."

"No, it definitely wasn't a date. Definitely not. No." I was shaking my head for emphasis, but doing a piss-poor job of convincing myself, let alone Mel.

She looked at me skeptically. "That kind of sounds like a date. Did you want it to be?"

"No, it's not like that," I said with a long sigh. "It's just . . ."

"Is this about Carolyn?" She set the Lego box down on the table, and gathered up the open instruction manuals.

"No. It's not Carolyn." Rolling the bottle between my palms, I let my head and shoulders slump down. How could I articulate this?

"I wish I'd never known Sarah before, you know?" She didn't know; I could tell. "Because then she could just be this remarkable woman I met at Charlie's a couple months ago. And there wouldn't be this . . ."

"Perception."

I nodded, setting the bottle on the counter. It was the first time I'd said any of this out loud.

"In every way that matters, I feel like I did just meet her. Before, I never had any occasion or inclination to get to know her. When it comes to my job, I'm very careful about distancing myself from my students and that was especially true at McKinley. I went to great lengths to avoid even the hint of impropriety."

"But you know how it is with teachers, Danny. It just takes one bad example to incite the mistrust thousands of great ones. It's unfair but it's never going to change."

"But *I'm* not like that."

"Of course you're not like that."

I rubbed my eyes in frustration. "I should just walk away from this." But it felt more like a question than a declaration of fact, and Mel knew it.

She pulled a chair out from the table and sat down, leaning sideways against the back of it. She just watched me sympathetically, well accustomed to the way my mind worked.

"So why don't you walk away?"

"I guess because . . . I like her." It was really that simple, or complicated, depending on your perspective. "She's smart, and she's fun, and she calls me on my shit."

Mel smiled softly, knowingly.

"I just admire her so much. She's amazing. And she's pretty and she's genuinely nice." I dropped my head to my hand. "That sounds stupid."

"No, it doesn't. It sounds pretty great, actually. In my experience, we never fall for the obvious choice. Or the convenient one for that matter. We fall for the one who makes us think differently—who makes us reconsider our own grand selves."

Mel's experience was exactly that. Jamie had represented a massive left turn in her life—the best one possible but at the time, it must have taken a huge leap of faith. She understood what it meant to risk something for the sake of your heart.

"I'm eleven years older than she is, Mel." That wasn't really the question, but a prelude to it, certainly. "And our past," I said, shaking my head. "Is it wrong?"

I needed the truth. And I appreciated that I always got it from her.

She processed me for a moment, and then answered solemnly. "No. It's not wrong. You're both adults, Danny. Free to make any choices you like. But that doesn't mean it would always be easy, either."

"Perception, you mean."

She nodded. "What's the saying? 'What people think of you is really none of your business.'"

"True enough, I guess. But doesn't it usually *become* your business?"

"Well, that's the thing, isn't it?"

# Chapter 6

**Danny**

I spent the better part of the next week at an offsite planning meeting for the Taft Middle School faculty. As the math and science department head, I was in budget meetings most of the time, trying to figure out how to squeeze yet another drop of blood from a stone. It was depressing knowing we'd never get the funding we actually needed, let alone the funding we wanted to make our program great. Such was the state of education in California. And it got harder every year.

By Thursday night, I was sick to death of looking at spreadsheets covered in red ink, and all I wanted is to do was head home for a long run. I'd felt restless all week, and I suspected much of that related my war of emotions over Sarah. I was so distracted at work, when that was normally never the case for me.

But I knew I'd be seeing her at the volleyball tournament in Half Moon Bay, and that's what I tried to focus on as I practically ran myself into the ground. I was drenched in sweat by the time I got back, and so goddamned tired I thought I might actually be able to sleep.

Sarah and I had traded a few texts while I was away, but other than that, we hadn't had any contact since I behaved tersely at the restaurant when she brought up the subject of my dad. That's not to say I hadn't thought of her often, though. And for the sake of my own sanity, I knew I needed to figure this out. Soon.

§

## Sarah

It was one of those points you love to watch in a sand volleyball game: the kind where the player makes a hail-Mary dive, arms outstretched, body flying sideways as if in slow motion. And miraculously, she gets her hand on the ball, just in the nick of time, and just before hitting the ground in an explosion of sand and sweat. The ball sails effortlessly over the net and the cheering crowd leaps to its feet in utter bewilderment.

My last shot of the day was just like that. Except that the ball hit the net instead of going over, and bounced back rather unceremoniously onto my team's side for the loss. The utter bewilderment was mine. And the cheering crowd, not mine.

Dan walked up as I was pulling on a T-shirt and grabbing my water bottle.

"Can I buy you a beer?"

Daniel Moore had had his own lengthy history with organized sports. Among other things, he'd played Division I basketball on a full scholarship for The University of Virginia. So he seemed to understand the competitive part of me that hated to lose even more than it liked to win. I'd bet he was exactly the same way. He didn't try to congratulate me for great play, or to try to make me feel better for missing that shot. He just tossed my gym bag over his shoulder, angled a bent elbow in my direction, and motioned with his head for me to take hold of it.

For many minutes, we walked along in companionable silence with no more talk of the match. Every so often, I'd sneak a sidelong peek at him as we made our way back towards the main building of the Ritz-Carlton hotel. He was handsome in a navy sweatshirt and beige shorts that showed off his tanned, muscular legs. His hair was a little ruffled from the ocean breeze, and aviators were hanging from the front of his crew neck collar.

Together, we probably looked like an Abercrombie ad—or at least he did. At the moment, I looked more like the girl who accidentally stumbled into the frame.

When he caught me glancing at him, he smiled warmly and pressed his elbow gently into his side, effectively pinning my arm between his torso and biceps. It felt like an intimate thing to do, and I realized this was the first time in our lives we'd actually touched each other with any real intention.

Of course, I'd thought about touching him a million times, but on the occasions we'd met up—Starbucks, our hike, breakfast, whatever—we'd always kept a professional distance. But something about tonight felt different. I didn't know why. He just seemed slightly less careful around me, slightly more . . . I didn't know what the right word was. Resigned? That didn't make sense, I know—the best I could say was that the dynamic seemed to be shifting, and it felt as if we were suddenly entering unchartered territory.

§

The Cliffs bar at the Ritz was a small, cozy place. It was surprisingly casual with dark wood tables and comfortable padded chairs. The real draw was the view, with windows that showcased the jagged Pacific Ocean coastline and rolling whitecaps below.

As soon as we found a small table inside, I excused myself to the restroom to freshen up. I needed to brush the sand out of my hair and wash my face, and I wanted to change into jeans and a top I had in my bag.

I was so unbelievably nervous all of the sudden. In the mirror, my cheeks looked flushed and blotchy.

*This isn't a date, right?*

Well, if it wasn't, someone needed to tell that to my heart because at the moment it was jackhammering inside my chest as my stomach put forth a respectable effort to claw its way up into my throat.

And it was brutally unfair that, back at the table, Dan looked casual and relaxed—like this wasn't the most confusing situation between two people who may or may not have been on a date.

But I noticed as I walked up that he was looking at me in a new way—his eyes traveling the length of my body. He stood, smiling when I arrived, and pulled the chair out for me with an exaggerated flourish.

*So . . . maybe a date?*

"You look really pretty," he said in a slightly awkward way that, for the first time, seemed totally out of character for the elegant, confident man I was getting to know. Was it possible he was nervous too?

I also noted this was the very first time he'd ever commented on my appearance.

*Jesus Christ—we were on a date.*

"Thank you."

I mean, yes, I had hoped we might go out after the match, and I chose an outfit to change into that I thought would be flattering. But until this very moment, I couldn't have said whether or not the effort was wasted on him. He was impossible to read.

As I sat in the chair he offered, I tried to hide the fact that my hands were now shaking a little with this possible new development. To make matters worse, the scrape on the side of my abdomen from that fruitless dive was rubbing against my denim waistband. It hadn't really bothered me before, but it was screaming now.

Dan noticed. His expression quickly turned to concern. "Let me see. Is it bad?"

"It's fine, honestly."

But Dan was nothing if not persistent. He left his chair to kneel in front of me. "Let me see." He was waiting for my okay.

Whatever the look on my face, he seemed to have all the consent he needed, and he moved my shirt gently away from my body to reveal a nasty scrape where my bare flesh had skidded across the sand.

"Jesus, Sarah."

I didn't think it was that bad.

He did, apparently. Rising from his crouched position, he walked to the bar and spoke briefly to the bartender. When he returned, he had a small first aid kit in his hand.

"Hold this away," he said, motioning to my shirt. He took a cleansing wipe from its foil packet, and brought his hand close to my skin. "This may sting."

He began gently wiping the area clean, checking my face to make sure the discomfort was manageable. But I wasn't even thinking about that. I couldn't seem to tear my eyes from the look on his face that was so intent and careful as he dabbed the scrape repeatedly.

It was a little dangerous the way that look made me feel.

When he seemed satisfied with his work, he blew lightly to cool the antiseptic. And good *god* I almost came out of my skin. It was the way he was being so tender about it, but it was also a wildly sexy thing to do. I was nearly overcome with the impulse to bury my hands in that decadent hair of his, and pull his sculpted lips to my body.

I thought it was just me until, softly and without warning, his fingertips brushed my bare skin, just to the side of the scrape.

I froze.

His hand was warm, compared to the cool of the wipe, and I could not breathe as I watched him study the drag of his fingers over my ribs. The contact between us was just a whisper, but it was enough to incite an almost desperate ache low in my belly.

And maybe it was the way my breathing suddenly accelerated or maybe it was the goose bumps on my skin, but he glanced up at me through those thick lashes, taking in what I'm sure was a look of pure desire on my face.

His own breath caught, and his lips parted fractionally.

I was powerless to control the riotous reaction of my body. I had to close my eyes to contain the utter craving that was seeping out of them.

I felt him reach up and run the back of his knuckles down my cheek. It was so unexpectedly intimate I leaned into his touch before I could stop myself. There were so many things I wanted in that moment, but I was motionless, unable to speak.

I opened my eyes to a face that was as intense and full of desire as I was—full of so many things I couldn't even begin to name.

But then he blinked and shook his head as if clearing it. He took a deep breath and his hand dropped from my face. As if nothing at all had happened, he bent to pick up the antibiotic ointment, carefully applying a thin layer, and then finished by gently pressing on an adhesive bandage.

"That should be okay," he said, though his voice was rasping and rough.

Something was definitely happening here, but damn if I was going to be the one to say what it was.

§

"Okay, favorite Star Trek episode," he asked around a mouthful of deep-fried zucchini. We were continuing a game of *Name Your Favorite* that we'd been playing for a while. "And don't say 'The Trouble with Tribbles,'" he added with a laugh. "That's just cheating."

"No. See, I call a nerd foul on that one. You're probably the only person under the age of fifty who's even seen all those episodes."

"That's probably true," he conceded, taking a sip from his pint. "My uncle loved Star Trek. We watched it together when I was a kid. I might be dating myself."

"How old are you, anyway?" I asked, setting my fork down.

It was just a curiosity, on my part—I couldn't remember if we'd ever discussed our ages. Well, okay, apart from the night at Charlie's when I shoved my ID in his face and then spilled my drink down his pants.

And showed him my boobs.

And my tampon.

"Thirty-three," he answered. He was picking at the coaster under his glass, and it didn't seem like he was thinking about boobs or tampons or anything else from that horrible night because all the humor appeared to drain from his face.

His eyes searched mine intently, focusing on something else entirely. "Does our age difference bother you? Or the fact that you were in my class?"

To me, this wasn't a big deal. He obviously knew my age—no need to relive that—and I assumed he was in his early to mid thirties. If anything, I thought he might find me too young or uninteresting because I was still in school and he was much more established. But the look on his face showed something more than ordinary concern that I wasn't sure he meant for me to see. There was a vulnerability there that surprised me, and made me feel eager to ease whatever it was that had made him ask the question.

I wiped my mouth with my napkin and shook my head. "I never think about our age difference." That was absolutely the truth and I knew he could see it because relief flashed briefly in his eyes.

"Is that a nice way of telling me I'm immature?" He was pulling out his self-deprecating humor that I knew was intended to break some of the tension suddenly gripping our conversation.

"No," I told him with a smile. "And, you know the funny thing is, when I think about you and I think about my eleventh-grade biology teacher, it's like you're two different people. I feel like I never really knew you before."

He didn't respond right away, just looked at me silently for several beats, again serious. Suddenly I began to realize there was a larger question at play here.

"Does it bother *you*?"

His eyes dropped away, and he took a deep breath. "I think about it sometimes." I could see in his expression that he did, maybe more than he was saying. "But for me, it feels a little late for second-guessing."

I didn't know what that meant or how to respond, and I didn't want to dig further into this subject if it meant stirring up something that was clearly an issue for him.

It was hard to say exactly what was happening between us, but I knew the look in his eyes earlier tonight wasn't just my imagination. It was real. And regardless of what anyone might have thought about our spending time together, I wasn't ready to give it up.

"Okay, favorite candy bar?"

"Candy bar?"

"Yes. What's your favorite?" That was the subject changed. I could see it register in his face with some relief.

"I don't eat candy bars." Of course he didn't. With a physique like that he probably never had. "How about you?"

"Butterfinger," I told him, to which he shook his head in disbelief.

"Does anyone actually know what's inside one of those things?"

"It's sweet and crunchy, and it's dipped in chocolate. Who cares what it is?"

He made a face. "You don't want to know what you're eating?"

"Not particularly."

"You're indiscriminate?"

"Must be why I'm here with you." I smiled at him sweetly.

Dan threw his head back and laughed hard. "I can't think of any other explanation."

§

When we finished our meal, he pulled my chair up next to his and handed me his phone so I could see a picture of what I thought might be world's homeliest animal.

"That's Ralphie, my bulldog," he said fondly. Ralphie had huge, smiling eyes, but his teeth were ridiculous—like nature had arranged them by randomly tossing a handful into his mouth. But it was entirely possible he was so homely that he was actually the world's cutest animal. It was a very fine line.

"What other pictures do you have of him?"

Dan's arm was around the back of my chair and I leaned in against the side of his chest so we could look together. This close, I could smell his detergent, and the faint, masculine scent of his soap. If I could have, I would have pressed my face into his neck to feel the warmth of his skin against my cheek.

Gently, he took the phone from my hand and our fingers grazed. Just a bit, but it felt magnetic.

He had begun looking for something in his photo reel when he scrolled by a picture of what was obviously a family. The two young boys had dark auburn hair like their father, and the mother was a beautiful brunette, almost angelic-looking.

"Who's that?" I asked.

There was something very familiar about the man, tall and muscular with a sizeable tattoo visible on his right forearm. I couldn't place him, though.

"I feel like I know him from somewhere. Stanford, maybe?"

I turned my face to Dan, who was so close now that I accidentally looked at his mouth.

His eyes dropped to mine too, just for a second. "Definitely not. That's my best friend, Jamie Callahan, and his wife, Mel."

That's when it clicked.

"As in *Cadence*?"

"As in."

It was so bizarre. I studied his face to see if he was bullshitting me. But as I did, he began to scroll through other pictures of he and Jamie together, and of him with the kids, or the rest of the band.

"He moved to here from Dublin when we were nine, and he was the coolest kid I'd ever met. He played the guitar, and was from somewhere exotic, at least to me. I think half my childhood was spent shooting hoops with him in my driveway."

"I have at least fifteen of their songs on my playlist. Right now."

Dan laughed. "He always claims he has a fan, but I just assumed it was his mother."

As we looked through more photos, he told me how they grew up together, and how he used to haul equipment for the band when they were first starting out. He talked about how gratifying it was to see them finally getting the recognition they deserved.

"You'll love Jamie and Mel," he said nodding, as if meeting them was something he'd already decided he wanted me to do.

It was a little stunning because it made me realize how much I *wanted* to meet them—how much I wanted to meet all the significant people in his life.

That was the moment I finally allowed myself to admit that I wanted to have some sort of a place with him beyond just the duration of our work on my fellowship essay. I would never have guessed it was possible.

§

The Cliffs bar closed early, so at about nine forty-five, Dan settled the check before I could even protest.

"Let's take a walk."

This time, he took my hand in his, and led me from the building. We checked my bag with a valet, and walked along the cliff next to the golf course.

It was a beautiful, clear night; a bit cold, but I barely felt it. His hand was enormous and warm, and my heart was racing.

"This is a perfect night for stargazing," he said looking up at the sky as we walked. "You can see everything."

I remembered how into astronomy he was. We did a major unit on it my junior year, including an evening seminar where he set up telescopes on the roof of the gym, and we took turns identifying various stars and planets.

"That's right, I forgot you were into all that astrology stuff."

There came that face again. The one from the coffee shop that told me he was having a major crisis of conscience over whether to correct me. Of course he wanted to, but he was too much of a gentleman to point out that astrology isn't science. But then he noticed my own expression and the look melted into a giant grin. "You're just fucking with me, aren't you?"

"A little." I couldn't help it. It was one of my favorite things.

"You're evil." The way he said it made me laugh out loud, and he tugged playfully on my arm.

Suddenly, something in the direction of the ocean caught his attention. He turned, and his eyes narrowed in the dim light. Following his gaze, it took me a minute to understand what we were looking at. The waves crashing on the rocks below were actually glowing blue. It was the most bizarre and beautiful thing I'd ever seen.

"What is that?"

"It's bioluminescence. If I had to guess, I'd say it's likely dinoflagellates—a type of marine plankton."

"Marine plankton can do that?"

"It's extremely rare to see an algal bloom like this in Northern California," he said excitedly, "but I did hear about one a few years back in Tomales Bay." He rubbed the back of his neck. "Damn, I wish I had my camera."

We stepped as close as we could to the edge of the cliff and peered over. "What causes this?"

"Well, dinoflagellates produce light in response to mechanical stress," he explained. "Most likely, there's a predator or something swimming in the area. The light is a defense mechanism."

As I listened to him talk, I had a momentary flashback, and was reminded once again of the odd circumstances in which I'd found myself. He was the same person I knew, but he wasn't. And I couldn't quite shake the sense of disbelief that I was standing here in this rather romantic setting with a man who, years ago, couldn't have been more out of reach if he'd been a Hollywood actor I was admiring.

"There are certain species that cause what's called red tide, where the water looks brown or reddish. In that case, the algal bloom is toxic to its environment. But in this case, I suspect it's a planktonic species you often see in marine mortality events."

He was looking at me as if this should all make perfect sense. Like, *sure, I know all about algal blooms and planktonic whatevers.*

"Meaning, what?"

"Meaning something big died out there, and a crowd has gathered at the mess hall." We both smiled.

"I've ever seen anything like that. I didn't even know it was possible."

"Yeah, well, that's the science behind it, in any respect."

I studied his strong profile as he looked out to the breathtaking sight below. "The rest is . . . art?"

"Nature is art," he said. "And maybe a bit of mystery too. In equal parts, I think. That's what I like about it—biology, I mean. Living things are so ingeniously designed for their environments. But they're not just functional; they're beautiful too, even when that's not strictly required for their survival. And beyond that, there's the whole X-factor—those things science will never be able to explain. Why dinoflagellates glow blue, for example," he said gesturing to the water. "Or why monarch butterflies migrate up to five thousand miles to Mexico. Did you know the lifespan of a monarch is less than six months, which means the ones that make the return journey can be many generations removed from the ones that began the initial migration? How do they know where to go?" He shook his head at the wonder of it. "We can understand a lot of things, but some biological imperatives will always be a mystery." He turned to me. "I think it's amazing."

It was amazing.

So was he.

He was unexpected in so many ways: smart and kind and generous with his time. He was so dedicated to teaching and to making a difference. And he was so beautiful to look at that he probably could've had any woman he wanted. But when we were together, he always made me feel like he believed he was the lucky one. Like my company was more precious to him than anything.

As we stared silently out at the glowing blue ocean, that thought made me shiver. Dan stepped behind me, wrapping his arms around my waist, and suddenly I was enveloped in warmth. I leaned back gratefully into his embrace and relished the feel of his solid weight at my back. It was a perfect moment—simple and unplanned and encapsulating absolutely everything I loved about being with him.

Resting my hands over his arms and feeling their strength, I held on to him as my chest rose and fell quickly with every pounding heartbeat. Something had definitely changed between us, and from here forward, this was all off book for me.

Softly—hesitantly, it seemed—he kissed my hair. Maybe this was all off book for him too. That first kiss was so gentle I barely recognized it for what it was. But the second time, the intent was there, and I closed my eyes and squeezed him to acknowledge it.

The moment was so surreal.

It was hard to imagine it was really happening. If anyone had told me I would've been standing here tonight with *this* man, in his arms, I would have said they were crazy.

Life can turn on a dime, surely. But it's not just tragedy that can do it; serendipity can do that too.

Slipping his hands down to my hips, Dan turned me in his arms. His expression was as serious as his green eyes were intense. And they followed the movement of my throat as I swallowed, and then came to rest on my lips. Slowly, as if he was giving me warning, he lifted his hand to my jaw, threading his fingers into my hair, and pulled me forward to press his mouth to mine.

His lips were the perfect combination of soft and firm, of patient and hungry, and he groaned a little when I opened my mouth and let him in. The vibration of that alone lit my body on fire and I moved closer, chasing the feeling.

He kissed me harder, then—no longer in the slow, careful way of someone asking a question. This was with definite intent and the wanting in that kiss made my knees weak.

And just when I thought he had stolen my breath, his lips wandered away to suck my jaw, my neck, my ear.

Any coherent thought I had simply vanished in the puff of breath that filled my lungs, then escaped my mouth.

Someone may have also let out a little moan.

And even though my eyes were closed, I could feel that his next kisses were delivered though a smile. I didn't even care that it was probably because of me.

"Your skin is flawless," he murmured. "Especially here." He bent to kiss the side of my neck below my earlobe, where my pulse hammered wildly.

"I didn't know that." I was breathing hard and leaning into where his mouth was now pressed.

I *ached* for him—ached for more than just the feel of his lips on my throat. I wanted to feel every part of him. I reached up to stroke his cheek while my mouth again sought his.

As though reading my growing frenzy just right, he deepened the kiss, fitting me tightly against his body, and gripping my hip securely. He felt firm from head to toe, every muscle taut, and the heat he generated drew me closer like a moth to a flame.

In seconds, the air around us was thick with desire. I finally allowed myself to do what I'd been dying to do for some time—I ran my hands up into his hair, tugging on the soft strands. He groaned low in his throat and his kiss became more raw need than practiced nuance.

We were not in a private place—anyone could follow the same path from the hotel, and stumble upon us. But I didn't care. Not even a little. I was unable to say sensible things to myself about making out on golf courses or how the sound of kissing is carried by the evening breeze. It was all just a crazy blur and I didn't want to think about any of it.

Suddenly, Dan was the one to pull back, and the effort it took was obvious. A mild chill rose on my skin where his warm fingers had been cupping my neck and jawline, and I felt myself deflate a little in the absence of the heat he generated.

"Jesus," he whispered. He was looking at me as though he was as shocked by the intensity of our chemistry as I was.

"I know." I stared into his face, suddenly fearful I might see some trace of regret there. But there wasn't any, and it buoyed me. "I think it was all that talk about dinoflagellates."

Dan blinked once, and then again.

Then he burst out with a laugh, running a hand through his thick, disorderly hair. "They are *undeniably* sexy."

"That's all I'm saying."

He studied me for a moment, still smiling, until his eyes curved into that look of affectionate amusement. "Have dinner with me tomorrow."

It wasn't really a question, but there wasn't much question I would say yes. "We can go out or I can cook. Your choice."

"You cook?"

"Let's find out tomorrow."

§

It was late and I was definitely shivering, though as much from nerves as from the night. We collected my bag from the valet and Dan walked me back to the outdoor lot where my car was parked, very close to his own. Even in the dimly lit space, I could see that his 4Runner was in pristine condition. I had a momentary pang of embarrassment that, by comparison, my car looked like it was from the Dark Ages. He eyed it too, for several seconds.

"Text me when you get home." His gaze was unwavering. "Don't forget, okay?"

"Okay."

He gathered me close, murmuring against my lips, "I had a really nice night with you."

"Me too." Honestly it didn't feel real. I was inches away from the handsomest man I had ever seen in my life, and it still didn't feel real. He bent to kiss me lightly again.

"See you tomorrow, sweetness."

"Sweetness?"

A crooked smile grew on his face as he stared down into mine. "That puts you in excellent company, you know; Walter Payton was called sweetness, for different reasons of course."

"A football player?"

He laughed. "Not just *any* football player—arguably the greatest running back in the history of the NFL."

Now I laughed. "You're such a man."

He lifted his hand from my hip to brush a mass of wind-swept hair back behind my shoulder. A look of genuine affection replaced the humor.

"And you're one of the nicest people I've ever known. You make me feel happy every time I'm with you. That's why I called you that, but I won't if you don't like it."

His frank simplicity stole my breath. Men often referred to women *baby* or *beautiful*, but that wasn't what this was. It wasn't about how I looked; it was about how I made him feel when we were together.

Happy. How great was that?

I answered him a little thickly, feeling genuinely happy too. "Coming from you, I like it."

# Chapter 7

## Sarah

"So you like him?"

Selene and I were lying on my bed on Saturday morning, catching up on the last couple of days.

Taking a deep breath, I admitted, "I do. He's pretty hard not to like."

"Well, if I had had a science teacher who looked like that, I might have chosen a very different career path."

I laughed. "I know. And you'd expect a guy like that to be an asshole or a player, but he doesn't seem to be, unless I'm just reading him wrong."

Selene couldn't offer any opinion, having only ever met him in passing, but she seemed to sense a bit of hesitation on my part. She knew my history with both types.

"And he obviously likes *you*," she said encouragingly.

"I think so. I hope so."

"A summer romance with an older man could be *hot*. And it's about time you got out there again. But tell him this for me—"

I already knew what was coming. I started to protest, but she held her hand up to silence me.

"Tell him if he pulls any shit with you, I will personally put his balls in a specimen jar."

"I'm sure he'll appreciate your newfound interest in science."

Selene smiled. "Okay then, if you're finally going on a hot date, we need to find you something absolutely irresistible to wear. And I don't think we'll find it in there." She motioned to my closet, which *was* a bit of a wasteland for fashion.

By contrast, Selene's closet housed enough clothing for a crowd of women. For our entire friendship, she had insisted on dressing me up for special occasions. I stopped arguing about it long ago; it just wasn't worth the effort.

Selene's family had a lot of money. They rented her a two-bedroom apartment near campus so there was room for them to stay when they visited. But when my relationship with my ex, John, went south, and I needed to move out in a hurry, she wouldn't hear of my going anywhere but her place. She said her parents preferred staying at a hotel anyway. It was lucky for me; I was literally homeless.

Selene emerged from her walk-in carrying three options: One dress so short I wasn't a hundred percent certain it was a dress; one blouse/skirt combo that would be stunning on her lithe figure, but on my more curvy body would look like something out of Maxim; and a third option I thought was perfect. It was a red, slim-fitting halter-style dress that showed enough leg to be sexy, but didn't come off as slutty, and highlighted my C-cups without side boob or excessive cleavage. With my summer tan, the color was very flattering. I loved it. She paired the dress with iridescent strappy heels, and gold and diamond drop earrings.

"I'm not borrowing the earrings." They looked way too expensive, and something I'd never be able to afford to replace if I lost one.

"Bullshit, they're costume. And they make the outfit."

I didn't believe they were costume. But they did make the outfit.

"I'm thinking hair down, smoky eyes and a soft nude shade on your lips. Oh, and we'll tuck these into your purse, just in case." She held up a couple of condoms, and wiggled her eyebrows, laughing at my blush.

"And no schoolmarm underwear," she called after me as I headed off to the shower.

# Chapter 8

## Sarah

Dan offered to pick me up, but I preferred to meet him at his house. The neighborhood he lived in was nice, but not overly affluent as much of Palo Alto can be. Trees lined the street on both sides, creating a canopy effect that was beautiful and quaint. Each house was well kept and, as expected, Dan's was no exception.

It was a beige ranch-style home with a stacked-stone façade and wide front steps. It was welcoming, and he clearly took pride in its appearance.

Before I reached the beautiful dark wood front door, it swung open and Dan appeared in the entrance. He was casually stunning in a crisp white dress shirt, untucked over dark jeans and that smile that threw me a little off-balance every single time.

"You look unbelievable," he said, pulling me to him and murmuring the words against my lips.

I was still getting used to the idea that this was happening between us, and still coming to realize how much I liked that it was. I'd never in my life had a man make me feel so appreciated. It wasn't that I hadn't had other men give me compliments, but somehow, it was different with Dan. With him, it was all in his eyes—not in anything he said or needed to say.

As he kissed me on the front stoop, I felt a heavy weight settle on my foot. I looked down to find the business end of a bulldog now seated there, while his toothy, flat face smiled up in my direction.

"And this is Ralphie." Dan sighed in a playful apology. "He's a bit of a Lothario. I'd tell you to ignore him but he'd never allow it."

Ralphie was even cuter in person. When I bent to scratch him on his head, he swung his rump around and covered my ankles in eager kisses.

"Ralphie, enough." Dan took my hand to bring me inside. Ralphie remained enthusiastically in tow.

The floor plan of the house was open and bright, and I was astonished by the extensive millwork in every room—thick, beautiful crown and base moldings painted a bright white, an ornate mantelpiece surrounding the living room fireplace, and elaborate woodworking around every door and window.

Everywhere in view, the floors were dark wood, and the walls were a warm coffee color. The living room had windows that were almost floor-to-ceiling, bathing the room in natural light. Centered in the space was a large suede sofa with two coordinating armchairs.

Dan showed me around, pointing out various details and things he was particularly proud of.

"How long have you owned it?"

"About ten years. I bought it with some inheritance right after I finished my master's. And then renovated it for about two years."

"You did all this yourself?"

"I didn't do the plumbing or electrical, but pretty much everything else." There was pride in his voice, though he downplayed it.

"And you knew how to do all this?"

"Not at all," he admitted. "At least, not when I started. I read a bunch of stuff, took some classes, made lots of mistakes, initially. But I liked it and I wasn't in a rush to finish. It turned out pretty well."

No, that was an understatement. The gourmet kitchen we were

standing in was stunning. And clearly not just for show. He did cook. And whatever he was cooking at the moment smelled delicious. "I'm so impressed."

"Let me show you the best part."

We stepped through the door onto a used brick patio, complete with a built-in barbecue, and tons of comfortable seating. But the star of the show was the lush landscape. There were huge Japanese maple trees that looked like they'd been there for decades, and shrubs in a dozen or more varieties—most I wouldn't be able to identify, except several hydrangea bushes, crammed with flowers. There were roses and lilies and loads of potted plants scattered around. It was like stepping into an oasis. I loved the house, but if I lived here, I wasn't sure I'd ever leave the yard.

"It's nice, isn't it?"

"Dan, it's gorgeous. How on earth do you have time to maintain this?"

"I don't do all of it myself. I wish I could but . . ." He let the thought trail off as he surveyed the yard. "My mom was the serious gardener in our family," he told me after several beats. "I always thought she would have felt right at home here."

Anyone who cared to notice would be able to hear the dull ache that lay beneath those words. But only someone who'd been through a tragic loss like his or mine would be able to recognize the lingering feelings of betrayal there too. They were always present, buried deep for people like us who'd discovered at an early age that the universe had no sense of fairness or justice, and no sense of obligation to grant what we thought we were promised—our innocence, maybe; the idea that if you did right, the world would do right by you. We'd both moved on from that, but I wasn't sure it was something you ever fully got over it. I hadn't.

Hearing in his voice what I'd felt so many times, I wanted to reach out and touch him—to offer some sort of acknowledgement or understanding. But my hesitation cost me the opportunity.

"Shall we cook?" he asked. The ache I'd recognized was gone now, replaced by a natural exuberance that only deepened my respect for the man behind the smile.

§

"What are you making?"

Dan poured two glasses of wine and pushed one in my direction. "You mean we?"

"Okay, what are *we* making?"

"Pasta from scratch. I've taken the liberty of making the sauce already. Come try it."

He lifted the lid to a pot, and dipped a spoon inside. Raising it to his lips, he blew gently and then offered it. But even as I tasted, I couldn't quite tear my eyes away from those beautiful lips. I nearly shuddered with the memory of what he could do with them.

"What?" he asked me, narrowing his eyes.

"What, what?" I answered as if I didn't know exactly what he meant.

"Don't look at me like that right now," he said with a wry grin. "Or we're going to end up ordering pizza for dinner at midnight."

Honestly, in my current state, I'd have been perfectly happy with a fistful of crackers if it meant we could get back to some kissing. None of that sounded bad to me.

"Here," he said, handing me a bowl. "You can work on the salad while I start the dough for the pasta. Grab whatever ingredients you like out of the fridge."

Even his refrigerator was unreal—stocked so full it was disorienting. He was just one person, but there was enough food in here to feed an army.

I was genuinely feeling like a massive underachiever at this point. I ate cereal more often than I cared to admit, and my fridge was so sparsely stocked that even if I got a wild hair to cook, scrambled eggs would probably be the most extravagant meal I could pull together on a moment's notice.

But Dan seemed very much at ease in the kitchen, like cooking was something he did often.

And somehow seeing him here, in his element, so many things made sense about him that didn't before.

I'd always thought of him as a stereotypical bachelor, but now I thought that assessment was wrong. He was someone who'd lost his home base, just like me, and had done everything possible to get it back. To find his center and to create a new home for himself under these circumstances he never chose.

In that light, watching him pull flour and salt from a well-stocked cupboard looked very different. And I understood what all of it meant—the renovations and the cooking and the garden filled with flowers. He had rebuilt. In the best way he knew how.

"Do you cook?" He glanced up from measuring flour into a bowl as I was setting some lettuce and a tomato on the counter.

"I used to do most of cooking for me and my brother, but his tastes were pretty limited. Since I've been at school, most of my cooking involves the barbecue. I do bake sometimes, though."

"Key lime pie?" he asked with apparent hopefulness.

"Yes. You like key lime pie?"

He nodded eagerly. "You can make it for me when I come to dinner at your place."

§

Together we mixed the ingredients for the dough and kneaded it thoroughly. When it was ready, we fed it again and again through the pasta maker until we finally had long, thin pieces of fettuccini. The kitchen was a mess by then—flour was everywhere. But Dan didn't care. Mr. Science was all about the experiment.

We threw the pasta into boiling water, watching its progress closely.

"You know how to check if it's done?" he asked me.

I shook my head. "I usually just eat one."

"No," he responded, as if it was the most obvious thing in the world. "You lay a piece across your nose. If it contours to your face, it's ready."

"What are you talking about?"

"How you check to see if fettuccini is ready." He should've just added *duh*, because it was right there in his voice anyway.

And this was where I got confused. I felt like maybe I missed part of this conversation.

"No one does that."

"Of course they do."

He removed a piece of fettuccini from the pot, blew on it, and began to drape it across my face before I could even stop him.

I was so stunned; I didn't know what to do.

So I just stood there.

With pasta on my *face*.

"Okay, give it just a sec," he said, and casually pulled the cell phone from his pocket. But the pasta on my nose was already getting cold. And it was kind of dripping. Was he setting a timer? Was that required? *What the fuck?*

Then he took my picture.

"Oh. My. God. You just totally *messed* with me, didn't you?" I demanded, as he went one hundred percent to pieces, right there on the spot. His whole body was shaking with laughter as I pulled the pasta from my nose and pinged him with it.

Oh, it was done, all right!

"Explain yourself, fiend!" I insisted, fists at my hips.

"I had to," that rat bastard wheezed, now clutching his sides in hilarity. "It was just too tempting. And I'm weak."

"You are no gentleman, Daniel Moore." But before I could help myself, I lost it too. He was the most fun I'd ever had.

§

Dinner was fantastic.

In spite of his shenanigans, the pasta was cooked perfectly al dente, and the sauce was outstanding. He paired the meal with my salad, crusty bread for dipping in the sauce, and a phenomenal red wine blend.

We talked easily throughout the meal about his love of coaching middle school basketball, the league he still played in, and projects he wanted to do around the house. I told him about my passion for music and my father's insistence (happily) that I took piano lessons from the time I was five. He watched me intently as I spoke, often reaching out in affectionate little gestures to let me know he was interested in everything. I felt contented in a way I hadn't in a long time.

§

When dinner was over, I rose to clear the dishes.

"Don't. I'll do them later."

"Let me just rinse things a bit for you."

I suspected he knew by now I could be a little stubborn, so rather than argue, he joined me at the sink. I had the sponge in my hand, and was rinsing a dish when it accidentally slipped, and a little water splashed his face.

"Sorry," I told him. But I was doing a poor job of containing my smile, and it was obvious I wasn't *that* sorry. He deserved it for his earlier crimes.

But then he dipped a finger in the running water, and flicked it squarely back at me.

"Hey! Mine was an accident—yours was way out of line."

"Mine was an accident too."

"Sure it was."

He was practically bursting with a mischievous grin, which inspired something very similar in me. In a spontaneous genius-turned-maybe-not-so-genius idea, I lifted the sponge in an attempt to wipe his face with it. But he foresaw this plan and grabbed me around my waist, taking the wrist holding the sponge and raising it high over my head. He was laughing, but his grip was still like iron; there was no way I could break free. I tried, but he bent me backward so the top half of my body was practically horizontal, with his hovering just above. By then, I was completely at his mercy. There was really no contest here—he had at least five inches, and a significant strength advantage over me.

His next move was to force the sponge in my hand closer and closer to my own face. I saw it coming, and grunted loudly in a futile attempt to halt its progress. The problem was that I was laughing hard too, and I couldn't maintain my position.

By now, his eyes were bright green and roguish—sexy as all hell, if I were being honest—and, in a flash, I devised a new strategy.

This one was absolutely brilliant.

*Or* it may have been incredibly naive.

Reaching my free hand up, I wrapped it around the back of his neck. A kiss.

That was my plan. A kiss to distract him. A kiss to regain my advantage. After that . . . well, I had no plan for after that.

I suppose I shouldn't have been surprised by how willingly he came—he offered no resistance at all. He was smiling just before our lips met, but the moment they did, that kiss was like a match to a pile of straw—fire. It was like everything pent up or unspoken between us suddenly found an opening.

The entire vibe in the room went from playful to scorching in a matter of seconds.

He dropped my wrist, and threaded his free hand into my hair, kissing me back desperately. I immediately dropped the sponge, dimly registering that it hit the floor somewhere in our vicinity. Every nerve ending in my body was now acutely attuned to the heat of his proximity, and to each point of contact between us. Everything else fell away—it was just the curve of my chest, my lower back, my pelvic bone, one thigh, our eager mouths.

I lost all capacity to think, instead I blindly focused on the wild, heady feel of his teeth on my jaw and neck.

He pulled me upright and crowded me against the counter. I could feel the lust radiating from his body. I could feel my own, nearly out of control.

Who was this girl I was with him?

My hands found the hem of his shirt, and I pushed them up underneath, desperate to finally touch the warmth of his bare skin.

And, yes, the feel of him was unreal. Every muscle in his chest and stomach was hard and taught, wrapped in the silky texture of his skin. I could trace the definition in his sculpted torso, and every ridge of his abdomen.

Each hungry sound he made slid into my mouth, and I savored them all, feeding on his raw desire.

As I consumed him hungrily, one of his hands moved from my waist up the side of my body to my breast, murmuring how perfect it felt in his hand.

Every single thing about this man turned me on, and tonight was a little gift I was going to give myself. If there were consequences, I'd think about them tomorrow.

Right now, I just needed to see him.

As though I was someone else entirely, my hands moved impatiently to the buttons of his shirt, fumbling and pulling in frustration. I finally understood why, in the movies, people tore the buttons off clothes. I, myself, was only a few desperate moments from scattering his across the kitchen floor.

He was much more successful, reaching for the zipper on my dress, and tugging it down in a quick, fluid motion. Then, he pushed it off my shoulders, and onto the floor in a puddle. I was wearing nothing but a strapless black bra, matching panties, and heels. I couldn't even imagine the expression on my face.

His breath caught as he took in my appearance, his eyes making a meal of me. That look alone made me feel more desirable, more feminine, than any words ever spoken.

He reached for me again, his hands cupping my face, and he took me in an ardent kiss. I was grateful that he angled his torso away just a bit in order to ease my progress with his shirt. But it was no use. My fine motor skills had deserted me. Finally, we both gave up and he yanked the shirt off over his head.

*Good. God.*

He was magnificent. But there was little time to appreciate as our mouths crashed together in a hot, desperate kiss.

If he wanted to have me right here in the kitchen, I would have let him. No question. Instead, he stopped abruptly, both of us panting.

He had one hand cupping my face, and the other holding my hip. His eyes were wide and clear, and when they met mine, my heart jerked hard in my chest. I couldn't look away.

"Yes or no, Sarah?"

My brain was so scattered, I didn't immediately understand what he was asking. I hesitated for a moment.

The clasp of his hand tightened on my hip and he repeated, "Yes or no?"

"Yes." The word was barely spoken. More of just a whisper. It could have just been a thought. But it was the best decision I'd ever made in my life.

He nodded slightly, seeming to understand.

Still, he continued to search my face, I think looking for any hint of doubt. There was none. That, I knew for sure.

# Chapter 9

**Sarah**

Dan lifted me from where I stood and carried me down the hall to his bedroom. There, he stood me on my feet, and crouched to remove my shoes.

"Jesus, I want you," he breathed. "I don't think I've ever wanted anyone this much."

I knew the feeling.

I couldn't allow myself to think about what was happening here, who I was with, or what happened next. Those thoughts were the enemy of my abandon. Pushing them farther away, I let him undress me, and then guided me down onto the mattress. My heart was hammering painfully in my chest, keeping pace with my shallow, rapid breaths.

Meeting my heated gaze, he removed his jeans and the look on his face mirrored mine: hungry and impatient.

Then his mouth covered me in exactly the place where my need for him was most acute.

I exhaled in a long, slow release.

I was lost. I couldn't watch him do that. I laid back and closed my eyes, swept away by the sensation of him, the realization of him. I could hardly think of anything other than where his mouth was, and how eager he seemed to want to give me pleasure. This man was no stranger to it. I'd never been with anyone so adept.

My whole body felt like it was on fire. A helpless cry tumbled from my lips as the warm, wet, velvet touch of his tongue silenced everything. I could *feel* it—feel it all—building in my belly so low and heavy, an aching ball rolling down my spine. My body clenched hard, and I didn't even need to open my eyes to know he was watching me come apart.

Then there was only quiet.

The bed shifted gently as he moved over me, pressing his wet mouth to mine. I could taste myself on his lips, and I breathed it in—enjoying it, as if this made him mine. At least for tonight.

His body was primal and demanding as he reached over to the bedside table and produced a condom. With a practiced ease I didn't want to think about, he rolled it on. But his hands shook a little with urgency and I was mesmerized by the sight, his neck and shoulders also straining with effort.

Then he settled again between my legs, wrapping a hand in my hair, and kissing my earlobe and neck. "Put me inside you," he whispered, and gave me another small kiss.

I pulled back just enough to examine his face. The message again was unmistakable: *Yes or no?* He was giving me the chance to change my mind. To stop here. To have no regrets. *Yes or no.*

I reached up, scouring my nails gently through his hair and he closed his eyes for a moment, groaning his pleasure. He looked nearly helpless with it.

The light burned in his eyes when he opened them again; he was primed, his body tight with anticipation, and absolutely glorious. Very slowly, I guided him inside.

"Holy fuck," he gasped. "It's never felt like this."

I might have agreed but I couldn't say a word—too afraid, I think, of what agreement might mean.

He watched every reaction cross my face, as if we were both discovering that my body had been designed exclusively for him.

"Tell me if this is okay. I want it to be perfect for you."

He was holding his weight on his arms and he leaned in, taking my mouth again with his. My entire world was reduced to the place where we joined, where the warm skin of his hips brushed against mine. I ran my hands over his back, feeling the hard bunching of his muscles as he thrust, over and over.

One of his hands slipped under my hip and lifted it, changing the angle. The result was breathtaking. There could be no more talking, only small thrusts that grew faster and harder. The space between us was filled with the quiet sounds of praise and urging. His teeth pressed to into my shoulder and I gripped his arms to anchor myself, fearing I might fall somewhere dangerous—somewhere new, where neither humor nor wit could save me.

"Sarah," he gasped, squeezing his eyes shut. And for several perfect seconds, his movements were fast and urgent, until he felt me come apart again, and then they grew jagged. He came with a low groan, fingers clutching me tightly.

Finally, he collapsed over me, with his lips planted gently against my neck.

"My god, Sarah," he said on a breath. "You wreck me."

He was still inside me when I dragged my hand up into his damp hair and cradled his head at my shoulder.

There's a subtle helplessness to a man just after orgasm. No matter how formidable, for one small moment, lying in a woman's arms, he is entirely vulnerable. Mortal.

I kissed Dan's shoulder lightly, and without looking up, he wrapped his arms securely around me.

# Chapter 10

**Sarah**

Lying in Dan's bed, I felt very much at home.

It was a rare thing for me to feel like that in a man's bed, and I didn't know if it should make me happy or uneasy.

We faced each other on our sides, just talking about everything. The sheets were around our waists, revealing both our upper bodies, but nothing about it felt exposed or vulnerable.

He seemed to like to play with my hair as we talked, twisting small sections around his finger and stroking it gently. I wasn't sure he even realized he was doing it, but I liked the familiarity of his touch.

Periodically, he would lie back and look at the ceiling or at me while we talked. And then he would get excited about something and be back up on his elbow, gesturing with his free hand for emphasis. He was beautiful to watch, and not just because this was the first time I got to freely look at his perfectly toned chest and muscular arms. He was just so vibrant and surprisingly playful. I still couldn't quite reconcile that with my impressions of him from when we knew each other before.

He was excited to tell me about the non-profit consulting work he was doing for Project Learning, an organization that provided after school STEM programs in lower-income areas. The funding proposal he'd been helping to write was successful, and now they were moving into budgeting and designing curriculum. It was illuminating to see how much this work meant to him, and what he hoped to accomplish.

He asked me about my family, places I'd been and wanted to go. He wanted to know all about Stanford's holiday concert that I was performing in later this year. It was still about four months away, but well worth the many hours of practice it would require.

"Okay, here's an easy one: Tell me a nickname you had growing up," I asked him, running my fingers through the light dusting of hair on his chest. I couldn't really imagine him ever being teased; he was *that* guy who hit the lottery of life, and ended up with looks, brains and athletic ability.

"'Danny.' I grew up here, so a lot of people still call me that."

"That's not a nickname. Give me a real one."

He thought for a moment and then his face twisted into an amused frown. "If I tell you, you have to promise never to call me this."

"Okay, I promise."

"Ken."

"Ken?" I couldn't make the connection.

"Yeah," he said distastefully, "like the action figure."

It took a minute to register and when it did, I burst out laughing. "Ken isn't an action figure, Danny. He's a doll. A *Barbie* doll."

Dan looked at me for a moment, trying to maintain a stern face. But even he couldn't hold it. His expression dissolved into a giant reluctant grin.

"I hated that name. And thank you very much, by the way, for further insulting my manhood."

I was shaking nearly uncontrollably by then and was powerless to control myself. It was just too good.

"Oh yeah, laugh now," he said, "but I'm still friends with the people who used to call me that. Just wait till they get a load of you."

He lifted his eyebrows as if he had just made the best point of all time.

The implication was one I couldn't really argue. I *had* been called Barbie from time to time in my life, and I always hated it. Mattel can make Barbie a veterinarian or an astronaut or a brain surgeon for that matter, but when people think of Barbie, they only think of one thing: a blonde with big boobs.

Period.

But something about what he'd just said made me oddly happy. I hated being thought of as a Barbie, but the idea of being Barbie to his Ken was something I strangely didn't seem to mind. And the thought that this . . . whatever this was between us . . . could extend beyond this night, beyond this bed, and out into the bigger circle of our friends and acquaintances, made my heart swell in my chest. I had to shut the thought down. It felt too dangerous.

I looked away, needing distance—needing space to rein in my wayward imagination. I quietly changed the subject as I watched my fingertips skip over the taught muscles of his abdomen.

"What's your favorite food?"

"Your breasts."

"Breasts aren't food."

"I'm pretty sure I could live on your breasts alone," he insisted appreciatively. "Put a little key lime pie on there and *fuuuuck* . . ."

His eyes rolled back in mock ecstasy.

He could always make me laugh. But when I met his eyes again, the joke was dissipating, and there was real heat there. I felt it low in my belly too, an acute desire for this impossibly beautiful man.

He reached out and ran his finger across my collarbone, and down to the sensitive peak of my nipple, his hand cupping and palming my breast.

Then he moved closer, and I could feel him hard as stone between us again as he nipped at my earlobe.

"Hungry?" I whispered, breathless.

"Famished."

And just like that, the conversation was over.

§

I must have drifted off to sleep for I don't know how long. I awoke when I felt the bed shift, and had the immediate and embarrassing thought that perhaps Danny was ready for me to leave. Truthfully, I wasn't sure exactly what the protocol was here—it'd been a while since I dated anyone. Plus, everything with him was so new and unpredictable.

As though answering my thoughts, he wrapped his arm around me from behind, kissing my shoulder gently. "I have a surprise for you, if you can stay longer. But you have to get up for it."

I turned to face him and in the dimly lit room, his warm eyes looked almost golden. He stroked a thumb down my cheek, and looked at each of my features in succession as though he was memorizing them.

Then he rose from the bed, giving me my first full view of his body. It was a stunning achievement of fitness and beauty. His broad torso was cut within an ounce of his life, right down to the deep V at his groin. There wasn't one bit of excess flesh anywhere to be found— probably the result of a lifetime of healthy eating. His abs were perfectly defined, and his arms and legs were long and muscular. Even his ass was perfect.

He pulled on a pair of gray sweats and removed a green and navy plaid flannel shirt from the closet, laying it on the bed beside me.

With an impish grin he said, "If you have any trouble with the buttons, let me know."

"You know, it's not very gentlemanly to point out a woman's misadventures."

"You thought I was a *gentleman?*"

He approached the bed, leaning over to brace his hands on either side of my hips. His green eyes held mine in an outrageously sexual way, while his tongue peeked out to stroke his lower lip.

"If I haven't divested you of that notion yet, we are clearly not done here."

Well.

The role of Sarah was now being played by a barn owl.

Wide-eyed and blinking, I noted to myself that I was very much okay with not being done here.

He laughed at my expression, and then sat on the edge of the bed, tucking a strand of hair behind my ear.

"Use anything you like in the bathroom, and meet me in the living room in five minutes."

Then he smiled a big boyish smile, kissed my forehead, and walked out of the room.

I just watched him go.

Snuggling deeper into the soft white jersey sheets and pillowy gray comforter, I knew could get used to being here and that scared me. What I felt for him so quickly scared me that much more. The whole night felt dreamlike, and I wasn't ready for it to be over just yet.

I could hear him in the kitchen, so I put his shirt on and breathed in the familiar scent of his laundry detergent. The flannel was warm and comfy and I was swimming in it. I felt sexy.

But heading into the bathroom, I nearly gasped at the sight in the mirror. Wow—not even sexy for a barn owl! My hair was rioting all over my head, and my lips were red and swollen—clearly not my best look. I rooted around in his cabinets, finding a hairbrush, some toothpaste, and some ChapStick, and decided that was about as good as it was going to get.

When I walked in the living room, Danny was kneeling in front of the fireplace, lighting a fire. The soft light cast alluring shadows across his back.

He turned when he heard me, straightening to a stand, with a book of matches lightly in his grasp.

For just a second, he seemed to lose his words. "You look stunning right now." And everything about his expression told me he meant it.

"What have you got there?"

A good-sized cardboard box was sitting upside down on the coffee table, and on it, drawn in a black marker, was a picture of two stick figures holding hands. The girl, presumably me by the long hair, was sporting a triangle dress and giant bow on her head. The boy—I guessed that was Danny—was naked and sporting a giant erect penis.

Of course, he was.

"I can see you're an artist, as well."

"And clearly, photo realism is my specialty."

I smiled. "Is this my surprise?"

He nodded. "Lift it up. Carefully."

Under the box was a three-layer cake on a clear glass plate. The cake was covered in swirls of chocolate frosting, and decorated with those hard sugar letters, spelling out my name. I honestly didn't know what I was expecting, but it definitely wasn't this.

And something about it was so sweet that, embarrassingly, my eyes filled with tears.

Danny's face fell instantly. He came quickly to me, pulling me into his arms.

"I didn't mean to make you cry." He tucked my head just under his chin, and kissed my hair.

"I know," I told him wiping away a tear and laughing a little to dismiss the concern I saw in his face. "It's just that the letters are lavender. Did you know that's my favorite color?"

"You told me at The Cliffs, remember?" I didn't remember. But it would be just like him to make a note of something like that. Ever the observant scientist.

"It's beautiful."

"No, it looks pretty lame but wait until you taste it—it's my mom's recipe."

We sat on the floor in front of the fire with glasses of red wine, and he sliced us a large piece of the decadent cake to share.

It *was* delicious. Plus, I loved to watch his boyish pleasure in efficiently polishing off the majority of it single-handedly, then neatly scraping up the remaining frosting with the side of his fork.

We were sitting side by side against the couch. The way the firelight illuminated every curve of his upper body made him look like a work of art.

"Did you ever want to be anything else, before you became a teacher?"

"I considered astrophysics for a while. That would have been a great job. The universe is mind-blowing, don't you think?"

He turned to me more directly, leaning his head against his fist with an elbow on the couch.

"I do," I answered honestly. Though I'd never met anyone more taken by the miracle of it all than he was.

"If I could meet anyone today, it would be Neil DeGrasse Tyson. Can you imagine the conversations you could have with that guy? It might be embarrassing, though. I might go all fan-boy on him." He laughed at himself, and then leaned forward to toss another small log on the fire.

"So why didn't you become an astrophysicist?"

"I had a teacher once," he said simply, and for a moment I lost him to a memory. "A Spanish teacher in high school. He made me want to teach."

"A Spanish teacher made you want to teach biology?"

He laughed. "In a roundabout way, yes. I was a sophomore at the time, and it was just after midsemester finals. We'd gotten our AP chem tests back, and I actually failed mine. A legitimate F, mind you."

Danny was the smartest person I knew; it was hard to imagine him ever failing anything. And as if confirming this unspoken thought, he told me, "I'd never failed anything in my life and I freaked. I was a straight-A student, Sarah, so this was end-of-the-world stuff for me. Plus, I knew my dad would have my ass on a platter if he found out. And, you know, that was around the time when we were all starting to think about colleges and where we wanted to go, and I worked myself up into thinking I'd just blown any chances of getting in somewhere good."

"With one test?"

"You were a teenager once," he reminded me, and the glint in his eye suggested he *did* remember the sullen, college-obsessed teen I once was.

He picked up my hand, and held it in his lap, running his fingertips over the lines of my palm.

"Anyway, I walked around campus for a while, just reeling from the shock of it, and feeling like I was going to puke. But finally, I showed up to Spanish—really late, and still pretty distressed. And Señor Lindo—that was his name—he was this older guy, towards the end of his career, I think. He called me up to his desk, and asked me what was going on. Of course, I was embarrassed to tell him, but he insisted. And when I finished, he just looked at me for a moment, and then said in the most authoritative way that I had no reason to worry. He said he had a strong sense about me—a premonition, he called it—that I would go on in my life to do an amazing thing."

"What was the amazing thing?"

"Point being—he wouldn't tell me. He said he didn't want to influence my path by saying, and he knew I'd find it on my own. But he asked me to keep in touch after I graduated because he couldn't wait to see how my life turned out."

Danny looked down, pausing from the story to brush a few stray ashes off of his sweatpants. When he glanced back up, the significance of the memory glowed in his face.

"Looking back on it, it sounds corny, right? But at sixteen, I thought it was true. And it made me feel so much better. All the sudden, the world wasn't ending, and I could imagine getting beyond this and going on to achieve something great. *He* gave me that.

"He could have been a dick about my being late. Or he could have ignored the state I was in and just went back to his lesson. But instead, he offered me exactly what I needed to hear—he helped me find some perspective on my failure. So, it didn't really matter if it was true or it wasn't—it was one of the kindest things anyone has ever done for me. And it made me want to have a career where I could have that sort of an impact too."

Danny shrugged the last thought off in his very modest way.

"That's a beautiful story." My voice felt a little thick. "Thank you for telling me."

He smiled. "Every so often I get to have one of those kinds of moments with a student. I imagine you have them too, in your line of work."

He looked at me in a way that told me he knew exactly why we both chose low-paying careers of little prestige. And it was one of the most intimate looks I had ever experienced. One of complete understanding.

"Kind of priceless, actually," I agreed.

A knowing smile curved his lips. Then he set the plate on the table, and pulled me with him onto the couch, settling me comfortably against his chest.

Taking my head in his hands, he very gently kissed my lips, whispering how happy I made him, and how good it felt to have me here. Those words, spoken in his raspy, soothing voice, filled me with unexpected pleasure. I snuggled into him, leaning my head against his fire-warmed shoulder, and breathed in his masculine scent.

It was as if we'd done this a thousand times—like something about him was so familiar I instinctively felt at home in his arms. I bent to kiss his chest, then again, and I felt his body react.

When I lifted my gaze, his eyes were focused on mine. In the firelight, they look almost golden again. He was so beautiful like this, so flesh and blood.

"You're perfection," he murmured, before running his hand reverently from the curve of my waist up to the column of my neck, watching its slow progression.

We laid together there, our limbs tangled, for a long time, neither of us wanting to break the magic of the moment.

Finally he spoke. "Stay with me tonight."

I was so content I could barely answer, but I reveled in the deep timbre of his voice, and the odd feeling of belonging in his arms.

§

I awoke the next morning alone in Danny's bed, which was warm and comfortable; the pillows smelled like him. Stretching muscles that were sore from the previous night's exertions, I found myself smiling as I replayed the evening in my head.

It was an incredible night. But now what? I had no idea if this was just a rebound thing for him, or maybe he was dating lots of other women right now. We hadn't exactly had *that* talk, but I was sure a guy like him wasn't hard up for dates. The thought made me feel a little self-conscious, and I had to remind myself that I was a modern woman, as capable of dating casually as the next person—even if, at that moment, I wasn't feeling particularly casual about him.

I smelled breakfast cooking and heard dishes being done, so I took a quick shower and freshened up before joining him. By the time I wandered into the kitchen wearing another of his shirts I'd pulled from the closet, he was sitting at the breakfast bar drinking coffee.

"There you are. You were snoring so loudly, I thought you might sleep till next week."

"Ungallant, sir!"

He grinned widely, standing to take me into his arms, and kissed me soundly before I could continue my protest. He was in his sweats again, with just a white T-shirt, and he looked sleep rumpled and yummy.

"Something smells great." I was very hungry all the sudden, and very eager to leave the topic of my snoring behind.

"I'll fix you a plate."

He returned to the bar with cheesy eggs, toast, fresh strawberries and turkey bacon. I raised an eyebrow at that one.

"Okay, I guess it's not *so* terrible," he said begrudgingly.

Sitting down at the bar, I realized I was a little sore. He noticed and his face changed.

"Was what we did . . . too much?"

"No, last night was really nice."

"It was really nice for me too." He reached his hand out to push a strand of hair from my face, as he seemed to like to do. "When can I see you again?"

His tone erased any fears I had that this was just a one-night stand. I didn't know what to call it, but I was pretty sure neither of us was ready to move on just yet.

"Wednesday? Do you want to come to my place for dinner?"

"Love to."

# Chapter 11

## Danny

I was early.

I debated whether to go to the door fifteen minutes ahead of schedule, or sit in my car like a douche and kill time.

Most women I knew hated when a man showed up early for a date, as much as they hated when he was late. Zero margin of error here. So, weighing my options, I decided to respond to a few emails on my cell, and then checked my social media.

Ten minutes early now. I couldn't wait to see her.

Sarah's apartment building was exactly what you'd think off-campus housing would look like. The complex was better than most but, clearly, no one lived here for too long, or put too much effort into making the outside nice.

I was so far beyond that point in my life that I had a moment of weirdness about dating a college student. When she was at my house, everything felt natural. But now, I wondered if being around framed posters and temporary furniture would make me feel like a relic.

I didn't want to think about it. Instead, I grabbed the flowers and the wine, and headed up.

At the sound of the doorbell, Sarah answered, beautiful as always, but looking a little flustered. In my head, I cringed at the impatience that had brought me to her doorstep early.

"I'm sorry." I made a face. "I kind of have a thing about punctuality. Sometimes I overachieve it."

She laughed. "Why doesn't that surprise me?"

Inside, her place was small with standard finishes, but everything was clean and neat. And surprisingly, it didn't have a typical college-apartment feel. The whole place was pretty stylish, actually.

"Maybe I'll give you the tour later," she said over her shoulder as she headed off to find a vase while I opened the wine.

Just then I heard Selene call from a back room. "When is the sex god getting here?"

Sarah emerged with a vase, looking suspiciously pink in the cheeks. I smiled at her, ready to give her shit for a reputation that apparently preceded me, but before I could get a word out, she raised her eyebrows, halting me in my tracks.

"She's not talking about you. I have another sex god coming over later."

I laughed. "*Another* being the operative word."

I decided to keep her company while she started the barbecue. She'd prepared a feast of marinated steak and vegetables. We walked down the cement steps into a small backyard, where an elderly looking grill was placed in the corner. I picked up the tongs and began rearranging the coals for better heat distribution.

"What are you doing?"

"Just helping get things ready for the meat," I responded naturally.

I'd only really known Sarah for a few months, but I was quickly realizing she was pretty strong-minded. And with that whole hyphen episode painfully fresh in my mind, I sensed perhaps I was entering dangerous territory here. And yet, god knows why, I pressed on.

"What I've learned is that if you arrange the coals like this, they cook the meat more evenly."

This didn't seem to go over particularly well, and the silence that greeted me was not reassuring. But I waited.

And waited.

Finally: "You've learned that from experience." Not really asked as a question.

"Yes."

"Experience as a teacher? Or a doctoral candidate, perhaps?"

I fought hard to maintain a straight face but it was a losing battle. Everything she did made me smile, even when she was teasing me mercilessly, which she often did. Being around her was *fun*. There was no way to hide it.

"No, smart-ass," I told her. "Not from my experience as a teacher *or* a doctoral candidate. From my experience as a barbecue-loving sex god who can make a woman come with just his giant roasted zucchini."

We stared at each other for a long, pregnant pause, but she cracked first, a smile splitting her gorgeous, perfect face.

"No one messes with my barbecue, understand?" She pointed her spatula at me for extra emphasis.

"Can I spank you with that later?"

My answer came in the form of a hard whack to the ass. With the spatula.

God help me, I was in love.

§

Selene left the apartment shortly after dinner to meet up with her boyfriend Kevin, presumably to give Sarah and me some privacy. I offered to do dishes, but she wouldn't have it. With time on my hands, I wandered around a little on my own.

I noticed what I thought was Sarah's bedroom down the hallway on the left. She'd offered to give me a tour later; I didn't think she'd mind if I took a quick look. The room was sparse, with just a bed, a desk, and some milk crates for storing books. What caught my attention was the red dress hanging on her open closet door. I thought back to the other night; she looked unbelievable in that dress.

But glancing into the closet, I was surprised to see that she owned very little clothing. In fact, she may have had the smallest wardrobe I'd ever seen for a woman. She always looked great to me, but it dawned on me as I processed the contents of her room, as well as the memory of that god-awful car, that she had *no* money. There were no extra things in this room. Just the basics.

I'd never really thought about it but, obviously, this room didn't merely reflect a student's budget; this was a *poor* student's budget. I hurt a little for her, though I knew she'd hate that.

Suddenly, several things happened at once. Glancing into the full-length mirror that hung from the inside of the open closet door, my eye snagged on a photograph, which was reflected from the opposite wall. I turned around to see it at the very same time I heard dishes drop into the kitchen sink.

Sarah, probably realizing where I'd wandered off to, came bursting through the doorway.

The photograph on the wall was mine—the one of the Golden Gate Bridge.

I couldn't make sense of that. Not at all. I stared at it for a long time, all the while with an awareness that Sarah was nervously watching me.

Finally, I turned to her. "How do you have that?"

Her face took on a pained expression before answering. "I bought it."

"When? How?"

"I bought it from Charlie's."

"But Charlie told me my photographs were sold to an Asian woman and a guy."

"The guy is a friend of mine. I called him after I ran into you that day. I'm sorry. I should have told you." She looked down at her hands, which appeared to be shaking. "But I bought it before we became . . . whatever. And, the fact is, when I bought it, I could never have imagined a scenario in which you would ever be standing here in my room."

My brain was on overload. I closed my eyes, and I don't know why, but the first thing to come out of my mouth was, "You paid three hundred dollars for this."

"Yes."

I was stunned. "If I knew you liked it that much, I'd have just given it to you."

A proud and defiant expression crossed her face. "If you knew how much I liked it, you could have charged me more."

I stared at her. None of this made sense to me. She seemed to have *no money*. Why would she do that?

As if I had spoken this out loud, Sarah went on, her voice shaky and tight, "I know you probably think I'm a nut job but I'm not. It's just that your photograph reminds me of how much progress I've made personally over the past five years, and also that the work I'm doing on myself isn't finished. And it's special to me because I remember a day when I came back to your class after school, and you were looking at this photo. You told me about your parents, and I knew you knew about my dad.

"I felt so alone during that time in my life. And it was comforting to me that someone else understood what I was going through and, even more, had managed to survive it. Knowing your story gave me the reassurance that my life would go on too. And it did. I'm sure you don't remember that day, but I never forgot it."

No, she was wrong.

I did remember. I'd been conflicted about hanging the image in my classroom because it was so bittersweet for me. The day I took that photo was the last day I ever saw my parents. Sarah had walked in in the midst of my decision and complimented the image, telling me as an afterthought that her father had been an avid photographer. I could see that referring to him in the past tense was still jarring for her, and maybe that's what prompted me to tell her my story. It was something I never did with anyone, let alone a student. But there was something in her face, a kinship of human experience I guess I'd wanted to acknowledge.

Maybe I told her about my parents that day because I wanted to let her know that I understood what she'd been through. Or maybe I told her because there was a part of me, still raw from my own loss, that knew she would understand what I'd been through.

And I remembered her reaction. It wasn't pity or discomfort. It wasn't the reaction people like us usually got when others learned our stories.

It was simple kindness.

It was empathy.

All at once, I understood why it had taken no effort at all to fall for her these past weeks, why I'd felt so at ease in her company. There were things she inherently knew about me without my having to say them, things she just understood because of our common experiences—the same things I'd had so much trouble through the years expressing to other people. And maybe the same was true for her.

"Danny, I—" she started. But I didn't need her to explain. Just the opposite—I wanted her to know I understood everything.

I went to her, pressed her against the wall, and kissed her with every ounce of emotion coursing through me. It was a confusing jumble of them, for sure. But I knew beyond all doubt there was no one else I'd rather entrust that photograph to than her—that photograph that reminded us both in different ways of everything we'd lost and all we had survived.

"You make me so happy," I whispered against her lips.

That statement nowhere near covered everything I wanted to say to her, and yet, it was the absolute truth. And more than anything else, that's what I needed her to know.

"Danny . . ." Her voice was so full of the very same emotions coursing through me. I shared that overwhelming need to be connected, body and soul. I pulled her skirt up and slid her underwear down her legs. In an instant, my jeans were open, cock out, and I was rolling on a condom from my pocket. I lifted her from where she stood against the wall, and she wrapped her legs around me.

With no real foreplay, I buried myself inside her and instantly felt a profound sense of relief.

*Mine* that feeling said.

Sarah moaned and clutched me tighter. It was all the reassurance I needed. I started to move, dragging my teeth along on her neck.

There was no place for words here. And no words equal to the task of expressing what our bodies already knew.

She ran her hands into my hair, pulling my head back hard. Then she pressed her lips to my throat, running her tongue over my Adam's apple, and across my jaw. It felt wild and unrestrained, and I loved it.

Honestly, the whole thing felt that way. I was thrusting against her so hard I could hear things falling off her desk. But I couldn't help myself. Sarah provoked some of the most overpowering emotions in me. When I was with her, I felt like I wanted to gorge myself in her—like I just wanted everything she would give me. Not just sex, I wanted it all. Every part of her.

The whole act took no time at all. Within minutes, we were both coming hard and I thought I might pass out.

I pushed her back flush against the wall for fear I'd drop her, and here we stayed, collecting ourselves, me still inside her. Her cheek was against my cheek and she smelled so good, like strawberries. Like mine.

I felt her shudder and eased her feet to the floor. But I wasn't ready to let her go just yet. Resting my hands on her hips, I leaned my forehead to hers. Neither of us said a word for the longest time, still processing a mess of wildly erratic thoughts.

This didn't look like making love, but it wasn't just fucking either. My feelings for Sarah were real, and looking into her eyes, I could see hers were real too.

I pushed all the hair away from her face with both of my hands and kissed her as softly as I could. I poured everything I wasn't good at saying into that breath of a kiss, and hoped she understood the enormity of its meaning.

Then with great care, I lifted her in my arms and carried her to bed.

§

Under her well-worn light blue comforter, we lay face to face, just digesting all of this and enjoying the pleasure of each other's touch.

As I took in her every feature, it occurred to me that this gentle creature could crush me. She had my heart in her inexperienced hands, and she was so young she might not understand how easy it would be for her to break it.

I didn't know exactly where this could go, but I knew I didn't want to be just some casual fling for her, which was so ironic considering that when I was twenty-two, every woman in my life was a casual fling. It was all about having these crazy life experiences.

But now, I found myself wanting more, and I knew I'd be devastated if it turned out that, for her, *I* was that crazy life experience. What if *I* was the thing she would someday laugh about with her friends—that time she was banging her former high school science teacher.

I realized, for better or for worse, I needed to clarify where things stood between us. My feelings for her were beginning to spiral out of control, and yet we had no defined understanding of what we were to each other. This was all new ground for me, and it felt far too precarious.

"Be with me, Sarah," I asked her. "Only me."

It gave me no comfort that she was some seconds in answering, and all the while she looked conflicted. Finally, she lifted her hand to my face and traced my features with her fingertips. I leaned into her warm touch for reassurance that this discussion wasn't going to end with my heart in shambles.

She was searching my face for . . . something. "My exes have always told me I'm closed-off and solitary."

I studied her, realizing in a flash that here I was worrying she might not *want* a relationship, when all this time she was worrying she didn't have the capacity for one.

Relief flooded my system. "I don't care what they've said."

"They're not wrong, Danny. I'm not good at this."

She looked so unsure of herself, so unlike the woman I'd come to know. And that filled me with unexpected anger for all the pricks who came before me—all the assholes who had no idea what they'd found in her. She was incredible. I was in awe of her.

"You don't know you're not good at it," I told her adamantly. "You haven't been with me."

"Danny—"

"We make each other better. Everything's better now that we're together. Don't you feel it too?" I bore witness to her self-doubt, fueled by too many relationships gone bad. I knew very little of her history, but regardless of the details, I understood the sense of failure. I'd had my share of them too.

"Be with me," I implored her.

It was as if my certainty bolstered hers. Her expression altered into the sweetest smile I'd ever seen as she studied me in careful consideration. "Okay," she whispered, her smile now spreading broadly across her lovely features. That smile was my heart's summer.

I grinned back at her, so happy I felt a little juvenile. And then I leaned in, sealing my mouth over hers. We'd kissed so many times, but this kiss felt new. And in a way it was. Because now the girl I was kissing was officially mine.

# Chapter 12

**Sarah**

Danny pulled up in front of my apartment at exactly six o'clock on Friday evening. Through the window, I watched him get out of his car, dressed in work clothes and dark aviators. He looked like a movie star.

He strode up the front steps, carrying a white envelope in his hand. When I opened the door, he dipped me for a deep kiss and then handed me the envelope without a word.

"Test results?" I asked him, glancing inside.

"I got tested on Monday. I'm clean. Not that I thought I wasn't, but I wanted you to know."

I went to my desk drawer, and pulled out my own results. I'd been tested immediately after finding John with another woman, and considering the circumstances, I hadn't been nearly as confident about the results. But luckily for me, they were negative.

"These are mine. I haven't been with anyone but you since I had them done. And I'm on birth control."

"Well then," he beamed, busting out that supermodel smile. "I want to take you to dinner to celebrate."

"We just found out we can have sex without a condom and you want to go *out* to a restaurant to celebrate?"

His face fell. "Well, when you put it like that, it does sound pretty stupid. On the other hand," he said, reconsidering, "I'm starving, and I bet you have nothing to eat here but cereal."

"We could order in."

But Danny wrinkled his nose at that. "Let's go out and consider it foreplay. I may not let you out of bed for the rest of the weekend."

§

In hindsight, we should have stayed in.

We arrived at Paul Martin's, a very popular hot spot for happy hour. It was crowded and loud, but it had a celebratory atmosphere that fit our mood pretty well.

And Danny wasn't kidding about the foreplay.

Throughout the evening, we snuggled close together in a booth. He had one arm draped casually over the back behind me, while the other was not so innocently working its way up my bare thigh. Engrossed in his wicked expression, I didn't notice when someone stopped in front of our table.

"Sarah?"

I instantly snapped out of my haze. Or maybe not as instantly as I had hoped.

"It's me, Jennifer Malcolm."

"Oh, wow, Jennifer! I'm so sorry. I just wasn't expecting to see you. You look so great!"

Jennifer Malcolm had been in my graduating class at McKinley. We'd spent a lot of time together doing various sports, and became friendly as a result. She was always very outgoing and social, and I was pretty much the opposite. But she was nice; I liked her, though we didn't keep in touch after we graduated.

"So do you. It's so great to see you!"

It was just at that moment that she glanced at my date, and then glanced back again, this time giving him a longer, more thorough look.

"Oh, my god! Mr. Moore?" She practically yelled this. "I can't believe it's you. Wait—are you guys, like, *together?*"

It would be pretty obvious to anyone looking in our direction that Danny and I weren't exactly having a business dinner. We looked cozy and affectionate. Maybe overly so, but I didn't dwell on that.

"It's nice to see you, Jennifer. And please, call me Dan." His tone was calm and professional, eerily so, but he was white as a sheet.

"I *cannot* believe this. Well done, Sarah!"

I was actually nauseous at this point because I knew Dan was secretly freaking out. This whole thing was mortifying. I didn't think it could get any worse.

"Wait, have you two been together since *high school?*"

Turns out it could.

Both of us gasped, "NO!" Maybe he said, "God, no!"

But I didn't think Jennifer was listening. Suddenly, she produced her phone and started to take a picture of us.

"Here, lean in!"

"Jennifer, no," I pleaded, but it was no use. She had the camera focused and pointing.

Both Danny and I forced some sort of contorted expression that probably looked more like constipation than the bliss it was not five minutes ago. I had no interest in knowing what we looked like in that picture. I just wanted this to end.

Mercifully, the phone rang in her hand. "Oh, shoot, do you mind? I need to take this." She said a quick goodbye, promising to get in touch, and rushed off . . .

Leaving the two of us just sitting there.

Silent.

*Crap.*

Without a single word, Danny signaled the waiter for the check and handed him a credit card before the bill even arrived.

The second he signed, he grabbed my hand and practically dragged me from the booth. I was cursing my shoe selection all the way to the car.

Once inside, it was torturously quiet. We didn't even put on the radio. I wasn't sure what to do because I'd never seen him like this. He was brooding. His hands gripped the steering wheel like death, while he stared straight ahead. His breathing was shallow, and his jaw was tight, which made the idea of breaking into his thoughts a little intimidating. So I just sat there. Absolutely still.

My place was empty when we arrived, and I couldn't have been happier that Selene wasn't home to witness this awkward strain between us. Danny sat down on the couch and scrolled through his phone for a full minute. At last, he closed his eyes and rubbed his jawline. Still not a word.

I sat down carefully, near to him but not touching, and watched him out of my peripheral vision. Finally, I couldn't take it anymore.

"Are you okay?"

"No."

"Are you mad at me?"

Hesitation. "No." *Okay.*

I was totally confounded at this point, and at a loss to know how to handle this. How to handle *him*. I suddenly realized how little I knew of him.

"Tell me what's wrong," I whispered.

He turned to me in a gesture of profound frustration, then fired up his phone and opened Instagram.

Without any explanation, he handed it to me. There in his notifications was that awful picture of us with the caption "Sarah Kyle and Mr. Moore getting some serious sizzle on at Paul Martin's!"

We were both been tagged in the photo, and although Dan and

Jennifer didn't follow each other, I thought she and I probably did, so the picture was likely to get around some. Checking my account, those suspicions were confirmed.

Under the posting on my feed were thirty-two comments and counting:

*Like! Like! Like!*

*You go, girl!*

*Mr. Moore gets 'em young!*

*Look who's into science NOW!*

*Private lessons in biology? Sign me up!*

And the worst of it:

*I always knew he was a dog!*

"I'll ask her to take this down, and in the meantime we can untag ourselves."

"That doesn't mean it isn't out there."

"I know. But nobody takes this stuff seriously, anyway."

He wasn't listening. He dropped his head to his hands and grabbed fistfuls of hair. "*Dammit!* How could I have been so *fucking* stupid?"

"It's not your fault," I tried, though I wasn't sure *fault* was even the right word. But it didn't matter; nothing I said helped.

"I'm a professional. I can't have this shit out there."

"What are you talking about?"

"*This,*" he said again in frustration, and inadvertently knocked a pillow from the couch. "This is exactly the problem. Shit like this calls my judgment into question."

"Your *judgment*? You mean being seen with me is bad judgment?" I could hear my anger growing.

He rose to standing, irritation radiating off his body. One hand was on his hip and the other was running through his hair, causing it to stick up absurdly in all directions.

"Don't act like that. You know what I mean."

"No, I don't have a clue what you mean."

"This is what I worried about from the beginning with you."

"Wednesday night, you told me you wanted me to be your girlfriend. Did you just mean behind closed doors? Am I some dirty little secret?"

This conversation had somehow gone so awry that I was now joining him in this loss of composure.

"Of course not."

"Are you ashamed of me?"

"What? No! I just . . . I can't have this." But he knew how that sounded. He knew it. That's why the next thing to come out of his mouth was a curse.

"You are an ass," I spit out. "Who *cares* what people say or think? We know we haven't done anything wrong. Or at least I do."

Sharp eyes narrowed in reproach. "You can't really be that naive."

That was the final straw. There were a lot of things that could be said about me, but naive wasn't one of them. Still, it made me feel young and stupid—made me question our dynamic.

"Get out."

I marched to my room and slammed the door.

But it was weird; the minute it closed, the adrenaline from our first real argument began to recede. I was gripped with sudden remorse.

I held my breath, willing him to come find me. Willing us to take back everything we'd said. Willing time to spin backwards to our kiss on the doorstep. Willing regret not to take the place of everything we'd found together.

But, instead, I heard the front door open and then softly close. A car engine started and my heart broke.

§

I lay in bed for hours, trying to figure out where everything had gone wrong. When my initial anger subsided, rational thought returned.

I remembered how Danny was in the classroom—stiffly professional, never smiling. He never joked with students or was familiar in any way. And yet, students still talked about him. They analyzed everything he did, looked obsessively for any trace of a misdeed. They loved the idea of a scandal.

Looking back on that now, he must have been aware of how people watched him, whispered about him. How hard must it have been for him to be a young, ridiculously handsome teacher in a high school? How did one survive the scrutiny, day in and day out? I'd never really thought about it like that, but it must have been terribly difficult. And it made me think about his question at The Cliffs.

*Does our age difference bother you? Or the fact that you were in my class?*

It didn't bother me. I hadn't given it a single thought. But even at the time, I could see it bothered him. How much? I didn't know. Maybe now I had an inkling.

The thought that continued to nag me, though, was that even if I let go of the hurt from tonight, even if I found the empathy to understand where these feelings came from, this ultimately wasn't *my* issue. He was the one who had to be okay with the implications of our relationship. I knew we weren't doing anything unethical. But did he?

The unfair truth was that I would always be the one to get the *You go, girl!* But he'd be the one to get the *I always knew he was a dog.*

He would be the one to shoulder the brunt of the judgment, however misplaced. And he had to decide whether our relationship was worth it.

I couldn't be with someone who had doubts.

With that restless thought, I drifted off into a fitful sleep.

§

I awoke to the ding of my cell phone, lighting up with a text at four forty-five. The room was dark and I felt momentarily disoriented.

*Are you up?*

*Yes. Where are you?* I replied.

*On your doorstep.*

I jumped out of bed quickly, now wide awake, and opened the door to find Danny in his running clothes, bathed in sweat. His hair was drenched, his cheeks pink, and he was leaning lightly against the wall.

"Come in." I searched his face for any indication of what to expect, but he was too masterful at keeping his thoughts concealed. His face was serious and carefully blank. As he stepped inside, he seemed to purposefully avoid any physical contact between us, which was disconcerting, to say the least. I found myself wrapping my arms around my waist in a revealingly protective way.

"How long have you been running?"

"A while." His mouth curled up just slightly at one corner, suggesting that *a while* was likely measured in hours.

"Do you want to sit down?"

"No, I'm fine," he said, and closed the door gently behind him.

"Water?"

He nodded. "Thank you."

I moved to the kitchen and took a glass from the cupboard, filling it with filtered water from the fridge. All the while he watched me wordlessly, as though absorbing every detail. Handing him the glass, I met his gaze. It was softer now, and slightly pained.

"Danny, I'm sorry for some of the things—"

"Don't." He shook his head, halting my apology. "You asked me when we first . . . met why I chose to teach middle school." The word *met* had a slight tilt to it and I understood what he meant. Yes, I was in his class five years ago, but I didn't feel like we actually met until we bumped into each other at Charlie's. Until then, we were strangers.

"What I told you was true," he said, "but it wasn't the whole story."

He paused to take a sip, and then set the glass on the counter, looking up at me before continuing.

"I was twenty-four when I started at McKinley and it was the best job I ever had. I can't tell you how happy I was to be teaching a subject I loved. But it quickly turned out to be . . . difficult." His brows pulled together in what might have been anger, or possibly regret.

"Not the teaching part; that part was second nature. But the kids were only seven years younger than I was, and it wasn't easy earning their respect. I realized very quickly I had to keep my distance, as much as possible.

"But even as bad as some of the students were initially, the faculty was worse. During my first week, one of the more senior staff stopped by my classroom under the pretense of *welcoming* me. It wasn't much of a welcome, I assure you." He shook his head, remembering. "He told me I'd replaced a tenured teacher, who was let go for misconduct after a lengthy process that most of the faculty thought was a witch hunt. They resented his removal, and they resented his being replaced by someone who was as inexperienced as I.

"Not only did they give me no help in getting acclimated, they routinely made cracks about various student crushes. Not just cracks, really—false insinuations about me or my character. I despised the way they toyed so loosely with my reputation, and in such an insidious way. So after four years at McKinley, I'd had enough.

"That's the reason I jumped at the chance to go to Taft. I do love middle school; I'd never go back to teaching the upper grades. But it shouldn't have gone down the way it did. And I guess seeing Jennifer just brought all that crap back in the very worst way. I wasn't prepared for it. And I didn't handle it well. I'm so sorry. It wasn't you."

"I get it."

But he shook his head. "I want to make sure you do. I'm grateful every single day that you came into my life. You have no idea how much."

Standing in the quiet of my tiny apartment, the echoes of our argument fell away. I was flooded with a deep sense of relief that what we had between us was real—and worth the fight.

"Okay."

"Okay? Do you mean it?"

"I do."

He let out a deep exhale and closed his eyes momentarily. I could feel in him a release of tension that no amount of running could've achieved.

Then he reached for me and kissed me deeply, cupping my face gently in his hands. He didn't break the contact for what felt like forever. He wrapped his arms around me and hugged me tightly, tucking my head under his chin. His large, solid frame was sweaty, and smelled of musky exertion, but I couldn't think of a single place I'd rather be.

Still, one question remained for me. I pulled back, looking directly into his somber green eyes.

"I know in many ways this is harder for you than it is for me. I want you to know I understand that," I said. *But I need to know you can deal with it*, I didn't say.

He shook his head. "I left the posting on my feed. And I'll gladly defend any criticism that comes my way from that, or anything else. That's what I should have said from the very beginning. It's my honor and my privilege to be with you."

"Danny—" I began.

But he bent to kiss my lips, silencing any intention on my part to ease his remorse. He wouldn't allow it.

"Will you let me stay with you for a few more hours?"

I'd let him stay forever.

He was undeniably wrecked and in need of sleep. I led him into the bathroom and ran the shower as he peeled off his soaked clothing and shoes. Taking out a fresh towel and placing it on the sink, I could feel him watching me.

He opened the shower door, about to get in, but stopped and gathered me again in a tight embrace. Very quietly, he whispered something into my hair.

With the din of the water, I couldn't quite make out the words. But some part of me knew what they were. I closed my eyes, breathing in his scent, and pressed my lips to his beating heart. It was strong and steady, and I hoped it would be sure enough to carry us over the unforeseen rough spots to come. Maybe I was even counting on that.

§

After showering, Danny climbed exhausted into bed. We wrapped ourselves around each other, and succumbed to a deep and peaceful sleep.

I woke up several hours later to find him still resting soundly beside me. His face looked so young and carefree, so unlike the tortured expression he wore when he finally came back to me last night. I thought about all the things he had told me. If even possible, it made me respect the man he was even more.

I loved to watch him sleep—and probably could have all morning—but I knew he would be very dehydrated when he got up. So quietly, I went to the kitchen for a glass of water and some Motrin. When I came back, his eyes were open.

"Hey there. Good morning."

"Good morning. Is that for me, by any chance? My head is pounding." His voice was gravelly and sleepy.

Nodding, I sat beside him on the bed, and stroked his hair while he raised up on one elbow and took the pills. Carefully, he set the glass on the nightstand and raised his eyes to mine.

"Are we okay?" He searched my face for his answer.

"Yeah. We're okay." And because I knew he needed it, I offered a small smile that seemed to relieve his concern that we'd done any enduring damage to our fledgling relationship.

"I really couldn't stand it if we weren't."

"I know," I said, running my fingers through the silky, wavy strands. "Me, either."

He reached up to cup my face and pulled me to him, pressing his mouth to mine. Then shifting, he positioned me beneath his warm body, enveloping mine in the alluring scent of sleepy maleness.

The bed was so cozy beneath me, his heat radiating from my flowered sheets. I ran my fingers up his muscular back and shoulders, enjoying the warmth of his skin. Slowly, he peeled off my tank and his mouth charted a course across my body. I closed my eyes, letting the sensual contact ignite every nerve.

"I absolutely worship you. Every beautiful part of you. I'm so sorry I ever let you doubt that."

Danny and I had been together many times, but it had never really been like this before—slow and deliberate. Like making love. Like a physical manifestation of his apology. It made me wonder if this was the way he was most comfortable expressing himself.

He rose over me, gentle but ready.

That's when an unexpected pang of fear griped my consciousness. I realized this was the first time we would do this with nothing between us. Being with someone in this way was a huge act of faith—of trust.

For me, the last time was with John, and his infidelity was a not only major betrayal of our relationship, it put me at physical risk in the most disrespectful way.

Danny seemed to sense my sudden anxiety and he stopped, pinning my gaze with his soft, loving eyes.

"Do you want me to wear something? I don't mind."

"No, it's just . . ."

I ran my hands again over his back as I scrambled to make sense of my emotions.

*What did I want?*

Danny waited for me, as if he had the patience to wait all day. I looked into his handsome face, felt the heavy, certain strength of his hips, and cursed my history for making me doubt what I'd found in him.

When I was with John, there were so many instances with other women that gave me pause, but he always seemed to have a reasonable explanation.

*I just happened to run into her.*

*We're working on a project together, and I lost track of time.*

*Her phone died, and she needed to use mine.*

It was such a common occurrence I started to believe maybe I *was* the jealous type, though I'd never been like that before. In fact, that's what he used to tell me.

When everything came down with him, it was so much more humiliating because it'd apparently been happening under my nose for god knows how long. How many people had been aware of his cheating? How many times did others snicker at my ignorance? And how many STDs had I so narrowly dodged?

I hated that I was on this precipice with Danny, who wasn't remotely like John, and I was struggling to push through this aspect of intimacy. Did I trust Danny enough to do this?

"Sarah? Talk to me." His expression was insistent, but his voice was soothing.

This man turned heads everywhere he went, and yet he never gave me one single reason to doubt he would be faithful. I didn't know why, but I felt from the very start that I could trust him. I *did* trust him enough to do this.

And I needed to get beyond these negative memories.

"I want you. Like this."

"Yes?" He'd always been so careful with me, always making sure I'd never do anything I wasn't one hundred percent comfortable with. Never asking for more than I was willing to give. It'd been that way from the beginning.

"Yes."

He paused a moment to assess my expression, and seemed to find the reassurance he was looking for.

He pushed inside and his eyes fluttered closed. Slowly, he started moving. Just exploring. I felt like I'd achieved a major victory over my past.

"Look at me," he urged. I did, and the look on his face took my breath away. "I know what this means to you, and I want you to know your trust is sacred to me. And what we have together means everything."

It meant everything to me too.

Our relationship was beginning to feel serious—substantive like no other I'd ever had. With the revelations of last night, I felt like I knew him better, like I could finally reconcile the man I remembered with the man I knew today. And maybe more importantly, he'd given me an insight into a part of his past I was guessing he didn't share with many others.

It wasn't just that I felt this could be a long-term relationship; it's that I thought it could be a meaningful one. I let go of any inhibition I might have harbored and pulled him closer to me, taking as much of him as he could give.

"Ah, god, it's amazing," he said, breathless.

He looked down, his hair falling across his forehead, and watched where our bodies connected.

The speed of his thrusts increased sharply, and I felt the familiar tightening in my own body. He was right behind me, shuddering almost violently, eyes closed tightly, and breathing rapid. When he finally looked at me again, those eyes were a brilliant green.

He smiled, bending to kiss my lips.

*We did it*, he seemed to say.

Yes, we did.

§

We finally got around after a long, luxurious morning, and I decided that leaving the bedroom was definitely overrated. But Danny's stomach was growling like a lion—a situation that could deteriorate quickly into extreme grumpiness. I got up to see if we had any food in the house, and when I came back to the bedroom with some crackers and cheese, he was looking at the piano-savings jar on my desk. It was mostly depleted.

"What's this?"

"Oh, it's nothing." I waved it off, hoping to distract him. But Danny was like a dog with a bone and he continued to wait for his answer. "It's just this silly idea I had, that's all."

"You're saving for a piano?"

"Not really. Even if by some miracle I could afford one, it's not like I have the room for it."

"What kind do you want?"

"Well, anyone who plays with any degree of seriousness would prefer a baby grand to an upright, but I wouldn't be picky. Right now, I'm lucky to just get a few minutes here and there with the piano in the choral room at school."

"What kind of music do you play?"

"All kinds, really. My father insisted I learn classical piano, but eventually I started playing show tunes, and now I prefer modern music or writing something of my own."

"I didn't know you wrote music."

"I have a program on my laptop that I mess around with. It's not serious."

He studied me as I answered. And then he glanced down as something else caught his eye. Dipping his fingers into the jar, he produced the white napkin from Charlie's with his email address written in that sprawling handwriting. He also pulled out the receipt for the purchase of his photograph.

"You used this money to buy my picture?" I couldn't quite discern the expression on his face.

"Like I said, I never really expected to be able to save enough for a piano."

I needed to change the subject quickly. I wasn't comfortable with where this was going.

"I'm putting the cash back in your jar. I'm not taking your money."

That's exactly where I was afraid this was going . . .

"You're definitely not. I bought it before we knew each other, and I would do it again."

Danny knew me well enough by now to know that pride was at stake, which meant my mind was made up. He narrowed his eyes, but didn't argue.

Two days later, the money was back in my jar. I didn't bother arguing, either. This was never I battle I truly expected to win.

# Chapter 13

## Danny

The palatial foyer of the Callahan's Mediterranean–style home *was* a little awe-inspiring. I was used to it, but as I closed the door behind us, I noticed Sarah playing absently with the delicate necklace at the base of her throat like she did when she was nervous. We'd slipped in unnoticed, and I took advantage of the momentary calm to reassure her once more. Wrapping my arms around her, I held her close, and felt her relax into my hold.

"I'm glad you're here," I said softly.

Her answering smile was dazzling and it took my breath away. But in the next beat, she glanced over my shoulder and pulled back from my chest.

"Those are amazing."

A set of four eleven-by-fourteen framed black-and-white photographs hung on the wall below the staircase. They were all close-ups of a hand, Jamie's hand to be exact, strumming a guitar, adjusting an amp, playing the piano, and grasping a mic. The images were tight, so the focus was on his hand and you just saw a portion of the instrument in the background.

"I played around with the exposure to keep the foreground sharp, and blur the background."

"You took them?"

"Yeah, at a music festival a couple of years ago. I gave them to Jamie for Christmas."

But before she could respond, a disembodied Irish voice called down from upstairs.

"If you like those, Sarah, you should see the hand shots hanging in my bedroom. I'd show them to you, but they're quite personal between Danny and me."

Sarah laughed. Yes, she and Jamie would get along just fine.

"You mind?" I called back. "I'm trying to impress this girl."

Jamie appeared at the top of the winding wrought iron banister with a giggling five-year-old Shane thrown over his shoulder.

"What were you thinking, bringing her here then, mate?"

He came down the stairs, firing a blazing, full-dimpled smile in Sarah's direction. Then, he turned to me, "How the hell did you get a beautiful woman like this?" But before the mini pair of jeans slung over his shoulder had a chance to broadcast his use of the word *hell*, Jamie chided, "Nobody likes a rat fink."

He tickled Shane mercilessly, and then set him down to consume Sarah in a massive hug.

I'd known Jamie pretty much my entire life, but it was interesting to see him tonight through Sarah's eyes. Of course, there had always been a lot of media fanfare about his looks. Some called him rugged, probably because of his strong jaw and the nose that had been broken at least once that I knew of. Some said he was charismatic—likely the accent. And the dimples. He smiled a lot. But I thought his true appeal was in his openness. He and I were very different in that way. Everything he felt showed on his face, so people came away from his shows or interviews feeling like they knew him.

He also kept himself in good shape. I had a few inches on him height-wise, but he was very fit, and he looked every bit the rock star with his tattoos and leather wristbands. As one might expect, he was a phenomenal performer. He had that voice, which was crucial, but he was also loaded with personality, which made him really entertaining to watch.

Sarah looked a little awestruck as they chatted. And for the first time in my life, I kind of wished my best friend were an accountant.

Jamie seemed to be soaking her in too—absorbing each little detail in a way that only an artist can. For him, everything was viewed through the lens of a song, and I could almost see him composing one for Sarah in real-time.

My guess was that hers would reflect her complexity. She had the sweetest face—so innocent and guileless. But he would recognize the grit in her. He'd be able to see that behind the gentle blue eyes was someone who knew more of the world than she'd wish to say. Sarah carried herself with tremendous dignity, and Jamie, of all people, would understand that dignity was often hard won. He'd love her all the more for those things.

"This bit of magic here is Shane," Jamie said to Sarah, placing a large hand on top of Shane's head and wobbling him around until he giggled. That's when I realized I'd lost track of their conversation. "Come, let me introduce you to my wife."

They both turned to me expectantly, and I nodded once in case there was some question hanging out there, waiting for my response. That seemed to do the trick, although I could almost feel Jamie giving me silent shit for whatever look of love may have crawled onto my face. I evened out my expression, and gestured to him to lead the way. He did, but not before those damned dimples made another appearance.

In the spacious, rustic kitchen that was the center of the Callahan household, we were greeted in the usual manner with a burst of affection from Mel. This was a very demonstrative family—I loved it, but it made me wonder if that's what Sarah was used to.

She seemed more surprised than she did uncomfortable; in no time they were talking and laughing like old friends.

In fact, my participation didn't seem particularly necessary, so I just leaned against the counter, chiming in here and there. At some point, Jamie came over to offer me a beer, along with a complex look that only twenty-five years of friendship could decipher:

*I like her*, he was saying. *And you _really_ like her. It's about time.*

I met his gaze with a look of my own: *Right on all counts.*

The noise level in the room was lulling, and I took in the whole scene in sort of a fly-on-the-wall way—Mel and Sarah exchanging stories, Jamie mixing some god-awful alcoholic concoction, and the boys helping to set the table for dinner.

In the middle of it all, I had this odd thought that I never got the chance to bring a girl home to meet my parents. No one rose to that level of significance while they were alive, and I realized now that I'd lost the opportunity. This, in fact, might be the closest I'd ever get.

It was one of those many random things that people like Sarah and me came to accept as our fate—those moments in our lives in which we realized something had been taken from us permanently and without our consent—experiences other people might just take for granted. We usually pretended not to notice. But we always did . . .

§

Having completed his job with the silverware, Paddy came over to lean against my leg in a little hug.

"You bored?" I asked him, ruffling his hair a bit.

He stepped back, nodding as he looked up at me with expectation.

"Did you bring us anything?" Sadly for him, all I brought for this visit was a woman, which was definitely less interesting to an eight-year-old than a fetal pig.

"Hmmm." I made a face. "Want to shoot some hoops?"

Paddy nodded enthusiastically.

I caught Sarah's eye. "How about a quick game before dinner?"

She didn't hesitate. "For sure. But I want them on my team," she said, indicating Paddy and Shane. And just like that, I added yet another item to the list of a zillion things I loved about Sarah.

Of course, Paddy looked at *her* like she was an alien.

"No way." I motioned with my beer to Jamie. "You get *him*."

§

Sarah and Jamie were the scrappiest of players—it turned out that pairing them was not such a great idea. They checked and fouled the boys and I constantly, like two ill-behaved peas in a pod.

When we were five points down, we made a new plan. As my uncle used to roughly quote, 'If you can't be a positive example, be a cautionary tale.' We abandoned all rules of decorum and just went for the win.

Shane jumped on Jamie's back while I grabbed Sarah around the waist, lifting her in a football-style hold. Paddy took the ball and shot repeatedly until he got something in. The game pretty much went to hell after that, with shirt pulling, and tickling, and hideous displays of goaltending. We were all in hysterics by the time dinner was on.

And dinner was no less of a ruckus affair. I blamed Sarah.

"So, how did you and Jamie meet?" she asked Mel, who was sitting directly across from her.

I closed my eyes and shook my head, knowing—just knowing—this was not going to go well for me. Jamie and Mel's origin story was actually a pretty great one, but *I* was a rather embarrassing footnote in it. And Jamie loved that.

He was sitting on Mel's right at the head of the table, and with some industrious chewing and a hasty swallow of Mel's phenomenal short ribs, he managed to insert himself into the conversation.

"I love that story!"

The kids groaned, almost in unison, and looked over to me as if I could do anything to stop this. Believe me, if I could have I definitely would.

"What?" Jamie asked innocently.

"First of all, you're the worst story teller," I told him. "Half your stories make no sense, and the other half are pointless."

"He's a spiral thinker," Mel acknowledged to Sarah, before Jamie could feign too much affront. "But eventually he does get to the point."

"*Second,*" I continued. "No one wants to hear that story anyway."

"Bollocks. Your girlfriend just asked."

*Girlfriend.* Hearing the word spoken out loud by someone other than me felt strange. It was definitely more official when someone else said it. I looked at Sarah to see if she was having an objection to the label, but she was just smiling—as though it was just another word in a whole collection of words. No different from any other.

"I would like to hear it," she said eagerly.

With elbows on the table, I leaned my forehead into my hands and felt Sarah squeeze my knee. When I turned to her, she was grinning. And now very interested.

"I have to say, it's quite a good story that happens to involve our friend Daniel here," Jamie began. "You see, one summer he was here visiting me from UVA, and he happened to come upon lovely Mel in distress at the market."

"Mel wasn't always the cook she is today. Right, M?" I teased.

Her answering expression proved you could, in fact, flip someone the bird with just your eyes. Turning to Sarah, I added, "She wasn't sure what was the difference between a scallion and a leek, and I helped."

"Yes," Jamie continued. "Our vegetable expert swooped in to provide some valuable assistance. *Unsolicited,* I might add."

I glared at him amiably. "They're both alliums," I told Sarah. "But leeks are generally cooked, and scallions are often not."

Sarah didn't seem particularly impressed with my knowledge of root vegetables, either.

"It was an extraordinary pick-up line," Mel said. "I could listen to a man talk about alliums all day long."

"It wasn't meant to be a pick-up line," I insisted. But then I laughed. "Well, I guess it kind of was. But I thought it was slightly more insightful than, *Come here often?*"

"So, Danny continues to follow Mel through the produce department, laying it on thick about being brilliant at basketball and great with small children and puppies, and the like."

"I *definitely* didn't mention children, but she did say she had a new puppy," I offered in my own defense.

Mel continued. "He told me about this barbecue he and his friends were having that night, and he said if I came, he'd grill some leeks for me to try."

With that, the entire table exploded into laughter. Okay—I'll admit, it wasn't my best work.

Mel looked at me sympathetically. "How could I say no to leeks? Plus, he was hot."

"Gross," Paddy grumbled, making a quick assessment of me and apparently finding me lacking.

"So, Danny spends hours in the bathroom in preparation," Jamie continued, "arranging his Ken-doll hair just so, applying several dollars' worth of Polo cologne, and selecting the tightest T-shirt he could find in his suitcase."

"That is not true," I protested. "It wasn't like that," I told Sarah. She wasn't listening.

"Anyway," he added. "Mel arrived, looking like an angel from heaven—in a *Cure T-shirt*," he said with emphasis. "And Danny and his cloud of cologne ushered her inside."

"There was no cloud of cologne. I smelled good."

"We were all pleased to see his cologne phase pass," Mel confided to Sarah in an exaggerated stage whisper.

"Very cute. Can we move on?"

"Gladly." Jamie leaned in as if this next part was so good it needed to be underscored with dramatic posture. "So, Danny is doing the full court press. He's showing off his best DJ Casper Cha-Cha Slide moves, and tempting Mel with his grilled leeks, and generally doing anything he can to entice her."

"Smooth," Sarah said to me, smirking.

"This guy was no better. He came outside with a guitar around his neck like he was about to break into song at any moment. It was the most incredibly transparent move to impress a girl I've ever seen."

"They were quite a pair," Mel agreed.

Jamie laughed. "It's true. But you can't blame either of us. She was the loveliest woman I'd ever seen in my life. And thank God she had an eye for me too, because she obliterated me the moment I saw her. I was determined to have her, even if Danny sulked about it."

"I never sulked. As I recall, my cologne and I were very gracious about you stealing my date."

"I can't argue there," he said to me, with the full depth of our friendship in his eye. "What do you think, Mel, have I about summed it up?" He looked to her, and then around the table for affirmation.

"There might have been a little more to it than that," Mel conceded to Sarah. "But he's right, I was smitten too. I have a thing for musicians."

"Hey now. Let's not go there, love," Jamie chided. Mel just laughed.

"It was pathetic." I shook my head, half laughing and half cringing at the dating rituals of twenty-two-year-old men.

Quite honestly, I'd always been glad Mel had the good sense to choose Jamie that day. Had she gone for me, she and I would've never become friends. I readily admit to having been an idiot at that age. I certainly wasn't in the market for anything meaningful.

"The truth is," Jamie began again, "I wasn't much of anything at that time in my life. A junior college dropout, struggling musician, piss poor. I had absolutely nothing of value to offer a woman like this." His smile waned slightly as his face clouded with some strong emotion. "Just a heart full of songs I instantly wanted to write about her. It didn't seem a lot."

He glanced at Mel as though looking for an answer to an unspoken question. Then, turning back to the rest of us, he added, "So yeah, I'd have embarrassed myself many times over if that's what it took to get her to notice me. She's still the most astounding woman I've ever met."

"Here, here," I said, lifting my glass in a toast to Mel.

The expression on Jamie's face as he looked at his wife was pure love. And for a brief moment, my two closest friends shared a silent conversation that felt as if it was the only one tonight that mattered.

I glanced at Sarah and smiled, and she squeezed my hand under the table. I wondered how many times she'd seen that same look on my face and recognized it for what it was. So many times I'd wanted to tell her. So many times. Ironically, it had always been the overwhelming truth of it that held me back.

§

At about nine o'clock, the boys headed off to bed. Jamie wanted to show Sarah his music studio, and Mel and I followed along.

The studio was pretty decked out with a wide variety of Jamie's instruments, recording equipment, and comfortable, distressed leather sofas. He would probably agree that his greatest extravagance in life was his collection of guitars, all lined up on the back wall. He said that every single one of them had its own set of songs. In fact, he still had the first guitar he ever owned.

Still, his pride and joy was the Fazioli piano. He was very competent on it, and most of his more recent songs were written on that piano. I was certainly no expert on musical instruments, but even to my untrained eye, it was quite something.

Judging by Sarah's reaction, she thought so too. Her eyes grew as big as saucers, and her mouth fell open slightly as she walked over to the enormous instrument.

"Go ahead. Give her a try," Jamie suggested.

Carefully, she sat down at it and almost reverently laid her fingers over the black and white keys. "I don't think I've ever seen anything so magnificent."

Gently, she pressed one, releasing a soft, sweet sound. She looked up at Jamie and smiled widely.

"Come on, now, don't be gentle about it."

She didn't need much more prompting from him than that, and launched into one of Cadence's early hits—a big, piano-driven rock ballad that Jamie had written for Mel early on. Jamie laughed when he heard the first few chords.

From there, she moved right into a classical piece, and her fingers flew expertly over the keys. I recognized the melody, but couldn't name the song for the life of me. I also recognized that Sarah was good. Very good. I had no idea.

Jamie looked over at me, and raised his eyebrows as if to say, *Really?* I just shrugged my shoulders back in amazement.

I studied her—the way she leaned into the piece, the way her hands seemed almost connected to the instrument, as though it was compelling her. She seemed so at ease in front of that piano, and so happy. I couldn't tear myself away from how she looked just then.

Bumping my elbow with hers and reminding me she was still standing there beside me, Mel whispered quietly, "I like her."

That small statement held a lot of weight for me. I knew Jamie liked

Sarah. Of course he would—she was an absolute sweetheart, and she was into everything he was into. But most importantly, Jamie liked her because I did. For him, it was always that simple. He didn't question it; he didn't need to know anything more.

He never asked for details; he just stood by me, no matter what. One hundred percent unconditional support. It was one of the best things about him.

But Mel was a different story. Maybe it was the lawyer in her, or maybe it was the mother in her, but she was much more contemplative. Mel listened and analyzed. She wanted to understand things and come to reasonable, logical decisions. She was protective of me, and I knew she'd spent a lot of time tonight watching Sarah and I together.

Her endorsement was carefully considered.

"Me too," I responded.

Mel easily saw the understatement in my answer and smiled, nodding. I put my arm around her and pulled her in close, feeling fortunate, once again, for the family I chose.

# Chapter 14

**Sarah**

"Did you have a good time tonight?" Danny asked me as we made the short drive back to his place.

"Definitely. They're such a nice family. Surprisingly down to earth, considering the band's success."

"Yeah. Jamie didn't come from much. His family was really messed up, so he appreciates where he's at now."

"I'd say where he's at now is pretty impressive." One glance out the window to the rows of impeccably manicured homes underscored that point. "Didn't Steve Jobs live in this neighborhood?"

Danny smiled. "He did. A few blocks away, I think. When we were kids, Jamie and I used to take the train up to go trick-or-treating around here. We always thought the people who lived in these homes had the world by the balls. I actually think that's why Jamie bought that house when he could finally afford it. For him, living here was the mark of making it."

"You said Jamie spent a lot of time at your house growing up—was he close to your parents?"

"My mom, yes. It was her personal mission to fatten him up."

"And your dad?"

He shrugged. "It wasn't that easy to be close to my dad."

"Why?"

He just lifted his shoulders again, keeping his eyes on the road, as headlights from a passing car moved across his face, giving sudden definition to his angular jaw and cheekbones.

"Were you close to your dad?"

I could probably guess the answer, considering the way he usually responded when the subject came up. And, tellingly, he didn't respond right away.

"Our relationship was complicated," he finally said, giving me only a brief, sideways glance.

This had been such a great evening, and I didn't want to ruin it by prying into an area he didn't seem to want to talk about. But I wanted to know him better, and I felt like I needed to understand this part of him in order to do that.

When I pushed him, Danny was always forthcoming about things. The problem was, he was a really private person and there was so much he didn't willingly share. It was the one thing about us I wished I could change.

So I waited. Expectantly. He knew I wasn't going to let it go this time. And in our silent standoff, he finally gave in.

"My dad didn't exactly approve of me."

"How is that possible?"

He shrugged defensively. "It's possible."

"But what does that mean?"

"There's nothing to tell, Sarah. There's no story here. It's not that interesting."

But it was to me. And every time we seemed to make a little progress, he threw up another roadblock. Unfortunately, before I could figure out a way around this one, he changed the subject with expert and calculated abruptness.

"So I was thinking," he said in a vastly different tone. "Can you stay tonight?"

We came to a stop sign and he glanced over, a new wolfish gleam gathering in his eye. It momentarily halted my thoughts with its blatant sexuality.

"Stay over?" I stumbled, suddenly caught in that look.

He reached across the seat to run his fingertips up the inside of my bare thigh, pushing the hem of my skirt higher and higher as he went, as if to underscore his intent.

"Okay."

For the record, logically I *knew* this was textbook distraction. I'd employed some form of it countless times myself over the years to avoid emotional intimacy. I was an expert here. And yet, even recognizing it for what it was, I still found myself powerless to fight it. His pull was *that* acute. He knew it. In these instances, his perceptiveness made me feel nearly transparent.

"Good." His smile was wolfish.

§

Danny and I were settled on the big suede couch in the living room, lying contentedly in front of a warm fire, his arms were wrapped tightly around me.

For whatever reason, I began to wonder how many girls, just like me, had been wrapped in his arms, just like this. I knew about Carolyn, of course, but he hadn't ever mentioned anyone else. This was *not* the right moment to ask. No one would ask that now. And yet . . .

"How many girlfriends have you had?" There. That didn't sound so bad.

Danny shifted uncomfortably behind me. "What do you mean by girlfriends?" he asked carefully.

*Crap. Maybe it was bad.* "Well, how many women have you . . . been with?" *I definitely just made it worse . . .*

"Do you really want me to answer that?"

*No.* "Yes. I mean is it like . . . a lot?" Even *I* didn't know where I was going with this. No, of course I didn't want him to answer that, but I didn't seem to be able to stop myself from asking.

I felt him lift an arm off of me, and run a hand through his hair. He inhaled a deep breath, as if deciding how to proceed. Then he exhaled, decision made.

"For a long time I wasn't looking for a relationship. I had a couple of girlfriends in college, a couple after college. And Carolyn, of course. But mostly I was . . . unattached."

Yeah, I got the subtext.

"Is monogamy difficult for you?" I couldn't believe I just asked that.

He laughed, thankfully. "No. I've never been unfaithful when I've made a commitment to someone. It's just that earlier in my life, I wasn't much into commitments. I liked my freedom."

"But Carolyn changed that."

"Yes. But maybe not for the reasons you think."

I was turned away from him, unable to see his face, but I felt his hesitation before he continued.

"When I was younger, my adversity to commitment was largely rooted in just wanting to . . . have some fun. I know how shallow that sounds."

"I'm not judging you, Danny. I just want to understand."

"I know," he said with a sigh. "But I also want you to understand that that changed after my folks died. It got harder for me to open myself up to people, or to allow anyone close enough to become important to me. It wasn't about me wanting to be a player."

"I get it." And I did—completely. "Losing my dad so abruptly made me feel like depending on someone else just opened me up to more loss. And I'm sure I protected myself by keeping most people away. I think I'm still guilty of that, really, but I'm trying to be better."

He hugged me tightly, kissing my hair and stroking it gently. He seemed to relax, his taut muscles softening against my back.

"We're very much alike in that way."

We were, and it sometimes scared me. Because the strength of a thing could also be its weakness.

"So, what changed for you with Carolyn?"

"Her brother is Jamie's publicist, and so we started hanging out a lot. Just as friends in the beginning, though I knew she had feelings for me. We were pretty close for about three years until one night when she kissed me. I was shocked; maybe I shouldn't have been. But I couldn't really think of a good reason not to go with it."

He paused, as if realizing how that sounded.

"Carolyn was good for me in many ways. She pushed me to take a step back from my work and my obsessive renovations on the house and just live a little more. At the time, I needed that. I really didn't think I had it in me to be a good boyfriend to anyone, but she was patient and she taught me a lot about being in a relationship. I owe her a lot for that."

He touched my hair as he talked, twisting it absentmindedly around his right index finger. I was almost afraid to move in any way that might interrupt this unusual candor.

"And I truly cared for her, loved her maybe, but I can see now I wasn't *in* love. I didn't really think I was capable of that. Any shortcomings in our relationship were mine, not hers, though. Truthfully, a lot of our issues stemmed from the fact that it was hard for me to open up with her." He paused again, thoughtfully, as though he was still chewing through this in his mind. "Plus, we were different," he said. "We just had different interests, different goals in life. Carolyn loves the whole society scene, and she always wanted me to have a more prestigious career path. She wasn't . . . Well, anyway . . ." He lifted a shoulder and then his arms flexed around me. "I think ultimately she thought she could make me into her ideal. She wanted me, but not really *me*, and I wasn't interested in trying to be someone I'm not."

His tone was matter-of-fact, but I suspected those words revealed so much more about him than just the circumstances of that single relationship.

Instinctively, I snuggled further into his arms, and he squeezed me to him a little tighter.

"Did you ever talk about getting married?" My voice cracked a bit, betraying the cool I was trying to convey.

He seemed to discount the notion. "It came up, but the timing was never right. I was putting in a lot of hours on my PhD."

"And then you broke up?"

"We both realized it was for the best."

It was hard to know what to make of all that. On one hand, it seemed like it was a fairly amicable split. On the other hand, how do people invest five years in a relationship where marriage is discussed, and then just walk away clean? And why would any woman give up this man without a fight?

"So, okay, now I want to know about you."

"What do you mean?" I turned in his arms so I was able to see his face. "You know I'm not seeing anyone else."

"I know *that*," he answered, brushing a hair from my face. "But I want to know about all the assholes who preceded me. The ones you're still pining over."

He smiled when he said it and his tone didn't convey jealousy, but something in his eyes told me this wasn't an entirely casual line of questioning either.

"There's no pining. It's a pretty short list. And I can easily say there's not even a close second in bed. Honestly, you've made that comparison a little unfair."

"Well that's a given," he said with no shortage of male smugness. "But tell me, anyway."

I took in a deep breath, and began to trace the beautiful lines of his lips with my finger. "Okay. Before you, there was John, as you know. We met at freshman orientation, and we dated for close to four years. But I wouldn't exactly describe it as true love. We were friends with all the same people; we were compatible. And it was easy until it wasn't."

"Before him?" he said, biting my finger gently at the knuckle.

"Ow," I protested, pulling my hand away. "Before him was Ethan. We dated for a short time during my senior year in high school. He was sweet. Too sweet, unfortunately for him. I was coming off a bad breakup, and I wasn't very good to him. I'm ashamed of the way I behaved."

Danny seemed to filter out ninety-seven percent of my confession, choosing to focus on only two words. "What do you mean by a bad breakup?"

"That was Seth."

"Seth *Abbott*? That idiot from McKinley?" Crap. I always forgot—he *knew* these people. His twisted expression left no question of his low opinion of my ex. Looking back, I would never have known he felt that way about Seth; Danny was never anything but neutral to all of us.

"Yes. It's not a big deal. We dated for like eight months, and it wasn't good for me."

"What do you mean? What happened?" He sat up, prompting me to do the same. His laser focus was a little intimidating, and suddenly, I was wishing I'd been more circumspect in my answer.

"What happened?" he repeated.

"It's just that he was a partier. We had a bad night and we broke up. I never talked to him again." I was looking down at my hands, but I could still feel the weight of his stare.

"He didn't . . . force himself on you, did he?" The words seemed to come out of him painfully, like shards of glass.

"No." I emphatically shook my head. "Seth was my first, and as firsts go, he was fine. Neither of us was very experienced, but he was gentle with me. This was several months later. He was just drunk and . . ."

I didn't know how to continue. This was where I always faltered. I had a hard time talking about personal things and revealing too much of myself. All my relationships, and even my friendships, had suffered from some form of this. But I wanted to be better with Danny. I really did.

So I steeled myself and prepared to continue.

It wasn't easy. Danny was now conducting himself like a statue on the couch next to me, bracing for something bad, though his posture was eerily calm. It threw me, especially because I had a pretty good idea of what his reaction would be. So, I sat with my hands in my lap and focused on my knees.

"He was really drunk one night and he came to my house. When I let him in, he started trying to kiss me. But he smelled awful, like alcohol and cigarettes. And he was rough; I didn't want to do anything with him so I told him to go home. He got really mad and he called me a cock tease."

There was no visible reaction from the statue next to me. I pressed on.

"I was young and stupid at the time, and I let my fighting instincts overtake my good sense. Instead of just getting myself out of the situation, I made it worse. I told him his cock wouldn't be a tease for anyone."

"Sarah," Danny finally breathed out, sensing, I'm sure, that this story got worse. "Sweetness . . ." He tugged one of my hands apart from the other and held it securely in his. The instinct to protect me was strong in him, even if all he could do now was to try to protect me from the memory of it.

"I know." I inhaled deeply. "He went into this *rage*, cursing and yelling; I'd never seen him like that before. It was scary." I glanced up at Danny just for a moment, but regretted it immediately. I couldn't lose my nerve now. "He picked me up by my throat, and slammed me against the wall. I was so mad; even then, I don't think I recognized the danger I was in so I did the only thing I could physically do, which was to spit in his face."

I don't know why I looked up at Danny again, but I did, just in time to see him close his eyes in silent fury.

"That was the final straw," I whispered. "He squeezed my neck like he was trying to strangle me, and with his other hand, he punched me in the face. Then again in the stomach."

"That cowardly motherfucker." The words sounded like they were spoken through helpless anger, and he made a sound of contempt, low in his throat. "What happened after that?"

"He dropped me like a ragdoll. I remember sinking to the ground. I couldn't breathe—he'd knocked the wind out of me. And I told myself over and over, *Don't cry. Just don't let him see you cry.*" The memory came back strongly for a moment, and I wrapped my free arm around my middle. "But my jaw was killing me, and my ribs felt like they were cracked. So, as soon as I could, I got up and scrambled away. I genuinely believed he would kill me. But, thank god, he just let me go. I locked myself in my bedroom, and he finally left."

I glanced at Dan again, and I knew he was seething. I could see it in the hard angles of his jaw. Still, he was working hard to let his voice convey only his unqualified support for me and a deep concern for my well-being.

"Were you able to tell your mother? The police? Anyone?"

I met his eyes once more. He might as well hear it all.

"By the end of my junior year, my mother was checked out. She was barely conscious most of the time, and this would've made it worse. My brother knew, but I begged him not to tell anyone. Believe me," I stressed, "our messed-up family didn't need the attention. And so that was it. I never looked at Seth or spoke one word to him again."

Danny was silent for a beat. "You were in my class."

"You couldn't have done anything. It was just one bad night, and then it was over."

"How did no one but your brother notice?" I knew what he was really asking, *How did I not notice?*

"Make-up, turtlenecks . . . I was very good at flying under the radar at that point in my life; I needed to be. If anyone had looked too much into my home life, they would've taken my brother away. Probably separated us both from my mom."

Danny was staring into the fire by now, and I wasn't sure he was really processing my words.

"Christ, Sarah." He rubbed his face with his hand. It felt like a helpless gesture. "You've been through so much. The thought of anyone hurting you is abhorrent to me."

His face was so pained that I reached out to caress his cheek. I wanted him to know I was okay. And he turned to me, perhaps seeing in me what he needed to see because his demeanor relaxed, and he closed his eyes, breathing into my touch.

"I know, Danny," I responded gently. "That's one of the reasons I love you."

The second the words fell from my mouth, my heart stopped beating. I froze, dropping the hand to my side. I was sure the look on my face reflected both panic and uncertainty.

At first, Danny seemed as surprised as I was with my admission. Long seconds passed as we just looked at each other.

Finally: "Do you need a do-over?" His tone was light, but in his eyes I saw a flash of vulnerability.

This was it. He was giving me an out. Every fiber of the old Sarah screamed to take him up on it, to make light of the moment. To give some witty retort or sarcastic comment that would make it pass without actually having to expose myself. It would have been effortless for me. I'd done it so many times before.

I thought about John, about how I rarely admitted to loving him. We were together for years, but he never really knew me. It was easier to keep things superficial and safe. In the end, I got hurt, anyway—and less from his infidelity than from the realization that after nearly four years together, our relationship was so easy to just throw away.

Then I thought about Danny. About his remembering so many small details of my life, and about the thoughtful things he did for me every day. I thought about how he made me laugh. I thought about his reaction to seeing his photograph in my room. I thought about how he understood me in a way no one had before him. I thought about how true happiness actually felt. This was a good man. A loving man.

This was the man I loved. And I needed to be brave enough to tell him so.

I inhaled deeply, gathering my courage. My heart felt ready to pound its way out of my chest.

"Just because I didn't mean to say it doesn't mean I don't mean it." I got the words out. They were inelegant and awkward, but they were a major victory for me. And he knew it. Of course, he would.

His eyes softened to the warmest green I'd ever seen. They were mesmerizing and reassuring, and I couldn't look away. Not for a moment.

He ran a finger gently across my cheek. "Say it," he murmured.

This time, I didn't hesitate. "I love you, Danny."

His expression showed it all, his love for me overflowing from his beautiful eyes. He took my face in his hands and kissed me, softly at first, and then more deeply until I could feel his complete certainty.

"God, I love you too," he whispered into my lips, like it was just the plain truth and he'd been dying to say it. "I love you like I've never loved anyone in my life. I've been trying to tell you but I'm not very good at that and I didn't know if you were ready to hear it from me."

He smiled, an embarrassed, vulnerable expression. Something about that boyish, unguarded look drew a lump in my throat. This man knew well how to pleasure a woman, but when it came to love, he was as much a novice as I.

"I think you may be every single thing I've ever wanted," he said softly.

If I had any words adequate enough to express what that meant to me, they were somehow missing in action inside my dumbstruck brain.

He studied my face carefully as I ran my hand over his cheek, but he didn't seem to need me to say anything more.

Instead, he took me in an embrace that overcame every ounce of self-doubt I had about love and relationships, clutching me so tightly to him that it felt as if we were one person. I just breathed him in, and let him fill me up with a happiness I hadn't known in years.

# Chapter 15

**Sarah**

"So when is God's gift to women showing up?"

It was Friday night happy hour at The Rose & Crown and Marcus was in a mood. Not surprisingly, I was already questioning my better judgment of introducing him to Danny.

"You promised me you'd behave tonight."

He leaned back in his chair, and rubbed the spot just under his lip. "I will. When do I ever not behave?" Those words would have been far more reassuring if they hadn't been drenched in his own special blend of sarcasm and wit.

"Don't make me even attempt to answer that question," I said, lifting a brow. He and I both knew we'd be here all night.

"I'll be a perfect gentleman."

"Oh, I'd pay to see your impression of a gentleman, Marcus," my friend Sheryl interjected.

Sheryl was in my major and we met in the dorms our freshman year. A few inches shorter than me with bright red curly hair, green eyes and a very voluptuous figure, Sheryl was everything I wasn't—gregarious, uninhibited, and right at home in the center of attention.

Marcus was pretty much her polar opposite. With dark hair and hazel eyes, he was also far slighter in build, and far less agreeable in personality. But for all his prickliness, he was one of my closest friends.

He was a year behind me in school, and was the epitome of a boy-genius. At present, he was developing an educational app that was very likely to become a full-blown business before the ink was dry on his diploma. It had been his obsession for as long as I'd known him.

He and I had met my sophomore year, and we became study partners almost immediately. Admittedly, I'd been aware that he'd developed feelings for me, but since I was with John for the better part of the last four years, it'd pretty much been a moot point. I valued his friendship greatly, and was thankful we'd never let anything get in the way of it.

I was certainly hoping that didn't change tonight.

But by the time Danny arrived after work, we were all on our second round. Selene and I were sitting with our backs to the door when he arrived.

It wasn't hard to notice the number of heads that swung appreciatively in his direction, and if I were the jealous type . . . well, thankfully I wasn't. Tonight, he was in a chambray shirt with the sleeves rolled up, and light denim Levi's jeans that looked like they'd been washed a thousand times, and then tailored for his athletic body. His hair was a little mussed and sexy, and his face bore the expression of a man who had no doubts about his place in the world.

When he caught my eye, he broke out that heart-stopping, megawatt grin.

"Wow," I heard Sheryl say quietly to herself; I could almost feel Marcus stiffen in his seat.

When I turned back to him, he was glancing down into his beer with a sour look on his face. I was assessing how bad this was going to be when Danny's strong hands gripped my shoulders.

"Hi," he whispered into my ear, giving me a quick kiss before bending to offer Selene a kiss on the cheek, as well.

"Did you forget your ascot in the townhouse?"

All of us turned to Marcus, conveying varying degrees of shock at his rudeness.

"*Marcus!*" I said.

"It was just a joke," he replied. Then he turned to Danny and added, "We're all friends here."

Danny brushed off the comment and graciously introduced himself to Sheryl, though the look in his eyes told me he'd made a rapid reassessment of the situation—and not in a positive way. He held his tongue, but he was clearly not going to be a fan of Marcus.

What I was coming to understand about Danny was that people usually saw in him what they expected to see—often to their disadvantage. I knew someone like Marcus would look at him and assume he'd never had a bad day in his life. Marcus would probably want to dismiss him as vain and superficial, and was treating him that way. Someone like Sheryl might assign too much value to his looks and not necessarily notice the substantive person beneath.

But the truth was, he was humble about his life in a way most people aren't—having experienced, like I had, the way fate can make even the most glorious among us just a postscript in a matter of seconds.

Fortunately, Selene and Sheryl jumped in to pick up the conversation, doing their best to ease the strain. I continued to stare pointedly at Marcus until he glanced up at me for just a moment, and then looked away towards the bar.

My heart sank.

I'd really hoped Danny and he would get along better than this, though I shouldn't have been surprised it didn't work out that way. I certainly wasn't going to condone Marcus's behavior, but to an extent, I had to admit to myself that I understood where it came from.

Danny had that trifecta of looks, brains, and athleticism.

Conversely, Marcus paired his looks and brains with cutting sarcasm and social awkwardness. Even in our circle of friends, he was viewed as amusing on his best days, and barely tolerable on others. His inclusion in our gatherings was usually my idea. I had a soft spot for him.

But I also knew that Marcus's best-kept secret—the one he guarded with vicious wit—was that at heart he was a really sweet guy. He was definitely not showing that side tonight.

Selene slid her chair over, and Danny sat between us. As he settled, he glanced in my direction with a reassuring look to say, *It's fine.* It wasn't, but I loved him for trying.

Danny ordered a beer, and engaged Selene and Sheryl in some conversation about school. Meanwhile, I tried to draw Marcus out, but he deflected my attempts at every turn, until finally choosing an unexpected moment to chime in.

Sheryl was asking Danny, "So when do you have to defend your dissertation?"

"A PhD?" Marcus whistled disingenuously. Danny purposely ignored it, but glanced at me in silent conversation that would've probably involved some colorful language if it hadn't been so blessedly silent. "I'm just curious," Marcus went on. "Do you find that's very impressive to younger women? The whole PhD thing?"

I'd just taken a swallow of beer, and nearly choked on it. I was seriously going to kill Marcus—as soon as I could breathe.

While I struggled to recover, Danny looked across the table flatly, his sharp green eyes locking squarely on equally sharp hazel ones. "I don't know you, Marcus. And I'm not especially concerned with what you think of me. But you do realize you're being disrespectful to Sarah, don't you? Since she's the one who invited me here?"

Marcus glanced quickly at me, and then back to his beer. The rest of the table fell silent. Sheryl was suddenly very occupied by an invisible speck on her sleeve, and Selene seemed to be watching the entire spectacle with no small amount of amusement. If she had had popcorn, her whole night would have been complete. When she met my gaze, she raised her eyebrows in an unmistakable *I-told-you-so* expression.

Yes, she did. I hated when she was right.

"Danny, Marcus is developing a K-through-8 app that allows teachers to track a student's progress in common core subjects and gives differentiated learning options," I told him in a transparent effort to make peace. "It's a phenomenal platform and he's getting a lot of interest in it." Looking eagerly between them, I suggested, "Maybe you could give him some feedback?"

Danny's enthusiasm for my idea was underwhelming, but out of respect for me, he responded coolly, "Be glad to, if that's what he's looking for."

This offer was met by a similarly underwhelming level of enthusiasm from the other side of the table.

And after another awkward moment of silence, Danny nodded his head towards the dance floor.

"Care to join me?"

*Hell yes.*

I took Danny's proffered hand and rose to my feet, glad for any excuse to get away from the table. This was not at all the way I had hoped this evening would go. Leaning in, I whispered fiercely to Marcus, "You're being an ass." I was livid. And he damn well should know it.

He didn't respond, but he did look a little shamefaced.

Good. He deserved to.

The dance floor was fairly crowded, and when we reached an opening in the masses, Danny pulled me in close to his body. He kissed me briefly, but thoroughly. His expression still carried the remnants of Marcus's unexpected ambush.

"I'm really sorry. I should have warned you about him. As you can probably guess, he doesn't have a lot of friends."

"I can't imagine why."

"I know," I sighed. "But he's been really good to me."

"That kid's a punk. He just wants to get in your pants."

"First of all, that *kid* is my age. Is that the way you think of me?"

"You know I don't."

"Well, just so you know, you sound very condescending. And second of all, that isn't why he's been good to me. I don't appreciate the implication that Marcus is only my friend because he's trying to get laid."

Danny held up his hands.

"You're right. I'm sorry. I meant no offense to you. I know he cares about you as a friend. Of course he would."

He appeared a little chastised, which he also deserved, so I let it go. I certainly didn't need to be fighting with him, while trying to referee something else between Marcus and him. It was all too exhausting.

I leaned my cheek against his chest, and he tightened his arms around me. We just swayed together for a bit as I sorted out my next words. When I leaned back to meet his gaze, he lifted his brows expectantly—like he knew there was more coming.

"Tell me," he invited.

"You need to understand about Marcus. After that whole mess with John, it was hard sometimes being around Selene and Kevin. Marcus and I spent a lot of time together. He always made me laugh, and he made me feel good about myself again. He used to tell me his most humiliating stories—times he was bullied, epic fails with girls—really awful stuff. But he would tell them in such an ironic way that we'd both end up laughing until we were in tears. I think he told me his stories so my own humiliation would be a little easier to bear."

Danny looked down at me and his expression softened. I could see twinge of guilt there for his unkind assumptions about Marcus.

"Then I guess I owe him a debt of gratitude for being your friend when you needed it."

He took my hand and brought it to his chest, covering it with his palm. His heartbeat was solid through the soft fabric of his shirt.

"He's not a bad guy."

Nodding slightly, he leaned in and gave me a quick kiss.

"Okay. I'll try harder to get along."

He nestled me close to his body, and his arms came around me again, enveloping me in his warmth. He smelled so good, that familiar laundry detergent-smell that I inexorably now associated with the man I loved.

But just as I began to relax into the moment, a voice to our right called out, "Hey, Redwood."

I felt Danny stiffen a bit, and then he muttered quietly, "Please say he's not talking to me."

His tone made me giggle, and I leaned back to see his incredulous expression. "I think he may be."

As in, he *definitely* was.

Danny closed his eyes momentarily, breathing deeply again, and then looked at me like he was trying to summon the patience of Job. He was likely to need it.

But before he could answer, Marcus added, now standing closer to where we were.

"You know anything about pool? Or are you more of a live-at-the-gym kind of guy?"

Marcus was wearing a slightly wicked, yet conciliatory expression, and I was happy at least that his tone had lost some of its bite.

Myriad emotions crossed Danny's face: strained equanimity, annoyance, gallantry—all fighting for mastery. He seemed to weigh the information I'd given him and finally he offered a slight nod. Decision made.

"I know a thing or two."

His lips compressed into a thin line, but there was a hint of resigned amusement there too. It appeared the high road had been chosen. For

Marcus's part, while his approach was no less offensive, I knew he was making an effort in his own weird way. And I was sure, like Danny, he was only doing that for my benefit.

I visited the restroom to give them some time to sort things out as only men can do. When I returned, Danny smiled reassuringly and gave me a wink.

As for Marcus, his demeanor had changed for the better. He was apparently pleased with his current position in the game.

Danny's next shot landed just left of the pocket and a flash of a smile curved his lips. Then it was gone. I didn't need to see the end of this game to know how it would play out. And as I watched the confidence grow on Marcus's face, my love for his opponent grew in equal measure.

# Chapter 16

## Sarah

I didn't usually love Mondays. But this particular Monday, I'd had a breakthrough with my patient, Joseph, who leaned his head into mine at the end of our session in an astounding gesture of affection.

When you work with kids with autism, you learn to appreciate every milestone in their journey, every small victory like this one. Kids with autism are extremely literal, but they can't always find the words to communicate. So you have to be sensitive to their body language, and to listen, even to the words they can't speak. Sometimes those words are the most profound.

Texting Danny with the news, I got an instant response.

*So proud of you, sweetness. And proud of Joseph, too.*

I headed out to my car, well aware of the idiot's grin plastered on my face. I was just getting in when my mom called. It was shameful to admit, but I hesitated before answering. We hadn't spoken in a while, and I instantly felt bad about that. I needed to make a point of checking in with her more often but . . . it was complicated.

"Hi, Mom."

"Sarah, I've been trying to get a hold of you. I never seem to be successful." Her tone was dripping with guilt.

"I know. I'm sorry. I haven't been home much."

"What have you been doing? I know the clinic isn't open 24/7."

I hadn't actually told her about Danny. I knew I should, but I found it easier not to get her involved in my life until I knew exactly where things stood. It was a month before I told her I'd moved out of the apartment I shared with John. But things with Danny were pretty serious, and it was time she knew.

"Actually, I'm seeing someone." Long pause. "You've met him."

"I have? Who is it?" She sounded surprised.

"Dan Moore. Do you remember him from McKinley?"

"No. He was in your class?"

I winced at the question I'd been dreading, preparing myself for what would inevitably come next. Taking a deep breath, I forged ahead.

"No, Mom. He was my teacher. My junior year."

The silence that met my words was deafening. I didn't have to see her reaction to know it wasn't good.

"How on earth did this happen?"

Yep. Not good at all. I closed my eyes and continued.

"It didn't *happen*, Mom. We ran into each other, and he was nice enough to help me with my fellowship essay, which was really generous. And as it turns out, he's a great guy who makes me very happy." And then for the cherry on top . . . "I love him."

There was another excruciating pause.

"Sarah, how long has this been going on?"

"A few months. I would have told you sooner, but I didn't know what you'd say."

"I think you knew exactly what I'd say. How old is he anyway? Thirty-five? Forty?"

"He's thirty-three. And it doesn't matter. He's brilliant, and he treats me well, and we have so much in common."

"I swear, Sarah, sometimes I just don't what you're thinking. What do you suppose your father would have said about this? You work yourself to the bone to get in to Stanford, to prepare for a career you've always talked about. And now, here you are, ready to throw all of that away? For a man?"

"What are you talking about—throwing everything away?"

"What do you think a thirty-three-year-old man wants? He wants a wife, Sarah. He wants kids. He's at a totally different stage in life, and he's not going to want to wait around while you finish school and start a career. What if you got pregnant? Then what?"

"I'm not getting pregnant!"

"You should be living the life of a twenty-two-year-old, not the life of a thirty-three-year-old. You should be focused on your career, and on enjoying this stage in your life. You don't need to rush into a serious relationship."

"Funny, Mom. You were fine with my living the life of a thirty-three-year-old when I was fifteen."

As soon as the words left my mouth, I regretted them. My mother and I had many weapons in our respective arsenals, and we both wielded them with surgical precision. Guilt, especially, cut both ways. I closed my eyes, and blew out a long breath.

"I'm sorry. That was uncalled for. I didn't mean it."

"I think you did," she responded quietly.

"I just wish you would be more open-minded about this. Danny is a really good person, and he cares about me. And he's very supportive of my career."

"He's old enough to know better, Sarah. Men like the idea of a younger woman because the chase is exciting, and it's flattering to their egos. But trust me on this: If marrying you isn't on his near-term agenda, then he's just having a good time. Eleven years is too much of an age difference to remain a non-issue for very long."

"I have to go," I told her, needing to end the call before I said anything more I'd regret. Why did I bother hoping my mom and I could have a better relationship? She was right about one thing: I knew this would be her reaction, and it was exactly the reason I didn't tell her.

"Will you come to Auburn for Labor Day weekend? It's been too long since I've seen you."

"I don't know. I'll see." We hung up quickly after that, and I drove to Danny's house with lead in my stomach. At some point, he was going to want to meet my mom again, and I didn't have the heart to tell him she didn't support the idea of us together.

§

I walked up the front steps of Danny's house, and let myself in using the key he insisted on giving me. When I reached the entryway, I could hear him on the phone in his office.

"No, this is unacceptable. You know my position, Bill. Every year, I expect you to come up with a new way to teach and assess every unit. I don't want to see the same lesson plans rehashed year after year. It needs to be fresh, both for your benefit and for that of the students. What you've given me here demonstrates a lack of effort."

I pushed the door open, and he immediately turned in my direction, giving me a warm smile that was in direct contrast to the tone of his current discussion. He nodded for me to have a seat in the comfortable chair that faced his desk, and held up a finger to say he was almost finished.

As he listened to what I imagine were protests on the other end of the line, I took a moment to look around this space. I hadn't really spent any time in his office, and I was fascinated by the way it reflected the man I'd come to know.

There was an entire wall of bookshelves, crammed with education and science-related periodicals. I didn't know how he could possibly keep up with all these. And there were photos of the basketball teams he'd coached through the years, as well as plaques of appreciation. There was an awesome action shot of him in his Cavaliers uniform jumping to block a pass. His expression was the epitome of intense determination. It gave me a small window into the kind of player he probably was.

Hanging on the wall off to the side in a less prominent position were not one, but two national teaching awards, both for his work at Taft Middle School. One was a Presidential Award for Math and Science Teaching, and the other was from the Science Teachers Association. These seemed like a big deal to me, but he'd never mentioned them.

Watching him at his desk was a reminder to me that as warm and funny as he was with me, this was a very accomplished man who had probably been intensely focused and goal-oriented his entire life.

"No, I'm not asking you to do anything more than I'm doing myself. I want to see new plans on my desk by Thursday. School starts Monday, and I expect you to be better prepared."

Hanging up, he turned his attention to me, immediately discarding any irritation from his phone call.

"Hi, beautiful! Great day today, huh?"

"It was quite a day," I mused, probably missing some of the enthusiasm he was expecting. He looked at me curiously, but he didn't push.

"You can tell me about it over dinner."

§

Dinner was a feast of succulent branzino, and a beautiful spinach salad. As we were finishing, Danny leaned back in his chair and looked me over.

"So, are you going to tell me what's bothering you?"

I debated just telling him I was tired, and avoiding the subject of my mom, but I knew when it came to intimacy, the right thing to do was usually the opposite of my natural instincts. I wanted this relationship to be much better than my previous ones. For Danny and I both, learning to be more open was a scary and difficult process. And I caught myself faltering often. But not tonight.

"I talked to my mom today."

"And?"

"And I told her about us." I didn't meet his eyes; he had a knack for seeing more than I intended.

"I didn't realize you hadn't told her. I take it the conversation didn't go well." His voice was gentle, and it broke my heart.

"I don't care what she thinks," I told him, glancing up into his face again, as his green eyes probed me softly. "She liked both Seth and John, so that shows how much she knows."

"What did she say?"

"It doesn't matter."

I was embarrassed to tell him. We'd only really known each other for three months. Any talk of marriage would probably give a mostly confirmed bachelor a nervous tic.

"Sarah." He lowered his head to hook my gaze once more. His eyes were tender, but insistent. "What did she say?"

I took a deep breath and exhaled. Oh, hell. The barn door was open, and the horse was probably in the next county by now.

"She said someone who's thirty-three is thinking about marriage and kids, and that I should be living the life of a twenty-two-year-old, not putting myself in a position to sacrifice my career because I'm with someone who's at a different stage in his life." There. If that didn't completely freak him out, I didn't know what would. "But like I said, she doesn't know you, and I don't care what she thinks."

"Then why does it bother you?" he asked carefully, searching my face for the truth.

"I don't know."

"I think it bothers you because a part of you knows she's right."

I stared at him incredulously. "How can you say that? She isn't right."

"I'm going to tell you something that might surprise you. Are you ready?"

I couldn't imagine where this was going, and no, frankly, I wasn't ready. "Okay."

"I would marry you tomorrow, Sarah. And nothing would make me happier than to have a family with you."

He was looking at me squarely in the eyes, and there wasn't a trace of humor in his expression. I knew without even having to ask that he was absolutely serious.

"How can you know that?" I whispered.

"Because when I told you I loved you, I meant it. I've never felt this way for anyone before, and I know exactly what I want with you. Your mom is right about that, so don't be angry with her. But you need to know I would never ask, or even want, you to limit a career that I know is important to you just because I'm at a place in my life when I'm ready. I can wait as long as you need me to."

"Danny." I didn't know how to respond.

He shook his head. "You don't need to say a word. I'm not asking anything of you. I just want you to know my intentions."

I was speechless and overwhelmed. I think my mouth opened slightly, and all I could do was blink at him. I couldn't begin to process all of this. There was no doubt in my mind that I loved him and that he loved me. But marriage? Family? We had so much to learn about each other still. How could he possibly know I was the one?

I was reeling. But then he smiled at me, leaning forward to brush a hair from my face.

"Now, where's my dessert, woman?" he barked, snapping his fingers for maximum effect. His eyes were alight with mischief, and it definitely broke the moment. If I was being honest, I was relieved.

I was pretty certain he knew that too.

# Chapter 17

**Sarah**

It was Danny's last week before the new school year started and we were spending the majority of it getting his classroom set up. I had no idea what went into preparing for students to arrive. The classroom itself had been painted and cleaned over the summer, so now he had to put everything back up, organize his supplies, and get books and lesson plans in order. In addition, because he had the added responsibility of being the department head, he'd been in meeting after meeting with his staff and administration all week.

By Friday night, we were both exhausted, and not prepared for the firestorm that was heading our way.

"So, don't forget I agreed to spend next weekend with my mom for Labor Day," I reminded him as we walked through the front door of his place.

"I didn't realize that was a done deal." He threw his keys and wallet on the table in the entryway and walked into the kitchen.

I followed behind, with Ralphie wheezing in excitement and begging for attention at my heel.

"It is. I need to spend some time with her. I haven't been to visit all summer, and with school starting in a few weeks, my schedule's going to get crazy."

"Okay," he said carefully. "You can take my car. I'll drive yours if I need it."

"No way." I brushed that notion off in a hurry. "I'm not taking your car."

Dan's car was really nice, and if I so much as dented a fender or scratched the door, I wouldn't be able to afford to fix it.

"How are you planning on getting there then?" He turned to me, and I stopped short at the look on his face.

"I'm driving," I answered hesitantly, confused by his question.

"You're not driving your car." He made solid eye contact, and for some odd reason, I felt like I was being scolded. I was so taken aback I didn't know what to say. And then he turned and walked out of the room.

I walked out right behind him and followed him to the bedroom. He was pulling off his black, pinstriped dress shirt when I walked in, and his bare chest almost distracted me from my point. Almost.

Standing in the doorway, I cut straight to the chase. "What's your problem?"

He turned abruptly at my question. "You really need me to spell it out?"

"Apparently."

"Your car's a piece of shit."

That made me bristle, lighting up every insecurity I had about my financial situation. I could feel my blood pressure rising steadily but I was trying to maintain a sense of calm.

Purposefully, I ignored his arrogant, insensitive, jackass of an attitude, and very calmly explained, "Well it may not be *fancy* like yours but it's perfectly fine, and I *am* driving it. I certainly don't need your permission to drive my own car."

"That's not happening," he said, plainly in no mood to be reasonable. "If you won't take mine, which is ridiculous, then I'll rent you one."

"Who do you think you're talking to?"

"I'm not arguing about this, Sarah."

"Really? That's how you think this goes? You make a proclamation and I fall in line like some student in your class?"

"Yes!" he said, giving me a glare that was downright arctic. "Because that car is—" he let out a harsh breath, "because one of us needs to be thinking like an adult."

"An *adult?*" I could not believe he pulled that card. "More like *one* of us—is acting like an ass! And just so we're clear, it's *you*. I *am* driving my car, and that's final."

I turned and stomped out of the room, down the hall, and towards the kitchen. And I'd almost reached it when he grasped my arm.

"For Christ's sake, Sarah! Why can't you ever just be reasonable? Why does everything with you have to be a fight?"

"What are you talking about? And did you really think I was just going to stand here and let you dictate what I can and can't do. Since when did you become such a tyrant?"

"A tyrant? That's what you think I am?"

"Yes!"

"Goddammit!"

The explosion of voices was followed by absolute silence.

Danny closed his eyes, and ran his hands through his hair again and again, as though he was struggling to regain his composure.

I just stared at him in shock. He was right in one respect; I *was* a fighter. But Danny rarely, if ever, raised his voice. It left me at a complete loss.

He was standing in front of me, with his head hung and his chest rising and falling with shallow breaths. I could practically feel him talking himself down. A part of me wanted to reach out to him because that was my instinct. But adrenaline was coursing through my veins and I was still reeling from how suddenly all of this had come to a head. I didn't know what to say. We just stood there. In silence.

"I don't want you to take that car," he finally said, very softly now.

And when he opened his eyes, his expression was filled with obvious regret and frustration. But there was something else there too. It took me a moment to recognize what it was.

Fear.

That's what it was. A fear that still lingered, even ten years later. My heart sank.

"I'm not going to get in an accident, if that's what you're worried about," I said in the same quiet tone.

He stared intensely at me for a long minute without answering. He didn't make a move to touch me either. We just stood there motionless as those words opened up between us, consuming all the oxygen. Finally, he turned and walked out. I heard him grab a bottle of Stella from the refrigerator and then he opened the sliding glass door to the yard.

To meet this man, you'd think he wasn't afraid of anything. But all of this—this sudden outburst, this need to control—was because he was afraid for *me*, and I had very mixed feelings about that.

I followed him into the yard, and found him sitting in one of the chairs, looking out at nothing specific.

"Can I join you?" I asked quietly. He didn't respond, but I sat in the chair next to him anyway.

"Dan, I service my car regularly. I promise it's far safer and more reliable than you think."

Still no response.

"Danny, I don't want to take your car because if I scratched it in any way, I couldn't afford to fix it. And it's against the law for you to rent a car for me. I wouldn't put either of us in that position."

"Then we can get you a train ticket. It takes about two seconds online."

"Yes, but it requires a credit card that I don't have," I said quietly, in an unsuccessful attempt to hide my embarrassment.

His eyes met mine and rather than pushing the idea of using his credit card, he honed in on what he correctly surmised was the bigger issue.

I didn't have a credit card.

"You don't?"

"I *can't.*"

"Why not?"

Looking down to my lap, I twisted my fingers together. I knew this would come up at some point, but definitely I wasn't prepared for it to come up today. I desperately battled back tears—to no avail. A drop spilled over and I quickly brushed it from my cheek, hoping he wouldn't notice. Of course he did. His demeanor changed in an instant.

With his attention now focused on me, he took my hands in his. His voice had lost the hard edge, and was now laced with concern.

"What's wrong? Tell me why you're crying."

The answer was something only my mother and I knew. I never, ever wanted to have to tell to anyone, least of all him. But he deserved the whole truth about me. It could very well affect him, at some point.

"I can't get a credit card. My credit is ruined."

His mouth opened slightly like he was trying to figure out what to say.

"By the time I was sixteen or seventeen, my mom had gone through most of our savings. She was drinking a lot and couldn't hold down a job. I worked as many hours as I could to make a little extra money but it wasn't enough. What I didn't know at the time was that she'd been taking out credit cards in my name. She maxed them out and never paid the monthly bill."

"Oh Christ, Sarah." He sighed heavily.

"I didn't find out until I was at Stanford and tried to rent an apartment. She'd been working to repair some of the damage by then, but it was extensive. So I'm stuck with the debt and the credit rating. If I reported it to anyone or tried to contest the charges, she could go to jail. She committed fraud."

"I get it." He nodded sympathetically.

"We've worked out a plan with the banks, and now that she's sober, she's been good about sending the payments in but it's going to take time."

"Let me help you. I have plenty of money, Sarah. Plus, I own my house and car outright, so I have no real expenses. I want to help. Call it a loan if you want, but you shouldn't have to live with the stress of that."

"No. Thank you, but no. We've got it under control. But that's why I can't do the things you're suggesting. I hope you understand."

He turned back to stare at the yard. "Then please take my car. I have insurance if anything happens to it and, frankly, I wouldn't give a shit if it did. But I can't . . ." He stopped and shook his head, his expression pained. "I know it's not rational, but . . . just . . ." He turned to face me again, his eyes searching mine, imploring me to acquiesce. "Please, just take my car."

I knew this was a big deal for him. And it was a big deal for me too. The fact that we'd both just admitted to some very painful secrets was a big deal for both of us. It felt monumental.

On top of that, I hated the thought of him worrying about me all weekend. I didn't want that.

"Okay."

"Okay," he said mildly. But relief was evident in his beautiful eyes, and that look alone was worth surrendering a considerable amount of my own stubborn pride.

He turned his attention back to the yard and took a long pull from his beer. He seemed a million miles away. He didn't say anything more, and it was hard to know if we'd actually achieved any sort of closure, other than my capitulation. But I didn't know what else to say, so I just let it go.

§

## Danny

I wish I could say Sarah's relenting on the car put the issue to rest, but the truth was, for me it didn't. The whole episode brought to the surface something I thought I'd long since buried: my own fucked-up demons.

The rest of the evening passed quietly. Dinner, some TV, and then we went to bed. I'm sure Sarah could sense something was going on with me, but she didn't pursue it. She just gave me space.

She fell asleep quickly, lying beside me in bed with the moonlight streaming in through the windows, but I couldn't sleep. I was restless and wide awake. I just watched her for the longest time, watched the way her golden hair spread out over the pillow, the way her perfect lips parted slightly, and her chest rose and fell with each breath. I watched her eyes move back and forth as she dreamed, wondering what visions she saw in her head. I watched the peace in her expression, and I wanted to feel that way again.

But I couldn't put out of my head the phone call I received ten years ago—the one that came out of nowhere, and sent my life into a tailspin.

I knew damned well this was totally irrational and I loathed the fact that the thought of her driving to Auburn would bring this feeling back so vividly, when I thought I was past it.

She was right that I was being overbearing. I *was* being an ass. Even *I* couldn't believe what was coming out of my mouth at the time. I mean, sure, her car wasn't great, but I knew it was fine for the trip. She went places every day, and I knew the chances of something happening to her were slim to none. I *knew* this.

But it didn't seem to matter. In my head, the ghosts of my past still goaded me, not with the statistical probability of what could happen, but with the reality that tragedy is *random*. There's no plan for it. Statistical probability doesn't apply. Life is just fragile, and it can be taken for no good reason—without discrimination, without cause.

It's not that I didn't worry about Carolyn and her safety; of course I did. But it never triggered this. Maybe because I loved Carolyn, but I'm not sure I *needed* her in the same way. My future with her never seemed quite clear. We'd been moving along, but I never had any idea where we were going.

With Sarah, I could see everything. I could see a future that felt hopeful. For the first time in my life, I wanted things: a wife, a family, a home. I knew who I was with her, and I *liked* that person.

My heart was thundering in my chest for reasons I couldn't explain. Sarah was still asleep beside me, and I reached over and touched her to convince my head that everything was okay; nothing was going to happen to her. Her hair was soft and beautiful, and her cheeks were smooth, like velvet beneath my fingertips.

The thing about tragedy is that when *it* touches you, you realize how close it actually is—every moment of the day. And you wonder how it doesn't reach you more often. But we can't live our lives worrying like that, always fearful of what's around the next corner. We'd go crazy. So, we turn away from it, push the random nature of life back, away from our consciousness, and pretend it isn't always breathing quietly right behind us.

Sarah awakened with my touch, and looked at me with a love that defined everything I wanted to be for her. I leaned down and kissed her lips, while her hands on my chest anchored me to a more level place in my head. With I need I couldn't even explain to myself, I moved over her, fitting her body perfectly with mine.

And as though she understood the dark place I was in, she opened herself to me, encouraging me with soft words and small touches.

I kissed her neck and touched every curve, every line, and every dip in her beautiful body. She pulled me to her, inside her—her touch providing a comfort beyond words.

She was so perfect beneath me. I began to move in and out in a steady rhythm.

My body was fully engaged, but the raging thoughts in my head remained a distraction I could not shake—they echoed with the realization that I had no control over what could come.

I couldn't protect her from everything.

I began to taste the fear, bitter as bile in my mouth, and my movements became more urgent. I needed more of her.

I rose up, pulling her with me so she straddled me.

"Yes, deeper," she whispered.

It was deeper, but it still wasn't enough. I needed even more. I reached for her wrists, wrapping my fingers around the delicate bones, and pulled them down alongside her body to restrain her as I thrust hard inside.

I felt her submit to me almost instantly. Here in my bed, she wasn't being willful; she wasn't being stubborn. She gave in to me, relaxing her arms and verbalizing her pleasure.

I pounded into her, throwing the full weight of my body behind it. Sweat was pouring off me.

I loved her. I *knew* this. But when did she become so necessary to me? When did it happen that I let myself *need* her? If I lost her, I wasn't sure I'd survive it.

Fear was inside me again like a monster. It was close now, even when I'd tried so hard to drive it away. I drove into her. Relentlessly. There was no ending and no beginning. It was all just a blur inside—a mass of contradicting emotions that scraped at the rawest parts of me.

Then finally, somewhere in that beautiful, fevered connection, the fear receded. She was *here*, and she loved me.

"Touch me," she whispered. "I'm so close." I released one of her wrists and pressed my thumb to where she begged for me.

"Ah, yes, Danny."

And then, gloriously, she shattered in my arms.

I needed this. I needed *her*. I felt my own climax gathering low in my spine and the rush began.

I let go. I let it all go: the fear, the doubt, the randomness. I pushed it all away.

A cry of profound relief ripped from my throat as I came copiously inside her, pouring out my love, pouring out my commitment, pouring out my need.

I had nothing left. No strength, no fight. Nothing withheld.

Rolling to the side with her draped over me, I held her close. I'd made a mess of her. I knew I should gather her in my arms and take her to the shower to wash her clean. But I didn't. I liked myself on her. As though I'd marked her in every way I could. As though I'd given fair warning to the universe that she belonged to *me*. This amazing and perfect, beautiful person was mine. This woman was my future, and she wouldn't be taken. Not on a car ride to Auburn. Not by some tragic twist of fate. Not by anything. Not ever.

I held her close, breathing her inside me—filling myself with the reassurance of her, flesh and blood. There, in her arms, I finally found my peace.

§

## Sarah

Awakening the next morning, every part of my body was sore and I was a wreck. As the haze of sleep began to recede, I could feel the ache in muscles I didn't know I had.

Danny was rougher last night than usual. I guess I'd never realized how much he held himself in check, always being supremely careful with me. And I never would have imagined that sex like that was something I would enjoy and even crave. But that's what he did to me, made me feel safe in a way I never had before. He obliterated my history, as though it were just a distant bad dream. With him, I was new. I was someone I never thought I could be: fearless, and open, and trusting.

I felt the bed shift, and turned in his direction. He was sitting up with the sheet bunched low on his waist, revealing miles of toned torso. To his face, he held small binoculars that he had trained on the far corner of the room.

"What are you doing?" I asked him, as though either he was crazy or I was.

He turned to me, but he didn't lower the binoculars from his eyes. Instead he began turning the dial at the center to focus on my face, and then shifted his gaze to my exposed breasts.

"I was watching a spider spin a very cool web on the ceiling over there, but this is actually much more interesting."

"You are a nut job."

An enormous grin split his face. "*What*? Everybody loves science."

Laughing, he handed me the binoculars, then leaned over and grabbed a second pair from the bedside table. Most people I knew stocked their nightstands with eyeshades, or books, or reading glasses. But not Danny; his was stocked with not one, but *two* pairs of binoculars.

"Seriously?" I asked him, with no small amount of disbelief. "You keep a spare set in your bedside table?"

"Those are good for looking at insects indoors," he explained, motioning to the ones in my hand. "This pair is best for watching hummingbirds out my back window. If you look very closely, you can actually see them fly backwards. But check out that spider."

With boyish excitement, he raised the binoculars to his face and directed them across the room to the spider. His enthusiasm for this activity was so contagious I found myself doing the same. How ridiculous we must have looked—me and the sexiest man alive, sitting naked in bed on a Saturday morning, watching a spider though binoculars from bed.

But this was the crux of my beautiful man. He was nerdy and gorgeous and perpetually curious. And he saw wonder everywhere around him.

I laid my head on his shoulder, comforted by the solid feel of his muscle, and the warmth of his tanned, smooth skin. He wrapped his arm around me and I sighed, contented and happy as we watched a remarkable little spider spin a miraculously complex web.

"Was I too rough with you last night?" Concern was evident in his voice.

"No, you were perfect," I answered with absolute sincerity.

In a million years, I could never have pictured myself in this moment. And yet here we were, binoculars and all. And the true joy of it was, there wasn't anywhere else in the world I'd rather be.

# Chapter 18

## Sarah

The Taft Middle School fall semester began on Monday, and as a result, Danny was swamped. Between school, his consulting, and the ever-present doctoral thesis, he was busy nearly around the clock.

Over the summer, he'd been pretty laid back. He was working hard on his thesis, but I got most of his evenings and weekends. Now, I had to share. So, as much as he might not have been happy about my trip to Auburn for the weekend, a part of him, I knew, was secretly relieved to have an opportunity to catch up on his work.

Saturday morning, he arrived at my house in his pristine car. He'd had it washed, serviced (again), and had put two new tires on it. All of this was unnecessary, but it made him happy so I didn't say a word.

Opening the passenger door to toss my small duffel inside, I found a large brown paper bag that appeared to be a care package for my trip. He'd decorated it in the same fashion as the box that had contained my surprise cake.

"More of your artwork, I see." He smiled.

On one side, he had drawn a stick figure of me—again with the long hair and the triangle dress. I was sporting an enormous grin, and holding a phone. The phone was apparently from the same era as my car, because it had a curly cord that wrapped around to the other side of the bag, where it connected to a phone in Danny's hand.

Thankfully this time, stick-figure Danny's giant penis was discreetly tucked in to a pair of stick-figure pants. Thoughtful, considering I was heading up to see my mother.

Both of us had speech bubbles filled with hearts.

"Look inside," he said.

As I might have guessed, the bag was filled with food. He'd cooked a full lunch that included two homemade chocolate chip cookies. Also in the bag was a Tupperware container he'd packed with cookies for my mom. It had her name on it. That made me want to cry. I had so many issues with my mom, and she apparently had her own issues with Danny. But Danny defended *her* at every opportunity, always encouraging me to be understanding and forgiving. Always gently trying to help me see things from her perspective. I loved him for that. And it also broke my heart.

At the bottom of the bag was a Ken doll. Or *action figure*, as I was given to understand.

"In case you miss me."

"I will definitely miss you."

"Text me from the road," he said, but quickly added, "but not *while* you're driving!"

"I know, baby. I'll be safe. I promise."

He smiled a full-on megawatt smile that I knew was meant to reassure me he'd gotten over his pique. But the smile didn't quite reach his eyes, revealing a bit of apprehension I suspected he didn't intend for me to see. If I didn't know him so well, I wouldn't have noticed it. I imagine most people would never guess that behind that smile was where he kept his secrets. I made a mental note to be considerate of causing him any unnecessary concern. He deserved that. He was a really good person and I loved him enough to want to give him anything he needed.

With a long kiss, a tight hug and several *I love yous*, I climbed into the car and waved goodbye. He stood in my driveway, looking simply delicious in jeans and a T-shirt, and watched me go. I couldn't believe how much I was looking forward to coming back.

§

The weekend with my mom went by quickly and without much incident. We largely avoided all talk of Danny. Occasionally, she made a sideways reference to him—"If you don't already have plans for the holidays . . ." or "It sounds like most of your time is occupied these days . . ." But for the most part, we kept the conversation on neutral ground. We went for walks together, watched her favorite TV shows, cooked some meals, did a little window-shopping, and talked endlessly about my brother, Scott. My mom and I were both overwhelmingly proud of him; this was rarified safe territory for us.

Danny and I spoke every night and traded some texts during the day. As I suspected, he was spending the long weekend buried in work, and taking a break every now and then to go to the gym or play basketball with friends. And, yes, it was only a few days, but I missed him like crazy.

When I pulled into his driveway on Monday evening, he came outside to greet me before I was out of the car. He swept me into a deep, lush kiss, perhaps not entirely suitable for neighborhood viewing.

"Are you hungry? I've got dinner prepped and ready to go."

"Yes, starving. Thank you." I was getting so spoiled. At least I knew it.

Over the course of dinner, I told him about the weekend, and how hard it had become to relate to my mom. I told him how it felt like with every passing year, there were more and more things we couldn't discuss, more and more shallow reefs we had to navigate. I told him it felt like our relationship had become a minefield, but I didn't know how to begin to repair it. I told him things I'd never told anyone. He was a good listener, and he never judged.

"You can't give up on your relationship, Sarah," he implored me. "Trust me when I tell you this is not something you want to leave unresolved."

The words he said spoke volumes about his own circumstance. "You have regrets about your dad."

It wasn't really a question—even with my limited knowledge, I knew he did, though he was rarely open to discussing it.

But tonight he nodded slightly, confirming my suppositions without his usual attempts to redirect the conversation.

"Do you want to tell me about it? I understand if you don't."

He frowned, his own struggles with intimacy articulated in every line of his face, and I silently willed him to open up a little, not just for my benefit, but because I knew better than anyone how important it was for *him*, and for us.

I didn't think he would do it, but then he looked at me with heartbreaking vulnerability.

"My dad and I clashed pretty much my entire life, and his disapproval of me was devastating as a child. It wasn't one thing in particular—it was just everything. He didn't like my friends. He didn't think I took my schoolwork seriously enough. He always thought I was too focused on sports. We just had nothing in common."

Danny paused, lost in a memory.

"I could feel, even then, that whatever that picture was he had in his head about what it would be like to have a son, it wasn't me. I could never figure out how to be enough.

"By the time I was a teenager, I was resolved to do what I wanted. If that happened to be the opposite of what he wanted for me, then all the better."

He took a sip of wine, and then set the glass down carefully, turning the base just so.

"Did the two of you ever try to work things out?"

Danny blinked a couple of times and I could almost watch him reliving something in his head.

"We just seemed to find so many points of contention—all the way to the end. And ironically, even after the end. I remember this one time," he said frowning. "My dad was dean of the law school at Cal while I was in high school, and then he accepted a job at Yale in the middle of my senior year. He wanted to move our family back east in January of that year, but I refused—said I'd rather live with Jamie and his family so I could finish my senior year here. Jamie's family was a disaster so, of course, we had a huge fight about that."

"What did you do?"

"My mom stepped in on my behalf and said she would stay in California with me until school was out. In the end, he allowed it because it was what she wanted, but he always resented me for keeping the two of them apart for those six months. He thought I was selfish. I thought he was selfish. We could never see each other's point of view. That's how it always was."

Danny shook his head in a way that made it evident that, among the many things we had in common, we both knew what it was like to feel an insurmountable distance from a parent.

"The thing is, Sarah, I have no idea whether we would've eventually worked out our differences. For most of my adolescence, I told myself I didn't care whether or not we got along. But the truth is, children always care, no matter how old they are. You may not feel like you can mend your relationship with your mom but, believe me, there'll come a time when you'll wish you'd at least tried."

The look on his face conveyed a sadness so great it felt tangible, and I wished desperately I had the ability to heal the wound beneath those words.

I reached my hand out and threaded my fingers through his.

"You weren't solely responsible for the state of your relationship with your father. You were a child, and he should have tried harder too."

He made a low, noncommittal sound in this throat, stroking my fingers absentmindedly with his own.

"Thank you for that. But what I'm trying to tell you is that it's not much consolation now. I understand what you're saying about how things were when I was young, but I was twenty-three when he died and at that age, I knew better than to let things go unresolved."

*I knew better.* At that very moment, I had pinned to my bulletin board a quote from Kierkegaard that said, "Life can only be understood backward; but it must be lived forward." I'd always felt the idea was a little unfair. Yet, suddenly, the words felt incredibly relevant. Like Danny, I knew better too.

It was yet another thing we shared.

I studied him for a moment, leaning back in his chair with his long arms stretched out before him, one hand holding mine and one hand toying with his wine glass. He seemed lost in thought, or maybe remorse. I wanted so badly to be able to say something to ease his mind, something to lessen the weight of the load he carried.

But as much as I might have wanted that, I knew the burden was his alone. Regret was lonely business. And we each had to find a way to carry our own, such that it didn't break us.

"I love you, Danny." It was the best I could do.

He met my gaze with a steady eye. Then a small smile formed at the edges of his beautiful mouth, and he leaned over and pressed a gentle kiss to my lips. His eyes were soft and unguarded, teeming with unnamed emotion.

"What man could want for anything more than that?"

# Chapter 19

**Sarah**

Danny's older sister, Casey Hanson, came for a visit in early October. She and Danny were obviously close, but living on opposite coasts, they didn't see each other very often.

He'd headed home to meet her right after work, but I was back in school and didn't finish class until five-thirty. By the time I arrived, they were sitting on barstools in the kitchen having a glass of wine. Danny smiled when I walked in, taking my backpack, and giving me a quick kiss. Then he introduced me to his sister.

As you might expect, Danny's sister was beautiful. There was definitely a family resemblance in their facial structure and features, but her coloring was completely different.

Casey was tall, probably around my height. Her hair was darker than Danny's, and she had brown eyes. She was dressed impeccably in gray slacks and a stylish ivory jacket, and she wore a stunning long, silver necklace over a shimmering ivory camisole. On her right wrist was a collection of expensive-looking bangles, and on her ring finger was the largest diamond I'd ever seen. I definitely felt underdressed, and frankly a little self-conscious, in my jeans and peasant top.

But Casey quickly rose from her barstool, her bracelets jingling as she embraced me. Her expression was warm, and it was clear the megawatt, supermodel smile ran in the family. I felt instantly more at ease with her.

As Danny worked on dinner, Casey and I got to know each other. She had a big job as head of admissions for NYU, and we talked about how much harder it was these days for high school graduates to get into college, let alone pay for it. She was very interested in my brother and his experience at CalTech, and we talked about her kids and their activities. Every so often, I would catch Danny's eye; he looked happy to see us getting along so well.

"So Case," he chimed in at one point, "Sarah and I have been watching all the old Woody Allen movies. She's never seen them."

"*Annie Hall* is his best," Casey told me.

"No way. *Manhattan*," Danny said.

Casey shook her head. "It's definitely *Annie Hall*."

"Says you."

"Says anyone, Danny. It's a fact."

"It's not a fact just because you say it's a fact."

Casey shrugged and made a face—a face that apparently also ran in the family. It was pretty funny to me. Danny could be a bit of a know-it-all, so it was refreshing to see him on the receiving end of this exchange.

"Do you mean like when I said you tried to feel up Brooke Decker at my sixteenth birthday?" Casey asked, taking another sip of her wine.

"Are you kidding me? You're bringing *that* up now?"

"I'm just saying that was a fact, even though you tried to deny it."

Danny paused in the dinner prep, kitchen knife in hand. "I did not feel up Brooke Decker. She was the one who tried to kiss *me*."

"That's not what she said. She said you came into the living room that night—I think you were wearing that Barney Rubble costume you used to wear all the time—and you pretended to trip on someone's sleeping bag, so you could put your hand on her boob."

Danny's ears turned red with embarrassment—or outrage, I wasn't exactly sure. It felt like I was being treated to a glimpse of the Moore siblings at their teenage best. I honestly thought just then that Danny's eyes might burn a hole in Casey's face, if that were even remotely possible. But she was completely unfazed. She returned the look with cool confidence.

"That is such a lie," he countered. "First of all, why are we even talking about that costume? One thing has nothing to do with the other. And, by the way, it was Tarzan, who is *cool*, not Barney Rubble. Plus, I wore that thing when I was like seven, not thirteen.

"And second of all, I did trip, because Brooke Decker tripped me, and when I fell, she grabbed me, and tried to kiss me. That's a *fact*."

"You were at least eight with the Barney Rubble thing. I have pictures of you in just your loin cloth at the grocery store."

"You do not."

"*Do*," she taunted, eyebrows raised, Moore-family smirk firmly in place. "In fact, I think I'll send them to Sarah." She turned to me with a whopping grin on her face.

I held both hands up. "I'm so not getting into this conversation. Although, a thirteen-year-old Tarzan at the grocery store—I would pay to see that."

"Seven! I was like seven! Maybe even six!"

I laughed. There really wasn't anything I loved more than teasing Danny.

§

The conversation throughout dinner was fun. There was a lot of good-natured ribbing between the two, and it was interesting for me to see the familial similarities in their personalities and mannerisms.

"How's the remodel coming along?" Danny asked at one point.

"It's looking great! You're going to love it. Here, I have pictures."

As Casey rose from her chair to grab the cell phone from her Chanel purse, Danny turned to me to explain.

"We're remodeling my parents' summer house in East Hampton. Casey's basically driving it since I'm too far away to be of much help."

Casey returned with her iPhone, and we gathered around as she began flipping through the pictures and explaining what we were seeing.

But I couldn't really pay attention to what she was saying; the photos, quite frankly, were a shock.

The *summer house* appeared to be right on the water with its own private beach. It had a Nantucket feel, and—I was no expert on the Hamptons—but I was pretty sure this wasn't where the poor people hung out.

She didn't have pictures of every room, but the kitchen alone was stunning. It was a huge bright space with gorgeous white cabinets, black countertops and sparkling stainless appliances. It looked bigger than my apartment.

"It's beautiful," I said quietly.

Noticing something in my voice, Danny looked up to meet my eyes.

"The house has been in my dad's family for a long time. He grew up on the East Coast. It's a great location, but it needed some work, so we've been updating it over the years. Casey and her family get to spend a lot more time there than I do, obviously."

He raised one shoulder like the whole thing was no big deal. But it *felt* like a big deal.

"You'll see it at Christmas," Casey said to him. "You should come too, Sarah."

"You definitely should," he affirmed, looking directly at me.

But I didn't respond, just glanced down as Casey continued the discussion of a bathroom remodel.

For starters, Christmas was almost two and a half months away, and we hadn't talked about the holidays yet. For all I knew, she'd just put him on the spot to invite me, when maybe he wasn't ready to.

Second, it was all a little strange. He'd never told me his parents had a summer home, or that he and Casey still owned it. Not that it mattered to me. I guess it just never came up. Still, I would think he might have mentioned it at some point.

§

After dinner, Danny took Ralphie for a walk while Casey and I tackled the dishes. I washed and she dried, making small talk about this and that. But at a lull in the conversation, she caught me off guard.

"Danny seems really happy."

She made solid eye contact as though she was watching my response. I'll admit, it was a little disconcerting. I was suddenly very aware that she and her brother were all that remained of their family, and the bond between them ran thick.

I set a wet saucepan on the counter, shutting off the water faucet, and turned to face her directly.

"We both are," I told her.

I wondered how much he'd told her about our relationship or if she would be at all curious about me—I'd certainly been curious about her.

Casey didn't respond, but smiled as though she was gratified to hear it.

And that seemed to give me an opening I hadn't realized I was looking for. I hesitated for just a beat, telling myself I shouldn't do this, but not quite able to stop.

"Can I ask you something? About Danny?"

She couldn't possibly know what I wanted to ask, and yet she didn't seem the least bit surprised I'd have questions. Her expression was sympathetic; apparently I wasn't the first woman to seek information about her brother.

"Of course. If it's something I can answer."

I took a deep breath. "Why was Danny's relationship with your father so strained?"

I was only half expecting her to tell me. If she were anything like her brother, she'd artfully avoid the subject. And maybe it was better she should. It wasn't really my business.

But she surprised me by sniffing out a small ironic laugh. "That's a complicated question."

"That's exactly what he said."

I felt a little disloyal getting information this way, but I wanted to know Danny better and I didn't know how to connect the dots.

Casey picked up a dishtowel and began drying the saucepan. Then, setting the pan down on the sink she replied carefully, "My father expected the best from us because he wanted the best for us. Or at least, that's how he probably would've liked to express it, if he'd had the skills.

"He was a good man, Sarah, and he loved us very much in his way. The only thing he ever wanted was for us to have a good life. But he had a limited vocabulary when it came to conversations of the emotional kind. My brother's the same way."

To say the least.

"They spent years fighting over nothing of any real importance—schoolwork, what my dad perceived as Jamie's bad influence, Danny's periodic irresponsibility. Had they both known how short their time together would be, I doubt either would've let any of it take on the magnitude that it did. But you can never see that when you're in the middle of it."

"There had to have been *something* to it, though. Right?"

She folded the dishtowel, placing it in the drawer by the sink, and pushed the stack of bangle bracelets back onto her wrist.

"Yeah, I guess. My dad was an intellectual and a workaholic. It frustrated him to no end that Danny could do so well in his classes without killing himself over it. I guess it was sort of a backhanded compliment. He just thought Danny wasn't living up to his full potential.

"Plus, my dad didn't revere sports. He felt sports created a distraction for my brother from a more certain career path. He wasn't particularly supportive of Danny's athletic career. That was a major disconnect between them.

"So, they constantly fought, almost from the time I can remember. It ripped my mom apart. I think it was the only thing my parents ever argued about. And the more my dad pushed Danny to do something, the more Danny wanted to do the opposite."

"But he can't have objected to the scholarship from UVA."

"Ah, the scholarship," she said rolling her eyes. "That was the final straw. Danny got into Yale, where my father was working at the time, and my dad insisted he go there. He wanted Danny to pursue environmental law. He thought with Danny's aptitude for logic and his competitive nature, law would be the perfect career for him. But Danny didn't want that. He didn't want to go to school where my dad worked, and he didn't want a job in a corporate environment. So, he and my dad clashed like titans, and my dad told Danny if he wasn't going to take that career path, then my dad wasn't going to pay for his education."

"Would your mom have allowed that?"

"Never." She shook her head in vehement negation. "It was an empty threat made in the heat of the moment, and everybody knew it. But that didn't matter to my brother. It was the principle of the thing. You know how he is."

"He took the scholarship so your father wouldn't have anything to hold over him."

"Bingo. The University of Virginia is a great school, but if he'd wanted to go Ivy League, he certainly had the grades and the test scores for it. The bottom line was he loved basketball, and the scholarship allowed him to cut my dad's purse strings. For him, it was the perfect solution."

"And they never worked it out?"

"No. They were both obstinate. There was so much conflict between them for so long they just couldn't get past it, and it got harder and harder to find common ground. There were too many things that set them off."

Casey paused, looking inward. When she met my eye again, there was more than a bit of regret in her expression. "I think they would have outgrown their differences once my dad saw how passionate Danny is about teaching, but they didn't have enough time."

My heart broke with the injustice of that.

"It's hard for me to imagine, given everything Danny accomplished, that your dad wasn't really proud of him."

"He was. I know he was." She thoughtfully twisted the bangles on her wrist. "But he was raised in a very traditional way, Sarah, and he believed that the way to parent a successful son is to push him. To never accept anything less than his best. It's the way my grandparents were with my uncle and him.

"The tragedy is that I know a part of him respected Danny's decision to become financially independent. Ironically, that may have made him prouder than anything. It was just hard for him to let go of his own goals for my brother."

"Does Danny know that?"

"We've talked about it, but I don't think he ever believed it. I think he just felt like a disappointment to my father for as long as he could remember. It broke my mom's heart that Danny was much closer to my uncle than he was to my dad."

"Your uncle—the Star Trek fan?"

"Yes, they were freakish together," she answered with a smile, and then it faded. "But we lost my uncle to cancer when Danny was still at UVA. When the accident happened—my parents', I mean—I had my husband

Michael to lean on. But I think Danny felt very much alone, and the experience changed him. That's why I love seeing him so happy now."

We finished the dishes, both of us consumed by our own thoughts. It was almost impossible for me to comprehend that Danny's father could have taken any exception to such an accomplished son. But I had to assume that his intentions came from a good place, despite the way they were communicated.

Still, I also understood how concern, frustration, and misaligned expectations—even when they stemmed from a parent's genuine feelings of love—could all feel like rejection to a child.

It was devastatingly unfair that Danny's relationship with his dad would forever be suspended in strife because fate didn't give them the time to make things right.

§

When Danny came back in the house with Ralphie, who was overheated but seemingly very happy from his mild exertions, I was still thinking about my conversation with Casey. And maybe it showed in my face because Danny cocked his head to the side in question.

But I just smiled brightly, not wanting him to know. He wouldn't want my pity. Still, he came over and kissed me, running his finger down my cheek.

"Everything okay?" he asked softly.

"Of course! I think I'm ready for bed, though."

I did my best to sound tired. I was, but more than anything, I wanted a little time to think about everything I'd learned tonight. Danny was just too perceptive when it came to me.

"I'll be in soon." A roguish expression crossed his face, and my heart skipped a beat.

§

As I was getting under the covers, I happened to hear Dan and Casey talking softly in the hallway. I didn't pay much attention until I heard Casey ask, "Have you discussed it with her yet?"

*Her* meaning . . . me?

This made me suddenly very interested in the conversation. I knew that eavesdropping is something you did at your own peril, but I couldn't quite help it—I held my breath, and focused on the muted discussion happening outside the door.

"No, not yet."

"Why not?"

I didn't hear the answer, but if I knew my boyfriend, it probably came in the form of a stubborn shrug.

"Danny, you shouldn't wait—not if you're serious about this."

He sighed. "I know. I will."

Shortly thereafter, he opened the door and came in. After brushing his teeth, and stripping down to his boxer briefs, he climbed into bed. I didn't mention what I'd overheard; I shouldn't have been listening anyway, and if it *was* something to do with me, he had to want to tell me.

But he was in a playful mood, which was my absolute weakness because he wasn't that way with most people. He pounced, tickling me and biting my neck.

"What are you doing?" I was flattened like a pancake, and gasping for breath as he reached under my tank to stroke my nipple.

"I'm having sex with you," he pronounced like he was a sultan.

"No, you're not," I told him. "Not tonight. I don't want your sister to hear us."

"I'm pretty sure she knows I have sex."

His eyebrow quirked up sardonically before he lowered down to take my earlobe into his mouth. I struggled to push him off, but it was no use—I might as well have been pushing a brick wall.

"Well, knowing it and hearing it are two very different things."

"Then you'd better be quieter this time."

He was busy divesting me of my tank top—despite my feeble protests—when suddenly we heard a blood-curdling scream coming from the guest room. Danny and I both leaped out of bed—he in his boxer briefs and me in my pajama shorts and molested tank.

We threw the door open to find Casey sitting in bed with the bedside lamp on. She was screeching and flailing her arms wildly as she shook her head and batted at her hair.

"What the *hell*?" Dan exclaimed.

"It's a spider! It was on me."

Out of the corner of my eye, I caught movement on the carpet, and Danny and I both turned quickly to see a large brown spider crawling across the floor. Dan trapped it under an empty water glass from the nightstand.

"Holy shit!" He turned to me with eyes wide and intense. "It's a brown recluse."

I'd heard of brown recluse spiders before, and I knew they were poisonous, but I'd never seen one. I wasn't sure what I was supposed to do with this information.

"Brown *what*?" Casey screamed.

"Did it bite you?" he asked her urgently.

"What?" She looked panicked.

"Did it *bite* you?"

"I don't know! I can't tell. I was lying in bed and I felt it on me!"

Dan grabbed her arm. "Shit! There's a bump here. Does it hurt yet?"

"Hurt?" Casey was in shock. "I don't know. No, I don't think so."

"Does it itch?"

"Itch?"

"Yes! That's a bad sign if the itching has started."

"I don't know. Yes, I think it itches." Casey began to cry.

"Do you feel dizzy or hot or confused?"

Looking very confused, she sobbed, "Yes, I think all those things. Is it dangerous?"

I was beginning to panic, myself. This seemed bad. Danny was carefully examining the bite, and Casey was nearly hysterical.

"Jesus, I think it's starting to swell," Dan said, turning to meet my eyes, which, I'm sure, were the size of saucers.

"What should we do? Should I go to the hospital?" Casey cried.

"I'm not sure we'll make it. Sarah, go grab my phone!"

I was so shocked. I just stood there. "Go!" he said urgently.

I ran to grab his phone off the nightstand in his room. When I came back, Dan was trying to suck venom from the site of the bite. Casey was as white as a ghost.

I handed him the phone, my hands shaking. He took it, and tapped something, which I assumed was 911. But then he held the phone up like he was videotaping poor Casey.

"What are you doing?" she screamed.

"In case you don't survive, I want our family to see how beautiful you were in your last moments."

Casey froze.

She was a mess—eyes running with mascara, hair wild, and pale as a ghost.

But in an instant, everything changed. I watched as her face turned bright red, and her eyes went from panicked to venomous.

Danny burst out in uncontrollable laughter, so hard he had to put his hands on his knees to keep from falling over.

"You little shit!" Casey screamed. "You are such a little shit!"

Danny couldn't respond. He was crying, he was laughing so hard. "*Should I go to the hospital?*" he said, in a rather unflattering girl voice.

Casey narrowed her eyes at him for a very pregnant pause. And then she, too, burst out in fits of laughter.

"I really hate you. You are the worst little brother of all time. I'm not even kidding!"

Then she turned to me. "See what I had to live with growing up? He's a monster!"

Danny regained some control, and wiped tears from the corner of his eyes, still smiling like a jack-o-lantern.

"You know, you're three times more likely to be killed by a flying champagne cork than you are from the bite of a venomous spider."

"No, nerd, I didn't know that. And I don't give a crap."

He sat down on the bed next to her, wrapping his arm around her, and kissing her on the head. "You love me," he coaxed.

"I really don't," she declared emphatically. "And, ew, gross, you're practically naked."

It was a funny thing to share a gene pool with someone. When I saw Danny practically naked, *Ew, gross* was about the last thing I would think. It would be right up there with, *Put some clothes on.*

"And look, you scared Sarah," she said pointing at me. "Now she knows what an ass you really are."

"I already knew what an ass he is. On our first date, he made me put a piece of pasta on my face. He claimed that's how you check it to see if it's done cooking."

Casey turned to Dan with renewed respect. "Did you get a shot of that?"

"I did!" he responded enthusiastically, and began scrolling through his phone for the photo. Upon finding it, both of them were rolling in laughter at my expense. And just like that, *I* was the butt of the joke. *How the hell did that happen?*

"You are both very annoying," I said, pointing at them.

Danny laughed unabashedly, and stood to grab me up in his arms.

"Ew, gross, you're practically naked," I grumbled.

"I'm about to get much more naked," he cracked as he dragged me back down the hall toward the bedroom.

"Come on," Casey shouted behind us. "I did not need to hear that!"

# Chapter 20

## Sarah

Every year in early December, Stanford put on its holiday concert, a spectacular culmination of four months of intense practice. This year, I was part of it.

In the crowded lobby afterwards, I located Danny—standing with his back to me, and his hands in his pockets. He was a striking figure in a navy tailored suit with his strawberry-blond hair and crisp white shirt. Some suits wore the man, but Danny's had definitely been brought to submission by his broad shoulders, and naturally confident bearing.

As I made my way towards him, I noticed a stunning brunette step into view. She was leaning in close, smoothing his red tie in what seemed to be a very intimate gesture. She was model thin, and dressed to the nines in a sleek, figure-hugging sheath dress in a rich, cabernet color. I couldn't quite place her ethnicity, but she looked very exotic—maybe part Russian or Eastern European lineage.

Over the past six months, I'd grown used to seeing women gawk, flirt, and get downright handy with my man. I couldn't blame them; he was gorgeous. And I wasn't usually jealous about these things, but something about this woman—this *particular* one—bothered me. I tried not to let that show as I reached them.

Danny instantly drew me into a tight embrace, and then tucked me to his side with his arm around me.

"I'm so damned proud of you," he whispered, while he eyed my body appreciatively in Selene's red dress.

Then he turned to the woman and introduced me.

"This is Carolyn Martin."

The shock of those four little words knocked me off balance for a moment, and I was thankful for his arm to steady me. I hadn't expected to meet Danny's ex here tonight. And she didn't appear any better prepared to be meeting me. In her expression, I saw a flash of something. But it was just a flash, and then she smiled widely and extended her hand.

"You were wonderful," she gushed.

I smiled weakly back at her, not sure what the protocol was when meeting an ex who may, or may not, secretly dislike you. Fortunately, the awkwardness didn't last long, as we were joined by Carolyn's date for the evening.

He was tidy and slight, handsome in a non-descript sort of way, and he seemed completely oblivious to any feelings of discomfort among the rest of us.

"Peter Gale, this is Dan Moore. Peter's a financial analyst with Columbia Management," she said by way of introduction. "And Danny is a *long-time* friend and PhD candidate here at Stanford."

The fact that she intentionally didn't introduce her date to me answered any question I had about her feelings towards me. And the emphasis on *long-time* was obviously there for my benefit.

Still, for Danny's sake, I made a conscious effort not let any hint of annoyance show on my face. What actually bothered me most was that she focused her introduction of Danny on his PhD, despite the fact that his primary occupation and great love was a nearly ten-year teaching career. *That* profession clearly didn't rank as highly as financial analyst in her book, and it spoke volumes to me about their relationship. It was obviously not lost on Danny either. I bit my lip with a strong urge to say something, and Danny squeezed my hip gently as if he could hear every thought.

Whatever he might have been thinking, outwardly he was calm and gracious, as always. He shook Peter's hand firmly and turned to me.

"Let me introduce my girlfriend, Sarah Kyle. Sarah was one of the performers this evening."

"Yes, of course," Peter said, shaking my hand. "You were terrific."

"So, you're a student, Sarah?" Carolyn inquired pleasantly.

But within the context of this conversation, her slight emphasis on the word *student* felt like an opening to the female version of a pissing contest I really wanted no part of. I realized I could just say *yes*, or I could explain further that I was planning a career working with children with special needs. But I knew she wasn't asking because she was actually interested in that level of detail about me. Her reaction to my presence suggested this episode was heading nowhere good.

So, rather than going down this path with her at all, I just smiled mildly. "I am." Then I turned to Danny, taking his handsome face in my hands and pressing a firm kiss to his beautiful lips.

"I love you," I said. *And I'm so proud to be with you.* I didn't need to say that last part out loud. He got it; I could see it in his expression. "I have to get backstage. I'll see you at home."

"Pleasure to meet you both," I said to Carolyn and her date. And then I made my way back through the crowd.

# Chapter 21

## Sarah

Selene and I had some last-minute gifts to buy, so we headed out to the Stanford Shopping Center with roughly a billion other people on the last Saturday before Christmas. Crazy, I know—but also the only opportunity I had to get through the rest of my list. Danny and I were leaving for my mom's the next day, and he would stay for a couple days before flying back east for the holiday.

After fighting crowds for hours, I was ready to get back to Danny's and put my feet up. But each time I texted him to let him know I'd be home soon, he sent back a request for this or that: Could I stop at the market for a couple of tomatoes and a package of coffee? Would I mind grabbing the sweatshirt he left at my place because he needed it for his trip? If it wasn't too much trouble, Ralphie needed dog food, or he'd run out while we were gone.

*Gah* . . . This was so irritating. But how could I say no? I could never say no to him.

Finally, I arrived at his place late in the afternoon with all of my bags, plus the tomatoes, coffee, sweatshirt and dog food. Jamie was just leaving, and Danny met me on the doorstep, taking the purchases from my hands. He set them down on the stoop, and cupped my face in his hands, pulling me in for a deep kiss that left me a little breathless.

"I have a surprise," he said, and in his expression was barely contained glee. "It's for you."

"What is it?"

"It's your Christmas present."

He looked nervous all the sudden, and I couldn't imagine why. If he'd done something crazy like gotten me a puppy, it was *his* house that would suffer the consequences.

"Okay. When do I get to see it?"

"Now. But you have to promise me you won't refuse it."

I had no idea what to think about that.

He put his hands over my eyes, and led me into the living room. Then he kissed my hair and whispered "I love you" in my ear.

When he removed his hands, I was standing in front of a magnificent ebony Yamaha baby grand.

I was speechless.

The piano and its matching bench were positioned in my favorite corner of the room that was bathed in natural light coming in through the floor-to-ceiling windows. The piano didn't look brand new, but it appeared to be in absolutely perfect condition.

And hanging on the wall just above it was a black and white photograph of me. It was a picture he'd taken months ago on our hike—a close-up of my profile in the grass. I was smiling and I look relaxed. It may have been the very moment I realized I was falling in love.

He had put this all together: the piano, the photo. This was *my* space. A sanctuary for me in his home.

No one had ever done anything like that for me before.

Tears began to stream down my face as the magnitude of his gesture set in.

"Do you like it?" he asked hesitantly.

I turned to him and threw my arms around his neck, sobbing in a very unladylike manner.

"Yes, I love it. I don't know what to say." I could feel his smile against my cheek.

"Well, the piano's all moved in here, and I hope at some point you might decide to join us."

"When did you do this?" I asked, pulling back to see his face.

"Jamie helped me." He wiped a tear from the side of my cheek and smiled warmly. "We've been looking for a while, but he liked this one. He had his piano guy tune and clean it so it's no longer squishy in the middle, whatever that means."

We just stared at the stately instrument together. "I can't wait to hear you play. I realized at the concert how much I wanted to hear the sound of that in our home."

*Our home.* I didn't know what to say to that.

"I love you so much." That was the best I could do, blinking back tears again. "I can't believe you did this for me."

"I did it as much for me. Having you here makes me the happiest man on the planet. You know that, right?"

But I was still too speechless to answer. And he didn't wait for that. Instead, he smiled at my uncharacteristic mute, and kissed me again.

"Now play me a song, woman."

He snapped his fingers at me, and I laughed. Again, how could I ever say no? And more importantly, why would I ever want to?

# Chapter 22

**Danny**

Midday on Sunday, Sarah and I left for Auburn. The plan was we'd drive up together, and then I'd fly out of Sacramento on a red-eye to New York on the twenty-third. She'd take my car back home after the holidays because I couldn't convince her to let me buy her a ticket to fly back and meet me for New Year's.

As you might imagine, I had many issues with this plan—being away from her for Christmas, chief among them—but I vowed to myself to keep a lid on it. We didn't need a rehash of the whole car argument. Plus, this was the first time I'd be seeing Carol in almost six years, and she didn't exactly approve of me, so that would be loads of fun already. Sarah was nervous about it, but I actually wasn't.

"How's your application coming for the master's program?" I asked Sarah as we drove. I knew she had to submit it right after the first of the year.

"Good. I made a lot of progress on it this week. It was much easier to do since most of the questions related to things we already worked on for my fellowship essay."

She was quiet again, but I got the feeling there was something else she wanted to say. I glanced over at her.

"What?"

"Nothing. I just had a thought." She paused for a second. "You know so much about educational policy and reform, and your perspective is different from anything else in the curriculum at Stanford. Have you ever thought about proposing to teach a class in it?"

"At Stanford?"

"I don't know. There or somewhere else. But you certainly have the contacts at Stanford—I bet Dr. Frick would support you, especially if you came to him with a detailed syllabus of your ideas. You could do a summer session class." She shrugged, sensing my hesitation. "Anyway, it was just an idea."

The truth was, I would *love* to do that. The idea of teaching a class on such a dynamic and controversial topic was very exciting for me; I couldn't believe I hadn't thought of it myself. I mean, it would be a long shot, but I'd have my PhD this spring, so I'd have the credentials. That, coupled with my public school teaching experience and ongoing work with Project Learning, gave me an interesting angle. I could imagine some very lively classroom discussions. Hell, who *wouldn't* love to teach something like that?

I spent a good bit of the rest of our three-hour drive musing about how I might approach a class syllabus, and I made a mental note to discuss the idea with Frick. Just out of curiosity.

When we arrived, it was dinnertime in Auburn and unseasonably cold, with the temperature at around thirty-five degrees. Carol greeted us at the door as we made our way up the front steps with our bags.

She was almost exactly what I remembered—an older, heavier-set version of Sarah, several inches shorter, with shoulder-length hair.

Carol gave Sarah a hug, and then turned to me with *great* formality, and offered her hand to shake. It was truly comical, but I played along like a perfect gentleman.

"It's an unexpected pleasure to see you again, Dan," she said, as though perhaps I'd been raised from the dead. She probably wished I'd go back there.

"And you, Carol. Thank you for having me."

For a very pregnant pause, we just took each other in, our handshake going slightly longer than was customary. She seemed to be sizing me up; she was probably counting my wrinkles and looking for gray hairs. She was gracious, but I would not say she was warm.

"Okay, then," Sarah said, clearing her throat.

Carol dropped my hand and turned to go inside. When I glanced at Sarah, her expression was unmistakable: *Isn't this gonna be fun???*

§

Carol's condo was nice enough, and situated on a corner lot, right across from a community pool and park. The complex was probably built in the mid-eighties. Her unit had two bedrooms, two baths, a small living room, and dining room. The kitchen was your classic eighties look, with brown cabinetry and cream-colored tile countertops with dark brown grout. The place wasn't fancy, but it was comfortable, and was probably all the house she really needed.

Looking around, though, I could definitely see a lot of deferred maintenance—cupboards that didn't close right, a sink that leaked, some peeling paint, god knows what else. And the place was *freezing*. Sarah noticed it right away too.

"Mom, why is it so cold in here? You need to turn the heat on."

"Well, unfortunately, it just went out. I've called someone to come look at it, but I'm not sure when they'll be here. We've been using space heaters."

Now, I didn't know Carol in the least, but I'd have put good money on a bet that she hadn't called anyone by the way she seemed to want to quickly change the subject.

"That's dangerous, Mom. When did it go out?"

"It was out when I got here last week." I turned in the direction of the voice to see a tall, skinny kid who was the exact younger-boy version of Sarah.

"Hi, Bear!"

Sarah and Scott shared a tight embrace that was really nice to watch. They were obviously very devoted to each other, and it was understandable given their upbringing. Sarah was like a mother to him during some very formative years.

Scott's Asperger's symptoms were mostly remediated now, but if you knew what you were looking for, you could still see small remnants of it.

"Hi, I'm Dan," I offered, extending my hand.

"Scott." He shook it briefly, and then broke the contact. He wasn't unfriendly—he just didn't appear overly comfortable meeting new people. Plus, I think he'd been waiting on us to arrive so Carol would serve up dinner, which seemed to be already on the table.

Carol had made enough food to feed twenty people. I wondered if that was for my benefit, and if she was expecting me to eat my weight at every meal.

But the conversation throughout dinner was surprisingly comfortable. Carol asked me about work, and we talked about the state of education in the U.S. She was definitely up on her knowledge of the subject, and we conversed in more depth than I would have expected about the role of unions, reform legislation, and educational inequality in poor areas. I now knew where Sarah got her analytical mind. Carol was sharp.

The more interesting thing, though, was what she didn't say. She was carefully watching every exchange Sarah and I had. And whenever I brought up something about Sarah's career or classes, she got sort of a skeptical look on her face like she wanted to challenge me, but she was trying to be polite. It was clear I had a lot of work to do here.

I insisted on doing dishes after dinner, and couldn't help but notice that the faucet leaked like crazy. It was nothing to fix something like this, and expensive to let it go on this way.

"Hey Carol, if you'd like, I can run to Home Depot in the morning and pick up a new washer for the sink."

"Oh, don't trouble yourself. I'll call someone."

*Right.* The same someone who was coming to fix the heater, I presumed.

"It's no trouble." I sincerely meant that.

"Mom, let Danny do it. He can fix almost anything. He's really handy."

Carol seemed to be conflicted, though, so I took a slightly different tack.

"Is there anything around here you'd like to have me take a look at? Something I can help with before I go?"

My guess was that the faucet didn't bother her much, but maybe something else did. And maybe she was short on funds to hire someone to take care of it.

"Well, I guess there is just one thing. The light fixture in my bedroom has started buzzing, and I'm afraid to turn it on. I was going to call someone, but I haven't had the chance to."

Bingo.

"Chances are the fixture's just bad. I'll take a look at it in the morning. And while we're at it, why don't you make me a list of anything else you can think of, and I'll knock them out tomorrow while you and Sarah do some shopping. Scott can help me, if he wants."

And just like that, I won my first battle in the fight for Carol's approval.

Unfortunately, I lost the second one in a far more spectacular way.

We were all preparing for bed, and it was obvious Scott had the couch for the night because Carol already had the blankets out, and he was settling in with the TV remote. The less obvious thing was who would be sleeping in the second bedroom. Sarah preempted the discussion by carrying both our bags into the room, and getting us unpacked while Carol was busy helping Scott put sheets on the couch.

I quickly changed into sweats and a T-shirt, and grabbed the toothbrush from my bag.

When I bent to give Sarah a peck on the lips, she took hold of the front of my shirt for a deeper kiss.

"You're aware that your mom already hates my guts, right? You know if you try to stay in here, she'll assume I'm defiling you under her roof?"

"*I'm* assuming you'll defile me under her roof," she said, running her evil hands up under my T-shirt and teasing my nipples. Then her fingernails drifted down my abdomen to the waistband of my sweats.

Of course, I was turned on; and these were *not* the right pants to be wearing if I was going to convince anyone of my intentions of being well behaved.

I grabbed her hands over my shirt. "That is *not* a good idea. I'm not *fucking you* in your mom's house. Period."

However convincing those words might have sounded, my body was arguing for the opposing side. And when Sarah took hold of me, all common sense seemed to get lost in the mass evacuation of blood from my brain to my dick.

"We can be quiet," she whispered, nipping my neck and tightening her grip around my length.

"Jesus, Sarah. When are you ever quiet? You're like a banshee during sex."

I forced the words out through gasping breath, just as her hand slid into in my pants, stroking me just the way I liked.

*Shit.*

She licked her lips to a delicious shine and stared up at me innocently. This woman was my undoing.

"Maybe you could just touch me for a minute," she continued.

*Goddammit.*

In the war between my head and my dick, my head was quickly losing ground. Could I do that? *Could I* touch her for just a minute? Before I even considered the negatives of the idea, I pushed my hand down the front of her little sleep shorts, and ran my fingers over the silky skin.

*Yes, I guess I can.*

And, *fuck*, she felt amazing.

I knew this was a bad, bad idea but I closed my eyes and gave in to the temptation anyway.

It was a moment of bliss. We stroked each other like experts, and I nearly groaned as her thumb passed over my tip.

I'd been with plenty of women in my life, but somehow with Sarah, *everything* was better. With anyone else, this kind of hand job wouldn't even rate, but with her, my level of excitement was already off the charts.

I leaned in to take her mouth, swallowing every banshee groan she made. She seemed to have no concept that her noises could wake the dead.

I was already panting when she broke our kiss, and pulled my shirt up with one hand so she could lick my nipple. *Fucking hell.* There was almost no chance now that this scenario wouldn't end with me losing my mind in her mother's guest room.

This was so jacked up.

But, fuck, it was exciting.

I finally just resigned myself to the idea that I'd become, in fact, every mother's worst nightmare, and I pushed Sarah's mouth more firmly against my chest.

If I was going to hell, I might as well thoroughly enjoy the ride.

There was absolutely no stopping this crazy train now anyway. We were headed straight for utter lunacy. Sarah was close, and I felt my own release gathering low in my spine. There was no way of stopping it. I let go of a deep exhale and just let it happen.

*Oh, fuck yes . . .*

"Sarah?"

Oh, fuck no!

Carol's voice sounded just as the door began to open.

The next moments were a blur of flailing arms, snapping elastic, and the hasty covering of parts that no potential future mother-in-law should ever see. If I wasn't *literally* coming in my pants as Carol stepped into the room, I might have even laughed.

But it was like everything was happening in slow motion.

Sarah was squeaking something about helping me with the dresser—whatever the hell that meant—and I was spinning around like I'd been shot, trying to hide my obvious pulsing erection.

Mercifully, this meant I didn't have to make *actual* eye contact with Carol, while my body finished its dirty business.

I braced one hand on the nightstand, and began straightening the lamp with the other, for lack of anything more convincing to do. I heard Sarah ask her mom what she needed, and her voice sounded very guilty, particularly to my guilty brain.

"Well, I assumed you'd be staying with me," Carol said politely. "Come, let's not crowd Dan."

*Yes, let's not crowd Dan. He needs to clean himself up after he's finished straightening the lamp.*

Fuck.

"Okay, I'll be right there," my traitorous girlfriend said, in an uncharacteristically compliant voice. She must have been so easy to bust as a teenager.

"Dan, do you need anything before I go?" Carol asked.

*Yes, some tissues and laundry detergent would be great.*

"No, thank you. I'm all set," I choked out, rubbing the back of my neck, and looking over my shoulder to face her. I was pretty sure my dick and my balls had crawled back up inside my body by this point. In fact, it was possible I'd become a girl.

"Okay, good." She stepped out of the room, and closed the door quietly behind her.

"Oh, shit!" Sarah mouthed, her eyes like giant spaceships.

"I cannot believe you talked me into that!" I whispered urgently. "I'm trying to make a good impression here."

"Well, you've definitely made an impression." She was laughing, and obviously not sorry at all.

"Christ, does your mom ever knock?"

"We'll have to be more careful next time," she said, still giggling.

"I don't think that will be a problem. I may never be able to have an erection again."

§

I wouldn't exactly say it was a restful night. I spent most of it torturing myself with various scenarios of my impending castration. It was bad enough I was going to have to keep my hands off of Sarah for the next two days before being separated from her for another week, but now I had to worry that her mother would be inspecting my every move for possible perversion.

Consequently, I was up before the rest of the household, and headed out for a run. When I got back, Sarah and Carol were seated at the kitchen table. I bent to give Sarah a *very* chaste kiss on the top of her head, and saw that Carol had made enough scrambled eggs to feed a small country.

"Morning, baby. Sleep well?" Sarah smirked.

I smirked back, and then worked the expression into more of a smile when Carol caught my eye.

"Let me get you some breakfast," she said, gesturing to the yellow mountain on top of the stove.

I wasn't a huge eater first thing in the morning, but I recognized that I had some penance to do for last night, so I resigned myself to suck it up and take whatever was coming to me.

I watched, a little nauseous, as Carol scooped spoonful after spoonful of eggs onto a plate, and then topped it off with bacon and some melon.

"Mom, Danny's not a linebacker. He doesn't eat that much."

But Carol was undeterred, and set the heaping plate in front of me.

I rubbed my hand across the stubble on my jaw, as I considered how the hell I could avoid offending her. This was the price for violating her daughter.

"Thank you, Carol. This looks great."

As Carol headed back to the sink, Sarah leaned over and snickered softly, "Are you trying to eat your way out of trouble?"

*Yes, actually, I think I am.*

"I don't think she saw anything." She was enjoying it all just a bit too much.

"Evil," I mouthed to her as Carol returned.

"Hmmm?" Carol asked me.

I brushed it off innocently, giving Carol my best good-boy smile, while Sarah's shoulders shook with an inaudible laugh at my expense.

§

I spent the entire day on Carol's list. If I had a nickel for every time she came back to me and said, "You know, there's just one more thing I thought of . . ."

But it was a win for both of us. I really did enjoy working around the house, far more than just sitting on Carol's couch while she grilled me, and she desperately needed the work done. Some things on her list were really unsafe.

She directed me to some old tools that had belonged to Sarah's father. They weren't great, but most were adequate, and I could pick up anything else I needed at the store.

And Scott joined me, though he didn't know much about home maintenance. His father had passed away before Scott was old enough to learn. But the engineer in him was definitely curious, and it gave us a chance to bond without a lot of forced conversation.

Together, we changed the bedroom fixture, sealed drafty windows, installed new locks, replaced batteries in the fire alarms, put new hinges on the kitchen cabinets, fixed the faucet, of course, and a number of other things, both big and small.

And then there was the matter of the heater. It was very likely original to the home and appeared beyond repair. But the ductwork was intact, so all she really needed was a new unit. I'd put a heater in my own house; I knew how to install it. The bigger question was the money. And for Sarah's sake, I didn't want it to be.

So when Scott and I were out, we stopped by a local HVAC supply store and bought one. His eyes bulged when he saw the total on the register.

"I wasn't planning on telling your mom how much the heater cost. Is that okay with you?"

Scott paused for a moment. "I guess so." He was a bit unsure and I felt a little guilty about that, but Scott seemed to understand like I did that pride wouldn't allow Carol to accept the gift, though she probably had no way of paying for a new heater herself. And she needed it. She couldn't weather the winter without one.

So we brought it home, and got it installed while Sarah and her mom were still out. By the time they came back, the condo was warm again.

"You fixed the heater?" Sarah asked in shock.

"We bought a new—"

"Fuse for it," I finished, and glanced at Scott.

Carol was beyond happy. She actually hugged me and thanked me for my help, offering to reimburse me for any costs. That, I declined. When she left with Scott to see the other things we'd done, Sarah looked at me with a level stare.

"What did you do to the heater?"

She didn't look mad; it was more relief, I thought. But I could also see her pride and her issues with money were right there, entangled in that look.

"Do you want me to tell you?"

She knew what I was asking. I wouldn't lie to her. But we both knew that my telling her would make her feel some misplaced sense of obligation to pay me back, which I would flatly refuse, anyway.

She didn't reply. Her eyes welled up, and she seemed very conflicted.

"I fixed the heat in the condo. And it's among the easiest things I need to do here." Then I kissed her. I'd do anything for this girl's happiness. After all, it was my own.

The rest of the trip went smoothly. Scott and I found unexpected common ground over Star Trek, and we both enjoyed pulling up a few of those old episodes online. And though Carol and I never quite got that *I love you, man* moment, I still put the visit in the win column. I think she could see how much I loved her daughter, and that I wasn't a pervert or a psychopath. She was still wary of my wanting Sarah barefoot and pregnant before her career got rolling, but only time could reassure Carol of that.

For my part, it was obvious to me that Carol worshipped Sarah. There were major issues between them, but Carol was trying hard to earn the right to be in Sarah's life again, and how could I not respect her for that?

§

As I was packing up for my flight, Sarah came into the bedroom with a wrapped gift. She looked as nervous as I felt when I gave her the piano.

"This is for you. For Christmas. I was hoping you could open it here."

She handed me the gift, and we both sat on the bed as I unwrapped it. Inside the box was a large scrapbook. I opened it to find that she had amassed an extraordinary number of clippings and photographs relating to my accomplishments from high school forward.

I was shocked. Where did she even get all of this? *I* didn't have most of it. There were newspaper articles about key games in the various sports I'd played in high school, awards I'd won, my acceptance letter and scholarship offer from UVA, loads of college basketball photographs, articles relating to various teaching awards, and newspaper stories highlighting many of the teams I'd coached through the years.

It was all right here. Painstakingly arranged and preserved. I couldn't begin to imagine how much time she'd put into this. And time wasn't something she had a lot of.

"Where did you get all these things?" My voice was rougher than I could help.

"Lots of places, really. I got some of it from the library and online newspaper archives, but a lot of it came from your sister. She was a huge help. Did you know your mom kept boxes of clippings about your achievements?"

I did know that. But after she died, it was too painful for me to go through it so I left it all with Casey to keep. As I flipped through the pages, I could see that many of the early articles and photos had notes indicating the date or occasion in my mom's distinctive handwriting. I ran my fingertips over one of them—thoroughly overcome by a sense of connection to her I hadn't experienced in years. It was momentarily stunning. And then the most random things began popping into my head—like the way her grocery lists used to look in that handwriting. I had a hard time pulling my hand away.

Flipping to another page, I noticed a photo that gave me pause. It was of my parents and I at the California State Science Fair, where I won first place in my category in eleventh grade. My sister must have taken the picture. My mom was standing on one side of me and smiling into the camera. My dad was on the other, his hand on my shoulder, and in the picture he was looking at me, rather than at the camera. And he was smiling too. I don't know why I stopped on that one, but I did.

"I had enough material I could've made this book three feet thick. Apparently, I have to become a private investigator if I'm going to learn of all your accomplishments."

I sniffed out a laugh. "I think you have it pretty well covered here. This is . . ."

I was at a loss for words. I just shook my head and clenched my jaw to keep control of everything I felt just then. When I met her eyes again, they were so beautiful and loving and affectionate. I saw absolutely everything I needed there. And that, in itself, was a gift.

"I love you so much. Thank you for this."

It was the most inadequate response, but it was all I was capable of in that moment. I knew she understood what I wanted to say. She knew me. Sarah knew me.

# Chapter 23

## Sarah

Towards the end of January, Danny was working so many hours that I was beginning to worry he was spreading himself too thin. His career was on fire; it seemed like he couldn't miss right now. Math and science standardized test scores for Taft came in at the highest in the district, and he was asked to document his department's curriculum and teaching approach as a blueprint for others schools in the district to emulate. Meanwhile, his consulting assignment with Project Learning was becoming more time-intensive, as they were less than six months from launching their pilot program. And on top of all that, he was finishing his dissertation and the summer course proposal he was submitting to Stanford.

Selene's parents came for a visit, giving me a perfect reason to leave Danny to his work, guilt free. Apparently, the San Francisco Symphony was hosting an all-Brahms concert with Iván Fischer and the Budapest Festival Orchestra at Davies Hall. Selene's mother, Helen, was a big fan of Brahms, and considered this one a *can't miss* event.

The original plan had been for Dr. and Mrs. Georgiou to take Selene and Kevin as their guests, but Kevin had a last-minute issue at the law firm where he worked and couldn't attend. I agreed to take Kevin's place.

The concert was lovely. Davies Hall was a gorgeous venue, and there wasn't really a bad seat in the house—particularly for a concert, which was more about listening than watching, anyway.

During intermission, I broke away from the group to use the restroom. The lines were crazy, and it took forever.

By the time I got to the front, intermission was almost over, and the bathroom was nearly empty. I was just finishing drying my hands when a stall door opened and Carolyn Martin stepped out. I saw her reflection in the mirror for just a beat before she noticed me.

Carolyn was so beautiful she almost didn't look real. For this occasion, she was wearing a very fitted knee-length black cocktail dress that gathered Grecian-style at one shoulder. Her shiny chocolate brown hair was swept into an elaborate updo I wouldn't begin to know how to achieve with my own hair. Her jewelry was kept simple, except for a stunning pair of gold chandelier earrings that amplified the gold flecks in her blue eyes. She was wearing killer black heels that made her at least six feet tall.

All in all, she looked polished and elegant.

As for me, I was in the same red dress she'd seen me in before— Selene's red dress that I seemed to pull out now for every occasion. When Carolyn glanced up at me in the mirror, I'm quite sure she noticed that too.

"Sarah, what a surprise," she said flatly, approaching the sink next to me. "I can't say I expected to see you here."

When I last saw her at the Christmas concert, she was at least *pretending* to be friendly. This time, there was no pretense. Her tone was unmistakably snide, and I knew I should just walk away.

*Do not engage*, I coached myself.

"Likewise," I responded, and congratulated myself as I made ready to leave for not taking the bait.

But that made her smile. And not the nice kind of smile, either. It was the kind that said, *Oh, thank you, Jesus. You've just made my day.*

"I'm the Senior Arts and Entertainment editor for the Chronicle. It's my job to attend these events. Or didn't Danny mention that?"

Her voice was dripping in condescension, and she could obviously tell that, no, in fact, Danny had never told me that. He hadn't really told me much of anything about their relationship.

"To tell you the truth, Carolyn, he rarely mentions you," I said, recovering quickly. I needed to get out of here.

"So, then, he probably never told you about our plans to be married?" she said, washing her hands.

"I know you didn't *get* married."

She smiled again, like she was enjoying the challenge.

"Yes, well, we both know Danny struggles with commitment." She met my eyes head-on in the mirror. "Plus, he was waiting until he finished his PhD. I think that's almost completed now, correct?"

"How does that make a difference for you?"

I didn't know where she was going with this, and I was working hard to keep my reactions from betraying an increasing sense of unease. As if she could read my thoughts, she turned to face me directly.

"Because I'm the one he'll come back to, sweetheart. We have five years of history, and many more as friends before that. What did you think this was between you?" She was almost laughing at me. Like I was somehow missing the biggest joke of all. "You're a nice little diversion, and good for you—but you can't honestly think you're more than a detour while he gets serious about his future and finally figures out what he wants."

She reached for a towel to dry her hands, with an unpleasant smile lingering on her face. And unfortunately, she wasn't even close to being finished.

"If I had to guess, I'd say you were a little gold digger, dressed in your retread outfit, just waiting to hit pay dirt with Danny. Am I right?"

I didn't understand the reference. But as I processed her words, I heard echoes of past conversations.

*I have plenty of money, Sarah.*

*The house has been in my dad's family for a long time.*

I was pretty sure she could read it all on my face. And she went in for the kill.

"Wait a minute—he didn't *tell* you he's loaded?" Her eyebrows were raised high, and her smile was triumphant. "I wonder why that would be? Maybe he thinks you're an opportunist, and he doesn't trust you enough to tell you? Or maybe it's because you're nothing more to him than a midlife crisis—a casual little fling with a much younger girl who strokes his ego and lets him pretend for an instant he doesn't need to get serious and settle down. How long do you think you can hold onto him, Sarah?"

I desperately wanted to leave this bathroom. But I felt like my feet were stuck to the floor and her venomous, superior gaze was pinning me in place. I couldn't look away.

In my stunned immobility, her words hit squarely on the mark.

"You're what twenty-two? And a *student*?" That drew another smile. "How long do you think you're going to be interesting to him? He's eleven years older than you, and his career is about to take off. He's going to be ready for a wife and a family. Can you give him that right now?"

Her tone suggested that she knew the answer was *no*. And all of my mother's words came back to me, further adding to the damage being inflicted on my self-confidence.

"I didn't think so," she said.

"Well, if he had wanted those things with you, he wouldn't be with me right now."

My words sounded logical—but somehow I couldn't quite put the conviction behind them to convey any confidence in their veracity.

Why would he not have told me he had money? It wouldn't have made a bit of difference to me. I'd never been someone who dreamed of being wealthy or wanted much in terms of material things.

But maybe he assumed, because of my circumstances, that I *would* have cared. Maybe he felt if I knew, I would try to manipulate him into buying me things or settling my debts.

God, is that what he felt had happened with heater? Or the *piano*? The piano was beautiful, but what I loved most about it was that I thought he bought it because he wanted to give me a special place in his home, in his life.

But maybe Carolyn was right. Maybe his earlier talk about marriage was just something that felt good in the moment. Maybe if he were really serious about us, he wouldn't have kept something so major from me. Maybe like my mom said, he was just having a little fun.

It wasn't as though I had such a great track record with choosing men.

Oh god, I felt like such an *idiot*.

And Carolyn was witnessing it all, bleeding right out of me. I knew it she could see it; she looked like a kid at Christmas.

"I guess we'll find out soon, won't we, Sarah?" she said. Then, she moved past me, and quietly left the bathroom.

I just stood there for the longest time. The lights flickered to indicate that the concert was beginning and, still, I just stood there. People came in and left again, and I didn't move. They probably thought I was on drugs. I was frozen. Nauseous and paralyzed with fear. With anger. With regret for my own stupidity.

I thought about calling Danny, but I didn't know what I would say. What would I ask him?

*Why don't you trust me? Why are you playing with me?*

Did I want to know the answers to those questions?

The bathroom door opened and an attendant came in. "Is it okay if I clean?" she asked hesitantly.

I looked at her wordlessly, and managed a nod.

Then I turned and walked out, finally making my way back to my seat under the merciful cover of darkness.

"What took you so long?" Selene whispered.

I struggled to contain the tremor in my voice. "Long lines."

But I couldn't contain it for long. There in the concert hall, my heart shattered to the masterful works of Brahms. The tears flowed silently, as the life I'd imagined came completely apart.

# Chapter 24

**Sarah**

By the time the concert ended, I'd collected myself enough to get through the motions of thanking Selene's parents for including me. I tried to give the illusion of being reasonably attentive to the conversation on the car ride home, but I failed.

"You seem really distracted. Is everything okay?" Selene asked me when we finally reached our place.

She looked concerned, and the very last thing I could handle right now was a lot of questions. So, instead, I regressed to deflection.

"I'm not feeling great. I think I'm just tired."

She looked at me skeptically, but nodded and rubbed my arm, too good a friend to insist on the truth.

"Okay, if you're sure. Sleep well."

I felt my cell buzz in my purse. It was about ten o'clock—the time I told Danny I'd be home.

As I walked to my room, I took the phone out and glanced at his text.

*I hear it's possible to play Brahms on the skin flute. Thought you might like to practice.*

The old me would have laughed, and responded with a witty retort.

The new me felt a little sick. I closed the door quietly and set the phone down on my desk. I was nervous and anxious. I didn't know what to do. I knew I should call him. Talk this out. Listen to his explanation, and be open-minded.

But I couldn't. I was pulled back to that moment of humiliation when I discovered my relationship with John was not what I thought it was. But this was so much worse because in this case I'd put myself out there. I didn't hold anything back from Danny. I fought my own issues with intimacy to open myself up in a way I never had before. Only to find out now that he hadn't done the same with me. It wasn't that I wanted or needed to know everything about his finances; it was the fact that his not telling me something of such significance made me question the true nature and depth of our relationship.

And that was devastating.

I had no idea how much time passed while I sat numbly on the edge of my bed. But finally another text arrived.

*Hey—still coming by?*

With shaking fingers, I answered. *I'm not sure that's a good idea.*

His response was immediate. *Why?*

*Let's talk tomorrow.*

*Why, Sarah?* he insisted.

*Because I think you broke us.*

After that, my phone went conspicuously quiet. I knew I didn't want to have a conversation like this over text, yet the silence felt ominous. The silence in our apartment was worse—oppressive, suffocating, unrelenting.

But it wasn't long before our buzzer rang. I heard Selene get up to answer it.

"Is she here?"

Danny's baritone voice filled our apartment, and moments later, he knocked softly on my bedroom door. He was wearing a black V-neck sweater over a white T-shirt and jeans. When he saw me sitting on the edge of the bed, he came over and sat beside me.

"What do you mean, I broke us?"

I just looked at him, expressionless. "Why didn't you tell me you had money? A lot, from what I understand."

Danny blanched, and I knew in an instant Carolyn was telling the truth. And if she was right about that, what else was she right about?

"Who said that?" he asked quietly.

"Your *ex*, when she accused me of being a gold digger," I answered, with as much disdain as I could muster.

I could see that was a blow. He rested his elbow on the desk, rubbing his face with one hand. "I was always going to tell you. I just . . ." He looked so lost—like he needed *my* help to come up with the words.

But I wasn't offering any help at all.

"Sarah, please. You have to let me explain."

"What are we talking about here? Millions? Tens of millions? More?"

I was baiting him, I knew. But at this point, I needed to know what price tag he'd put on our relationship. How much money was worth keeping a secret that could put at risk what we had together?

"Around twenty million dollars in investments, plus the property," he said, carefully watching me for a reaction. I wouldn't make it that easy.

"We've been together for more than seven months. Did you not trust me? Did you think I was the kind of person who would care one way or the other? Or that I would use you for your money?"

"No!"

"So, it was just that you didn't think our relationship was going to be long-lived enough to merit the discussion? Or am I just a fun little screw on the road to someone else more meaningful?"

He looked like he'd been punched, with an expression of bewilderment so desperate as to be almost comical. His eyes were wide, and he was shaking his head emphatically back and forth.

"No! It's not like that." He reached for me, but I pulled away. "Sarah, you know I never thought that."

"I thought I knew. But to be honest, when I look at you now, I'm not sure what I know and don't know about us."

"That's not true. You know me. You know *us*."

I didn't respond. How could I?

There was total dismay in his face, and he stood up in frustration, or maybe anxiety. He rubbed the back of his neck and started to pace.

"Let me explain." He took a deep breath and swallowed hard. His hands were trembling, and he crossed his arms over his body, tucking them away to hide it. "The money is inheritance from my parents' deaths. I never wanted it. I hate it because, for one, it's ill gained. And, two, it was given to me out of spite."

I understood the first part. I didn't inherit anything from my dad except his camera, but I could understand feeling like money was no compensation for a loss of that magnitude.

The second part, I didn't understand. But I was tired of pulling information reluctantly out of him. Instead, I just sat still, making no eye contact.

But he knew exactly what I was thinking, and he continued.

"Casey told me you asked her about my father. And you may have guessed that his family was wealthy. What you may not know is that his ultimatum to me was a breaking point for us. He tried to use money as leverage in our relationship, instead of respecting me enough to let me make my own choices.

"He never saw me, Sarah. Not once. All he could ever see was someone who wasn't him. So, when I rejected his ultimatum, I wasn't just rejecting college tuition, I was rejecting all of it.

"And he knew that. He knew how I felt about the inheritance. Yet he gave it to me anyway. He couldn't even respect that choice."

Danny breathed in, and then purged the breath audibly. Like maybe just speaking the words relieved some of the burden they held.

I remembered our conversation from Labor Day weekend.

*We just seemed to find so many points of contention—all the way to the end. And ironically, even after the end.*

"Maybe he gave it to you because he wanted you to know he loved and respected you," I replied softly. "Maybe he just didn't know how to communicate it."

Danny didn't respond. He was standing with his hands on his hips, and his head hung in regret. "I've never touched one dime of that money. Not a single dime."

"What about your house?"

"My uncle passed away of lung cancer when I was finishing up at UVA. Most of his estate went to charity, but he also left something to Casey and me. We were close, and his generosity never came with any strings. I knew his bequest was his way of showing how much he valued our relationship."

"You should have told me about this, Danny, because it's not a small thing to you, obviously."

"I know. I do know. I just don't like to think about it. I try not to most of the time. But since I have this money, I decided that someday I'd really like to start an educational foundation—make something good out of something bad. It's a big part of why I'm getting my PhD. But in order to make a difference, you have to know the system. You have to know how to negotiate the unions, and the politicians, and the red tape. That's why I'm also doing the consulting work—because I need to learn those things and make contacts. Otherwise, the money will be wasted, or ill-used, or tied up in bullshit."

Hearing this explanation rush out of him, I just stared in disbelief, searching his face for something that was familiar.

"Why have you never told me any of that? That *that* was the intent of your PhD and your consulting work. Or that you were interested in running a non-profit. I just don't understand."

That may have actually been the most painful admission so far. Not because it was a bombshell, but because it *wasn't*. In the scheme of things, it was a rather harmless bit of insight—one that anyone of the rank of casual friend might be entitled to. And yet, he'd never shared it with me.

I tilted my head towards the floor, letting my hair fall around my face for a brief moment of privacy. The hem of my red dress peeked out between the front flaps of my cream-colored wool coat. That coat felt like the only thing holding my insides together. I sensed him studying me, and the silence was heavy and pregnant between us.

"It wasn't a secret." His voice sounded uncharacteristically quiet and unsure. "It's still so far off at this point, and I just figured I'd tell people when or if it became something."

I lifted my face to him once more. It was as though I was listening to a stranger, and not comprehending a word of this.

"*People?* Is that who I am to you?"

"No! You know what I mean, Sarah. It may not happen for a long time, if ever. It's a lot more complicated than just having money to spend. And I haven't had any time to organize my thoughts around the kind of organization I'd like to set up." He ran his hand through his hair over and over again, frustration and despair raining from his tense frame. "I didn't mean to hurt you. I wasn't thinking of it in that way."

"I know." *God, did I know.*

With his uncanny ability to hear the words I didn't speak out loud, he took my hand hesitantly in his.

"You're my heart, Sarah. Isn't that obvious to you?"

The last words were spoken as though they were a plea. I knew he meant them in his way. But still . . .

I pulled my hand from his.

"I love you, Danny. But I can't stand the fact that you rarely tell me anything. And even when you do, I never know if I'm getting the whole story."

He didn't respond, but his expression was drowning in remorse. I ached for him, but I needed to say this.

"I felt embarrassed and guilty as hell for having to ask your sister about you and your dad. But at least in that case, I knew enough to know what questions to ask. I look at you tonight, and all I can think about is that I have no idea what other things I don't know. And don't know to ask. Carolyn said your plan was to get engaged as soon as you finished your PhD. Is that true? You made it sound to me like the subject just came up in passing."

"No, I . . ." He closed his eyes, struggling to explain. "It was more like . . ."

But nothing else came.

"Don't bother," I said, feeling resigned to his reticence.

"Sarah—"

"Let me finish," I interrupted, holding my hand up to silence him. "I'm so sorry that you grew up not feeling valued for who you are. The stories you told me break my heart, and make me angry on your behalf.

"And, believe me, I know better than anyone how hard it is to truly let yourself be close to another person. I struggle with that every day. I struggle at it with you. And I'm far from perfect. But, Danny, I can't be in a relationship that I believe is one thing, only to find out it's something else. And I need time to think about whether two people like us, who both have issues with intimacy, can really make this work."

"Sarah, please. Don't do this."

I was crushed by the look of devastation in his eyes, and I was afraid he could sense my own resolve faltering. So summoning every ounce of strength I possessed, I continued.

"I need some space to process everything you've told me. You need to give me that."

"Sarah, don't walk away because of this. I swear there's nothing else you don't know. Please give me a chance."

All I could see in my head was Carolyn's smug face. *What did you think this was between you?*

"I'm exhausted. Please just go tonight, and we can talk tomorrow. Please."

Thankfully, something about my voice or demeanor told him not to push me further. He wanted to stay; he wanted to persuade me to forgive him. But it wasn't really a question of forgiveness, and I think he knew that too.

So it was with visible pain that he leaned over and kissed me gently on the top of my head, stroking a finger softly down my cheek.

"I love you," he whispered, his words choked with emotion.

I couldn't meet his eyes. I needed time. Slowly, he withdrew, and I heard the door close behind him.

A minute or two later, Selene knocked gently. She didn't pepper me with questions. She just sat down beside me, and wrapped her arm around my shoulder. The tears came easily. And this time, I didn't try to hide them.

# Chapter 25

**Danny**

Walking out of Sarah's apartment nearly killed me—it was so difficult that I found myself sitting in the car outside her building for a very long time.

*What the fuck just happened?*

Many times, I started to go back inside, desperate to make her understand that my not telling her these things was about *me*, not an indictment of what we had together. It was largely about my messed-up relationship with my dad and the baggage I guess I still carried from it. And I was pissed at myself that, even ten years after his death, I was still doing battle with him. Now the collateral damage was my relationship with Sarah.

I knew I should have told her myself about the inheritance. I meant to. It just didn't occur to me that something like that would make her question everything about us. Maybe she didn't have every detail about my life, but she knew the most important things. She knew how much I loved and needed her, how much I respected and believed in her. It was a naive assumption, maybe, but when it came to our feelings for each other, I guess I thought we were beyond doubting. Christ, I thought we were on exactly the same page.

I have no idea how long I sat there in my car, just reeling from the turn of events. But after a long while, I started the engine. With a painful last glance at Sarah's front door, I reluctantly shifted into gear.

The streets were quiet, nearly deserted for a Sunday night. But inside my head was pure chaos. I was so angry. At everyone. At myself, most of all, for being such an idiot; at Sarah for doubting me; at Carolyn for exploiting the situation for some unknown purpose. That wasn't the Carolyn I knew—or maybe it just wasn't an instinct I'd ever seen in her before.

Our breakup had been tearful and difficult, but I assumed it was more because we'd been together so long. And maybe also because we both just expected that one day we'd get married, for better or for worse. But the relationship wasn't healthy. We were different people to begin with, and that became increasingly apparent over the years until we began to just tear each other apart. Yes, it should have ended sooner, but I thought it had ended in time to preserve the long-standing friendship we'd shared. If nothing else, I thought we had that.

On pure impulse, I dialed a number I'd called thousands of times before. Carolyn answered on the first ring.

"What the hell did you say to her?"

"What are you—?"

"Don't. Just *don't* lie to me."

After a long pause, she exhaled into the receiver.

"It's not my fault you still can't bring yourself to let people in on all your precious secrets, Danny. God knows, I put up with your silence long enough."

Angry with her as I was, I knew she was entirely right about that. That blame was squarely mine.

Still . . .

"You were trying to stir up shit and you know it."

"Maybe this is a *good* thing. Maybe it should tell you something about your relationship that you can't even be honest with her about the basics. I still don't understand how you could be satisfied going out with a child."

I laughed spitefully at that. "My relationship with Sarah is not subject to your understanding. And for the record, what you did says far more about you than it does about her. Sarah would never do anything so mean-spirited."

Carolyn didn't answer. Instead there was a long silence on the other end of the phone and I could hear her breath in the receiver, short and shallow now—not like she was angry, more like she was . . . struggling.

"Christ, Carolyn," I said hanging my head into my hand. "I thought we were friends."

"That's funny," she answered quietly, "because for the longest time I really thought we were in love."

Driving alone through the empty streets, the full impact of those words hit me head on. Carolyn and I had always said our breakup was mutual. But now I could see that had just been her pride. The truth of what transpired between us was evident in her voice, and it wrecked me.

I breathed out a deep sigh. "Fuck."

For many long minutes we hung on the line together, neither of us saying a word. And all the while, I thought back on the conversations that had led up to our breakup. I wondered what I could have done or said differently to have prevented the hurt I heard in her voice. Or maybe it was inevitable. I had no idea.

"I'm truly sorry if I hurt you," I told her. "I never wanted to do that."

"I know," she answered softly.

She didn't need to say that not intending to hurt her did not make up for actually doing it. And now I could see the parallels of my failings in both relationships: the way I'd so naively—and maybe insensitively—handled things with Carolyn; the way I'd so poorly handled things with Sarah.

This was what I'd always found so difficult—relationships weren't like science. In science, there was a right answer to discover. And to find it, you could read books, and follow procedures, and conduct experiments. The worst failures usually took the form of a ruined beaker, or a minor explosion, or a complete lack of any measurable result.

But relationships were something else entirely. There were things at stake that mattered. There were consequences that couldn't be undone. And there was no playbook for any of it. Some people had instinct as their guide, but I wasn't one of those fortunate people. I *sucked* at this. And I hated myself for it.

"I wish I knew what to say. I just thought . . ." I exhaled deeply. "I thought we were okay."

I heard her sniffle hard, and then clear her throat. "God, this part is awful, isn't it?"

A small, ironic laugh bubbled out of me, but there was no humor in it. "Yeah."

"I guess I thought I was ready to see you with someone else; obviously I'm not." She let go of a heavy breath and held there, soundlessly. And the quiet spoke more than anything she could say. Finally, I heard her inhale. "You weren't unkind to me, Danny. You just didn't love me the way I loved you and I don't think I've gotten over that."

She went silent again and it felt heavy.

"Carolyn—"

"Maybe at some point we can be friends again but for now . . ."

"Carolyn—"

She hung up quickly before I could add anything more, though I wasn't sure what else there was to say. It was all such a mess. I had hurt two people I cared about and I wasn't in a position to fix things with either one. It was the most helpless I'd ever felt.

When I reached my house, I texted Sarah one more time.

*I'm so sorry. I love you.*

She didn't respond. I didn't really think she would.

§

I spent the next many hours in a kind of a fog. I desperately wanted to do something, but I had no idea what. Sarah had asked me for time. And I think it might've been the only thing I could offer her that she'd have taken from me.

Over and over in my head, I relived the look in her eyes when I walked into her bedroom. It was a searing, punishing memory of hurt, humiliation, and the absence of trust. I used it to flog myself repeatedly throughout the night.

# Chapter 26

**Danny**

By four o'clock in the morning, I couldn't lie in bed any longer. I headed to the gym to lift, doing a full circuit until every muscle in my body was fatigued. Driving home, I remembered the first fight we'd had after we ran into her high school classmate. I'd acted like a prick, and she was so goddamned mad, I thought she was going to tell me to go fuck myself. But in the end, we'd worked it out. We talked. We made love. It was okay. What worried me now was that this one didn't feel the same. Last night, she wasn't furious, she was hurt. And, god, that was so much worse.

§

In the hours I spent at work, I was barely able to concentrate. My lectures felt dispassionate and disjointed. I took great lengths to avoid social interactions, opting for lunch at my desk under the guise of grading papers. For the most part, my colleagues left me to myself.

"Hey."

At the sound of a familiar voice, I glanced up to see Tom Ryan, my friend and a math teacher in my department, poking his head in the door.

Tom and I joined Taft the same year, and became close right away. He was just a hell of a nice guy—big into basketball—with two young kids, one of whom had Down Syndrome. Tom was the kind of person who never said an ill word about anyone, and who never seemed to falter in his appreciation for the life he had.

"Hey, man." I tried to muster a little enthusiasm, but I was worn out and not really up for the conversation.

"I thought maybe you were sick today. Everything all right?"

His gray eyes were serious and compassionate, and I had the disquieting sensation that I was as transparent as glass. I started to look away when my attention caught on the glint from his wedding band as he clasped the partially open door. For some reason, it further deflated me.

"Yeah. Just . . . not feeling it today, I guess."

Tom sized me up, then walked in and rested his long torso on one of the lab tables at the front of the room. Stretching his legs out in front of him, he crossed his arms over his chest.

"What's up?"

"You don't have to mother-hen me, Ryan. I'm fine. Just a little off today." I tried to keep the tone light, but I could tell he wasn't buying it.

"Everything okay with Sarah?"

Of course, he was exactly the guy who'd zero in on that and I was feeling far too raw to be able to deny it. Resting my elbows on the desk, I ran both hands through my hair.

"Is it that obvious?"

He just shrugged, still eyeing me closely.

"We had an argument last night, and she's not answering my calls at the moment."

"Women have been known to do that when they're mad."

"Yeah." I nodded and bit at a spot on my lower lip, probably betraying my nagging doubt that this wasn't just one of those things

223

that women do. Sarah wasn't most women, first of all. And second, when she was mad, she fought.

I didn't know what she did when she was hurt.

"You don't think this one will blow over," he responded, correctly surmising my thoughts.

"I don't know. This wasn't like other fights we've had. I messed things up and I'm not sure how to make it right."

He looked at me sympathetically, and rubbed the small, dark goatee on his chin. "Well, take it from someone who's been married long enough, and screwed up on enough occasions to know, sometimes an impasse like this is good for your relationship. Sometimes you have to hit a wall in order to break something loose, you know? In order to force yourselves to address something that's not working."

I absorbed this bit of advice with a mixture of skepticism and concern. If that's what was going on here, it was unsettling to me because I guess I didn't realize something wasn't working. Admittedly, I hadn't always been successful in my relationships before Sarah, but to me ours seemed almost perfect. In fact, it was the very best thing in my life; I'd never been happier. Was I missing something here? Had I been so obtuse as to overlook a larger issue between us?

"Yeah, maybe," I finally responded, realizing he'd been patiently waiting while I processed this possibility.

He stood up to leave and patted my shoulder. "You two will figure it out. I know you will. Let me know if you want to grab a drink this week."

"Thanks." I nodded, now more distracted than ever by a torrent of conflicting thoughts.

I pulled the phone out of my pocket. Still no word.

*Fuck.*

§

That evening, after a particularly punishing run, I showered, wrapped a towel around my waist, and grabbed my phone off the nightstand. Resting back against the headboard of my bed, I brushed my thumb over the list of Sarah's recent texts. There were so many of them: *xoxo*, and *can't wait to see you*, and little smiley, winky faces.

How in the world did we get here?

Not twenty-four hours ago, I was working on my dissertation, awaiting her text that she was on her way over. But now, everything was a mess. We'd gone from happy to estranged, and I was at a loss to know how to get past this.

Before I could second-guess myself, I touched her name on my cell and it began to ring. My heart was pounding in my chest as I prepared myself to leave her a message. What more could I even say?

But then she picked up, and the sound of her voice hit me like a freight train.

§

## Sarah

His hopeful relief made me feel instantly guilty. He sounded tired, and I could almost picture him rubbing his eyes like he did when he was feeling stressed.

"I'm so glad you answered," he said in one long breath.

"I'm up in Auburn. My mom took a fall on some ice last night, so I drove up early this morning."

"Auburn." I could feel his brain chewing through the implications of that.

"I'm sorry I didn't tell you I was leaving."

"It's okay," he murmured softly. But it wasn't. We both knew it. "How is she?"

"She's banged up, but she'll be all right."

"I miss you." The rough timbre of his voice told me everything I needed to know about his state of mind. I fought to keep my eyes from welling up with tears.

"I miss you, too."

He breathed in deeply, and then let out a small sound that conveyed a world of regret and frustration.

"I'm so sorry, Sarah. The last thing I ever wanted was to hurt you."

Despite all of the vile things Carolyn said, I did know that he loved me. I never really believed I was a midlife crisis. He'd been far too good to me for that. But it hurt. The whole ugly episode really hurt.

"I need to ask you something. When Casey was here, I overheard your conversation about whether you had told me yet. Is this what she was referring to?"

There was a long, conspicuous pause. "Yes."

That was exactly what I was afraid he would say, and I felt my anger resurfacing again.

"So, it's not that all of this just slipped your mind; you made a conscious decision not to tell me."

"No," he groaned into the phone. "Sarah, I didn't tell you that night because bringing up all this shit with my dad is depressing, and that night with you and Casey . . . I was just . . . I was happy."

My heart squeezed tightly in my chest—torn between feeling like I'd do anything for his happiness, and fearing that I'd be sacrificing part of my own to accept his ongoing reticence.

"That was four months ago."

"I know. It's no excuse, but time just got away from me. I was waiting for the right moment to bring it up."

"In seven months, you couldn't find the right moment?"

"Sarah—"

"Because I feel like I somehow found the time to tell you everything, even things I'd rather not have." The tears began to flow, and I was so mad at myself for losing control.

"I know. Sweetness, I wish I knew the words to tell you how sorry I am."

"What do I have to do to earn your trust?"

"No, Sarah," he said in a helpless breath, the anguish in his voice coming through clear as day.

The truth was, I loved this man dearly, but I was so hurt and so angry with him. Was this what it would always be like to be with him? That I'd just have to stumble upon those pieces of him that he kept from me? Or, worse, that I'd have my nose rubbed in my obvious exclusion from his confidence by some ex-girlfriend I ran into in a public bathroom?

Was I really okay with a relationship like that?

"I have to go," I said weakly.

"No. Don't do this. Be mad at me, yell at me, call me every name in the book. But *deal* with me. *Please*, Sarah. Don't use this as an excuse to push me away."

I swallowed hard, knowing I was weak when it came to him. But I needed some space to think about everything that had happened. I didn't say anything for a long pause.

"When are you coming back?" His question had enough force behind it that I knew if I wanted any time to process my feelings, I needed to maintain my physical distance from him. Otherwise, he'd just overwhelm me with his determination.

"I don't know," I hedged, glancing around my mom's guestroom to a small picture she had in a frame of he and I smiling in front of the Christmas tree. Danny's enormous presence in this small apartment filled the space to bursting.

"I want to come to you, then."

"I'd really rather you didn't." I put as much conviction as I could muster behind those words, and prayed it would be enough to mask how vulnerable I felt.

I could practically hear the debate raging in his brain. Danny was someone who tackled his problems head-on. He didn't do well when he was asked to be passive.

Finally, he said, "It feels like you've already decided to end things with me."

"I'm not saying that. I just need a little space."

"Can I at least call you tomorrow?"

"Let me call you next."

"When?"

"Soon." The word came out at the end of a long exhalation, and as soon as it crossed my lips, I knew it was a lie.

# Chapter 27

**Danny**

After a short time.

Before long.

Rapidly.

Those were my definitions of *soon*. Sarah's was something else entirely.

For weeks, I waited—trying to give her the space she needed. I called periodically and left messages. I texted just to let her know I was thinking of her. No fucking response.

At first, I told myself Sarah would come around after she'd had a little time to cool off. But it was clear to me now that I was mistaken. It seemed we were really over—with no discussion, no real explanation. Just done.

The shocking finality of that brought on such a range of emotion for me that the distraction of work was a godsend. The university accepted my proposal to teach a special summer session course on education reform, thanks in large part to Dr. Frick, who convinced the Board of Trustees that I could offer something unique to the current curriculum. They granted me the opportunity, providing I finished my doctorate this spring. If the course was successful, Frick said they'd ask me to teach an evening section in the fall.

So, I was spending every free moment finalizing my dissertation, leaving no time to dwell on our breakup, or to acknowledge how dead I'd become inside. I got up, ran, went to work, lifted in the gym, came home, and locked myself in my office, working until I was too exhausted to see straight.

I avoided the living room at all cost. That goddamned piano was like a sucker punch every time I saw it. I had to take the picture down. I couldn't bear to look at it.

I wasn't interested in doing anything social, but at the same time, I despised my own company.

So, it was like choosing between the lesser of two evils when Jamie asked me to come with him to a benefit concert Cadence was headlining at the Fillmore in San Francisco. Mel and the kids were out of town visiting Mel's parents and Jamie seemed a little lonely in her absence. Ultimately, I agreed because he wanted me there, and there wasn't a single thing he could ever ask of me that I wouldn't do. It had always been that way between us.

Plus, The Fillmore was a good distraction. It was one of those classic San Francisco music venues that was just cool be at. It had great bones, and a forty-year history of performances that read like a who's who in music: The Grateful Dead, James Brown, Jefferson Airplane, Prince, The Cure. Jamie always got a little misty when he talked about The Cure, and playing on the same stage once occupied by them was a surreal experience for him.

Cadence played a set of ten songs, and every one was tight and spot on. Since there was no seating on the main floor, the audience was on their feet for the entire show, pushing towards the stage in a massive crush.

I was spared that—I happened to have the best view in the house from the balcony near the bar above, reserved for associates of the band.

Cadence did a few of the early hits, and then moved on to some of the more recent material. Jamie was in rare form at the mic—teasing and taunting the audience into singing along, taking off his shirt at one point to a deafening level of screaming, and shaking his sweaty head into the front row of girls. They loved it. He was really playing up his Irish accent, too, which he did just for effect, though he'd never admit it. Not to be outdone, Greg was thumping on his bass, and hamming it up with Jamie, Killian, and Nash. All in all, it was another great show—and I'd seen *a lot* of shows.

Backstage was already a zoo by the time I made my way there at the conclusion of the set. At Cadence's own concerts, Jamie was very specific about not letting groupies hang around after the show. It was one of the things he did for Mel's benefit. The rest of the band could do whatever they wanted in the privacy of their own trailers, but not backstage. Jamie was adamant about that.

This show, however, was another story. Since they were sharing the stage with a bunch of other bands, there were girls everywhere.

"Dan!" Greg called to me. "What's up, man? What'd you think of the show?"

I walked over to him and extended my hand. "You guys sounded great."

Greg was a really good guy—more reserved than the rest of the band, though who was I to talk? He and Jamie started Cadence fourteen years ago, and the two of them collaborated on all of the songs. Creatively, he was a genius, with all the musical talent that went along with that.

"That blonde over there is checking you out," he said, finishing his beer.

I glanced in the direction of the girls he was referring to. There were about six of them, all partying and having a good time. The blonde was dressed in a skin-tight white tank and a black leather skirt so short I doubted she could bend over without giving a full view of her ass. Maybe that was the idea. She was wearing thigh-high black boots that looked like they'd be part of a dominatrix uniform. When she noticed me looking in her direction, she smiled back and raised her eyebrows in invitation.

"No thanks," I told him. "I'll leave that for Killian."

Greg laughed. "Good plan."

Christ. I just needed to get out of here. I made my excuses to Greg and stepped away, pulling my phone out of my pocket. But the next thing I knew, the blonde was at my side with one of her giant breasts pushed up against my arm.

"Hi, handsome." She smiled at me, giving me a full view down her tank. I took a step back and told her I had to make a call. It was kind of rude, I know, but I just didn't care.

Everything about that girl was fake. Rather than tempting me, she reminded me of what I no longer had.

Unlike these girls, Sarah's lips weren't smeared with heavy lipstick. They were full and supple, a feast for my mouth and teeth. And her eyes weren't hidden under dark liner. They were bright and sincere.

Sarah made me laugh—so often and so hard that nothing in my life ever seemed that bad when we were together. It was so much a part of our dynamic from the very beginning that I often forgot that no other relationship in my life had ever been like that. *I* wasn't usually like that—lighthearted and easy-going.

I didn't know what it was about her that made me want to dive right off a cliff into the murky waters of love and commitment, actually admitting my desire for marriage and a family. I barely recognized myself.

But with Sarah, it was so *easy*. I was in awe of her. Not just her beauty and her talent, but her strength, her fortitude, and her bravery. For someone so young to have been through so much, and come out of it with such grace and dignity, she was amazing. I'd never known anyone like her.

I'd spent a lot of time over the past weeks thinking about why I didn't tell her about the money. Mostly, I thought I didn't because telling her meant admitting to the wreckage of a relationship I had with my dad, and exposing every regret of my early life.

With her, I could be beyond all that. I was exactly the person I wanted to be, and she accepted me unconditionally for it.

It was never a question of trust.

And I *knew* I had screwed up. I took full responsibility for that. What I couldn't get over, though, was how easily she just threw our relationship away like it meant nothing.

Did she not understand I would have done *anything* to make her happy? I loved doing things for her. I loved being the person who gave her comfort, who made her smile, who took care of her. I wanted to look out for her, and stand up for her. I wanted her to need me, and I wanted to know I was as necessary to her happiness as she was to mine.

But she fucking gutted me. I was not prepared for that.

§

Someone dropped a bottle nearby, abruptly reminding me of where I was. When Jamie walked up and squeezed my shoulder, I realized I'd probably been staring like a zombie at my phone for an uncomfortable amount of time. He'd changed into an R.E.M. T-shirt, and was carrying a bottle of water.

"Hey brother, how'd we do?" If he noticed something in my mood, he didn't mention it.

"That may have been was one of your best shows," I told him, slipping the phone back into my pocket.

"We've come a long way from when we were the fluffers at these sorts of gigs."

I laughed. "You were definitely the consummators tonight."

Jamie smiled. "It felt good. The crowd was going *mad* the entire time."

He looked over my shoulder to the packed room and I watched as his eyes absorbed the party, which was now in full swing around us. Then his smile faltered a bit.

"I wish Mel were here."

I winced a little inside to hear that. Because that's what it was like to be with *the one*. When you wanted to share your every success with them. When you looked out into a room full of people and it felt empty because your one important person wasn't in it. That's what I thought I had with Sarah. I wasn't sure I'd ever find it again.

I forced myself back to our conversation, though, not wanting to dwell on that just now.

"I videotaped the show so you guys can watch it together tomorrow. Maybe you can take your shirt off and sweat on her a little to set the mood." I smiled at him, not wanting my poor temper to detract from his deserved sense of satisfaction.

"Brilliant." His eyes lit up and he laughed. "Thanks, brother." Then studying me carefully like he did, and no doubt noticing that I wasn't really feeling up for this scene, he said, "You want to get out of here? Go hang out for a while?"

And that right there was the true meaning of friendship. It wasn't about finding your next thrill, and it wasn't about crowing your career success. It was when you missed your wife or you'd lost a great love, and you didn't have to explain it or hide it or feel like a pussy about it. You didn't even have to talk about it if you didn't want to. Because what really mattered was right there in those small moments of camaraderie—playing hoops or catching a game together. That's when you knew there was someone out there who was willing to let you go through the hard stuff in your own way, but who wasn't willing to let you go through it alone.

# Chapter 28

## Sarah

I woke up Saturday morning to find a tiny Valentine on my pillow like the ones I used to give out as a kid. It was a little brown owl surrounded by a pink squiggly border, and inside it said, "Whoooo loves you, Valentine?" My immediate thought was Danny, but it took only a sobering moment of wakefulness to remember he hadn't reached out to me in two weeks. Why would he? I gave him no reason to believe I would be receptive. I opened the little card from Selene, a sweet and painful reminder of the mess I'd made.

After a few days in Auburn, I'd returned home, having convinced myself it would be best for us to take a break. I told myself it didn't matter what we felt for each other if I couldn't live with our one-sided communication—if I couldn't reconcile his deliberate secrecy with his insistence that our relationship was more than just a casual thing.

But the truth was . . . the real truth was, I just ran. I ran because I was scared that I'd overinvested in a relationship that might not be all I'd imagined it to be. I ran because if that were true, the hurt would be worse than anything I'd ever known. I ran because self-protection was my fallback. It was where I went when I felt my life slipping again out of my control. It was my habit, though it had never served me well.

I knew my failing to stay and face our issues was wrong. It was a strong signal of my own issues and I owed Danny more than that. I owed myself more, too.

§

My mom stopped through town for lunch on her way down to Pasadena to visit my brother. We celebrated my acceptance to the master's program, and the generous fellowship I'd been granted. I was truly ecstatic about it. Still, it was difficult to think about my acceptance and not think about Danny. He was so thoroughly entangled in that process.

As she was gathering her things to go, she noticed some pictures I had in the living room—in particular, a selfie of Danny and me from Thanksgiving. I was wearing that stupid red dress—the one I now wanted to burn—and Danny was in a blue and red plaid dress shirt.

His eyes were bright and full of joy, and he was wearing his million-dollar smile; I was laughing.

My mom paused for a moment to look at the picture. "He sure is handsome, isn't he?" I just nodded weakly, and bit my lip to keep from crying. "I've always thought he looked just like a younger, taller Robert Redford."

"When he was a kid, they used to call him Ken. Like the doll."

My mom laughed. "I can see that."

Neither of us said anything for a long time.

"He's been good for you, Sarah. I was wrong for the things I said."

"Mom . . ." The tears came streaming down my face, and there was nothing I could do to hide them.

My mom came immediately to my side, and wrapped her arms around me, just like she used to do when I was small.

"I knew something was wrong when you were at my place. Do you want to tell me what happened?"

In that moment, I had flashbacks of being ten years old, and coming to her after having a fight with my best friend. It reminded me how much I missed the time when we were so close I could tell her anything. I realized how much I wanted that again.

So I sucked in a deep, ragged breath, and painstakingly told her the whole damn story. Every detail. She listened, stroking my hair and rubbing my back as I talked.

My mother and I had never really talked about our own past. We'd never been able to have a constructive conversation about what happened in those difficult years. We'd had arguments, but neither of us could see past our own pain to be sympathetic to the other one's suffering. I wasn't sure I was ready to tackle all of our issues just yet, but opening up to her about Danny felt like a good place to start. It was the first time I'd brought her into my confidence in many years.

"Sarah, does knowing about the money change what you think of him as a person?" she asked me carefully.

"No, of course not."

She took my hand and looked me in the eye. "And do you believe his explanation for not telling you?"

I nodded, thinking about her question. "I do believe his explanation. But what if we're both too guarded and closed off to make a relationship work? It's not just him. My response to this whole situation was cowardly and appalling."

"From what I can tell, you've both come a long way. You've had a setback this past month, but in any good relationship that'll happen from time to time. The important thing is that you recognize your part in it and learn from that. Have you learned from it?"

I met her gaze and nodded. But I couldn't shake the very real fear that my learnings had come too late.

She cupped my chin in her hand, and smiled at me kindly. "You two seemed happy when you came to my house at Christmas, happier than I've seen you in a long time. I think you just got scared. And that's okay—natural even. It's a risk to love someone. But look at this picture and tell me it's not worth it."

I stared long and hard into Danny's beautiful face and I knew deep in my heart she was right.

"What if he won't take me back?"

For just a second, she considered this with a mother's practicality. "I think the better question is, are you brave enough to try?"

# Chapter 29

**Danny**

The lecture hall was packed. I was sitting at a small desk in the front with four other professors to my left, waiting to give students a brief synopsis of the course I was teaching at Stanford this summer. Since most of the classes discussed tonight weren't offered during the regular school year, students were here to get a preview of the schedule before making their final selections in a couple weeks.

I looked out over the sea of faces as Dr. Frick introduced each one of us, either new or guest professors. I was definitely feeling the pressure to justify his confidence in me. But I also knew I was well prepared for this, and that I was ready to take on a new challenge in my career.

I was the second to last to give my course overview, and as the speaker ahead of me launched into his PowerPoint my phone buzzed with a text. I'd neglected to turn it off. As I reached to do so, I discreetly glanced at the message. I was stunned to see it was from Sarah.

*I think your fly is open.*

What the hell?

I hadn't heard from her in nearly a month, and the last time we talked she was breaking up with me. And now this? Was she messing with me?

Was she *here*?

I looked around the hall, scanning the crowd for her face, but I didn't see her. There were too many people. And I couldn't decide if I'd even *want* to see her. Sometimes, I was so angry with her I couldn't stand it. And other times, I missed her so very much . . .

Plus, *was* my fly open? It would be embarrassing, to say the least, to stand up at the lectern with my dick hanging out. But I was sitting in front of a hundred or more students. How could I check without being obvious?

*Shit.*

As discreetly as I could manage, I felt for my fly under the pretense of bending down to pick up a pen. It was closed, thank god. When I straightened, another text.

*Ok, Mr. Science, why don't seagulls fly over the bay?*

Moments later, *Because they'd be bagels.*

She *was* messing with me. Furthermore, that was a horrendous joke. Unfortunately, it sparked a tiny inward smile and that truly pissed me off. She was definitely here. But *why*? Why would she come here? I knew she wasn't taking classes this summer.

And how could she think we could just pick up where we left off—or worse, pretend that our breakup never happened?

The applause for the prior speaker was winding down, and I rose to the lectern to begin my presentation. I scanned the faces again as I talked, but still couldn't locate her. I guess it was morbid curiosity—I just wanted to know whether our time apart had been half as difficult on her as it had been on me.

I finished my synopsis to more clapping and a few questions from interested students. Then I took my seat.

*Your class sounds amazing. I knew it would be.*

This text knocked the wind out of me. I stared at it for a long time. Her kindness was unbearably cruel. She had no right. If an offer of friendship was what this was, I wasn't ready for it. I didn't know if I could ever be.

I put my phone in sleep mode and dropped it into my coat pocket. I knew she could see me, wherever she was, and this was my way of sending a message back. *You left.* I didn't look at the audience for the rest of the night and instead, focused on the job I came here to do.

§

## Sarah

He looked amazing. And he looked terrible. Watching him in front of the standing-room-only lecture hall, he appeared self-assured and capable in his bespoke navy blue suit and crisp white shirt. He walked through his presentation, passionate and engaging. This was a man who was born to be at center stage. He was knowledgeable, authoritative, charismatic, and absolutely in control. He was mesmerizing.

But as I studied him closely, I thought he also looked tired. There were circles under his eyes and a tightness in his expression. He appeared a bit thinner too, although perhaps more muscular at the same time. I was probably the only one who would notice, but then I'd painstakingly committed every detail of him to memory and had tortured myself with those memories over the past month.

I'd missed him. Desperately. Countless things reminded me of him. Countless times my mind had drifted back to the warmth of his skin, his touch, and his laugh that I loved so much, every moment we spent together. Each precious instance played over and over in my head in an endless loop. For the past month, I'd felt like I was drifting. Like I'd lost my true north.

I went through all the motions: I studied, I saw friends, I called my family. But it was all hollow, mechanical.

I used to find comfort in my ability to distance myself from others.

My invulnerability was my superpower. It protected me.

But tonight, I didn't feel invulnerable. I felt scared and exposed. I was oscillating wildly between wanting to crash my way to the front of the room and throw myself into his arms, and feeling terrified that it was too late. That I'd lost him.

Our comfort zone had always been humor. So I thought perhaps I could break the ice between us by texting him tonight in the same spirit of teasing we'd both enjoyed countless times before. But as I watched him read my texts, I couldn't tell what he was thinking. He was too guarded. I had no idea if he was happy to hear from me, or if my intrusion was unwelcome.

I sent him one more text, this time just going for honesty.

*Your class sounds amazing. I knew it would be.*

I watched for his response, unable to breathe. I saw him stare at the screen, his eyes blank and his face impassive. His jaw tightened and he picked up the phone, dropping it into his suit coat pocket.

*Ouch. Ouch. Ouch.* My breath caught and my eyes filled with tears. I was desperately clinging to a tenuous composure—this was not the time or place to lose it. But suddenly, I couldn't hear anything but my own heartbreak. It ripped through my body with indescribable violence. I put my face in my hands, needing privacy for this profound undoing.

I had an urgent need to leave this room. I wanted to get up and run.

*What am I doing here? What have I done?*

More memories: The stick-figure drawings, his quiet wisdom, so much laughter, our passionate lovemaking. My world was colorless until he came into it. *He* brought me to life again.

Suddenly, I realized people were getting up to leave. I lifted my face from my hands to the awkward stares from people around me. It was embarrassing, but I didn't really have the capacity to care.

I had a decision to make. One decision—perhaps one of the most important of my life: *Now or never?*

When I lost my dad, I was devastated but I didn't have regrets about the way things were between us when he died. Losing Danny would be entirely different. And that regret was one I didn't think I could ever get over.

I made my way down to the front. His proximity felt surreal. I'd thought about almost nothing *but* him since I sent him away a month ago. His back was to me and he was speaking with a student. She looked all too interested in what he had to say.

I moved closer, my heart banging in my chest. A huge part of me wanted to walk up and wrap my arms around him like I'd once had the right to do. But I gave up the right, and that humbling fact sent a crash of panic through my body.

Someone accidentally bumped me and I stumbled forward, my hand reaching out to a nearby chair to steady myself.

Danny turned towards the commotion and when he caught my eye, I saw in a flash the countless emotions that passed over his face. And then they were gone.

I straightened myself slowly and we just stared at each other. It could've been that an entire conversation happened in that instant. It could have been there was nothing said at all. I'd never seen him more guarded. I had no idea how to proceed.

He turned back to the student.

"Thank you for coming tonight and for your interest in my class." He smiled at her politely, but dismissively.

Coming here was a bad idea. His lack of acknowledgement told me my presence was unwanted. Or worse.

I started to leave.

"I'll be a moment and then we can speak privately."

I looked up and realized he was talking to me. His eyes were flat. His tone of voice was not one he'd used with me in nearly six years. It wasn't the warm, caramel-covered husky tone that was my safe place. It wasn't the one that said, *I love you. You're my everything.* It was cold and detached. It wasn't my Danny. It was Professor Moore.

My heart sank. "*Run! Run now,*" my head said. But before my feet could move, Danny excused himself from Dr. Frick, grasped my elbow lightly and led me out rear door of the lecture hall.

It was cool outside and I gratefully inhaled a deep breath of the late winter air. We walked silently down a corridor to a small courtyard where students normally hung out between classes. It was empty now, and the eerie quiet seemed to fuel my growing sense of apprehension.

Danny stopped by a low wall and folded his arms across his body. There was an indifference in his expression that I'd never experienced before in his presence.

"Why did you come tonight?"

The question came out sounding harsh, almost accusatory. And while I was expecting him to ask, I was suddenly worried I didn't have a good enough answer for him.

"Because I miss you terribly and I fear I've made a horrible mistake."

My heart felt like it was clawing its way out of my chest as I awaited any response. It wasn't like me to be so direct with my feelings, but then again, I'd been someone else entirely since the day we met.

He was giving nothing away. "I tried calling you, texting you. No response."

I looked down at my feet, and fought to hold back my scattered emotions. I'd been so unfair to him. So cruel.

"I know. I'm so sorry. I had to get my head together and work some things out. And I needed to spend some time alone in order to do that."

"That's bullshit!" His vehemence startled me, and his eyes were furious and filled with hurt. "You were punishing me. You just didn't have the guts to say it. I was wrong for not confiding in you; I know that. But I was more than willing to face up to my mistake and make things right. At least I was trying, Sarah. You just cut and ran. You gave up on me. You gave up on *us*."

"No, I *didn't*. I've just never been good in relationships. I was confused about what we had and I was afraid."

"That's a fucking cop out. I begged you not push me away. I gave you every chance. I would have gone to hell and back for you. I did, in fact—waiting for weeks on end for you to see fit to at least talk to me. Or to end this, if that's what you really wanted. But you didn't even show me that minimal amount of consideration." He stared at me intensely and then ran a hand through his hair. "I told you I loved you, Sarah. Do you have any idea what that meant to me?"

I took in the angry, smoldering presence before me. He was nearly vibrating with energy, but his body was eerily still.

"Yes! I do . . . because I feel the same way. And I messed up. I'm so sorry I handled all of this so badly but it didn't mean I stopped loving you. You have to believe me."

My voice was weak and pleading, tears spilling down my face. I searched his expression for some kind of recognition that what I was telling him was true. But his posture was carefully neutral, as though he was examining my words with an acute sense of detachment—turning them over and over in his mind.

"I do believe you love me," he replied at last. "I can see it in your eyes, Sarah." He reached out as though he wanted to touch me. For a brief moment, my Danny was back. "But it's not enough. I realized after you left me so . . . callously, that you didn't need me the way I needed you. You wouldn't have been able to do what you did, otherwise. I'm not sure you'll ever allow yourself to need anyone that way and I can't live like that."

The impact of his words left me speechless. *Needing* someone else was a luxury I hadn't afforded myself in years. Not since I learned how easily those whom I needed could be taken from me.

I thought that was my strength. But in his eyes, it was my weakness.

I reached for him, but he stepped back, shaking his head.

"You know, when we first crossed paths again, I thought the hardest thing we had to overcome was our age difference and the awkward fact that I'd been your teacher." He laughed a bitter-sounding laugh—not the one I loved, at all. "But ironically, I think it was the connection we shared over our parents' deaths that was actually our downfall—the very thing that brought us together in the first place. Because I think our connection is that, at heart, we're both solitary people who just happened to recognize something similar in the other. Maybe it fooled us into thinking we could find completion together. But solitary people are probably better alone. I think you may have been right, Sarah; maybe we never really had a chance."

There were no words to describe the silence that followed.

I can only say this: Though I'd never been stabbed, in that moment I could truly imagine how it felt. The blade slides in with such precision, such sharpness that at first, there's no pain—not even a full realization of what has transpired. Then slowly, as it recedes, the dawning occurs— a shocking, detached understanding of one's own frailty. And with it comes the evidence that life is now free to flow from the body, painfully and unchecked, until there's nothing left to give.

Danny stared intensely at me for a long moment, almost as though he was memorizing me one last time. The idea of that was horrifying. Then he turned back toward the corridor to leave, drawing a figurative blade from my body without sound or ceremony.

"Danny . . ." I said desperately. It was all I could manage as my breathing became shallow and I battled back a deluge of emotion.

I wanted to argue with him that he was wrong, but the words just didn't come. The truth was, I wasn't sure if he was wrong. So I just stood helplessly by as the most important person in my life walked away from me for good.

# Chapter 30

**Danny**

It was Thursday evening. And after a long day at work, and the hardest run I could possibly put myself through without resulting in actual death, I found myself inexplicably seated on a barstool at The Rose & Crown.

No matter what I did, I couldn't shake the restlessness I'd felt since I left Sarah standing in the courtyard two nights ago. I had imagined a meeting like that with her a thousand times. In some scenarios, I'd take her in my arms, we'd ask each other for forgiveness, and I'd tell her I wanted her back. She'd tell me it would be different from now on, and I would believe her.

In some scenarios, I'd say all the things I practiced: that she gave up on me, that she didn't need me, that she *couldn't* need me, and that I had to move on. I'd walk away feeling like I'd achieved closure and I'd be able to get back to my life and feel good for maintaining my resolve to end things between us.

But the scenario I was in now—the one that actually went down—well, that one was shit. I said all the practiced words—the ones that were supposed to make me feel better but they didn't. They made me feel empty.

I rubbed my eyes again and again, trying to ease the ache caused by weeks of stress and sleeplessness.

And somehow, being so deep in my own head, I was oblivious when the seat next to me became occupied. I heard someone cough, and looked up.

"Hey, Redwood. You look like crap."

*Oh, fuck me.*

I closed my eyes again, and soundly cursed the universe for having a really shitty sense of humor. Then I desperately tried to remember what I ever did to deserve this. Unfortunately, a few things did come to mind, and that pissed me off even further.

I turned to face Marcus squarely so there could be no misunderstanding between us.

"Can you please just not speak to me right now?"

By silent mutual agreement, Marcus and I rarely talked throughout my relationship with Sarah. On those occasions when we went out with Sarah's friends, we might have offered each other a quick nod, but that was about it. It was better that we avoided each other.

He gave a soft grunt of agreement, and I turned back to my beer, doing my best to pretend I was alone.

"I just need to know something first."

*Oh, for Christ's sake.* I glared at him. "What?"

"Why'd you let me win at pool that first time we met?"

That was definitely not the question I was expecting. It had been months since that night—why bring it up now when it no longer mattered? I breathed deeply and focused my attention on the contents of my glass.

But this guy was actually waiting for an answer. Finally, I rubbed the stubble on my jaw.

"What makes you think I let you win?"

"Because I'm not an idiot."

"That's debatable."

I could almost feel his eyes boring into the side of my head. "You sank all the hard shots and missed the gimmies."

"The hard ones are much more fun." I turned to meet his gaze, and he smiled shallowly, nodding.

"So was it my sparkling personality that won you over?"

"That wasn't exactly it, no."

"You love her, then."

It wasn't a question. But it felt a little irrelevant considering the last conversation Sarah and I had had effectively ended all future ones. I didn't bother answering.

"She told me you broke up. Is that why you look so depressed? I thought maybe they discontinued your hair gel."

If I'd had just a little more fight in me, I would've seriously contemplated a physical resolution to this conversation. Instead, I scanned the bar for any other possible place to sit. With no other alternatives, I turned back to him.

"What is *wrong* with you? Honestly, do you just enjoy being a dick?"

He raised his eyebrows as if I'd missed the obvious, and instead of answering, took a deep pull on his beer. He swallowed and then made a face as the carbonation burned going down.

I couldn't resist. "Sure you're old enough for that?"

"Fuck you," he said casually. He dug through the bowl of nuts, knocking a few over the side, and came up with a cashew that he tossed in his mouth. Licking the salt from his fingers, he went back in for another.

*Gross.*

"Well, for starters, I recently lost the girl I was in love with too."

Marcus and I were hardly confidantes. He must have known that I was truly not interested in his dating woes. In fact, I would have paid good money for someone to make him disappear at this very moment.

But, short one magician, I turned my attention back to my own pint, and made a mental note to avoid bar nuts.

"Well, I guess *lost her* isn't really accurate," he continued uninvited. "She wasn't my girlfriend—she's my friend. She's just never going to be more than that."

In spite of myself, I turned in his direction as the meaning of his words opened up. But he wasn't looking at me; he was carefully pulling the label off his bottle. I took a deep breath, suddenly very uncertain— and a little wary—at the direction this conversation was heading.

"Anyway," he continued. "She fell in love with this *a-hole*."

He looked over, catching my eye again, and smiled wryly. I just stared at him for a moment, and then a small chuckle bubbled out of somewhere it'd been hiding inside me for weeks.

"And that pretty much ruined my chances with her," he finished. "If I ever had any." With one last pull, he peeled the label clean off the bottle in one piece. "I didn't deal with it well at first."

"You think?" I scoffed. But, oddly enough, I could relate.

He huffed out an ironic laugh, and tilted his head back and forth in acknowledgement.

Although he was making light, I got the sense that Sarah's feelings for me had been harder on him than his pride would have him let on. Of course he would have been in love with her. Who wouldn't? Marcus was a handsome guy, but his personality was repellent.

Her breakup with John must have seemed like it opened a door for him in a way. And all the time they spent together probably made it feel like there could be something between them. Sarah wouldn't knowingly lead him on, but her kindness and her ability to see the best in people probably made him feel hopeful. And then I showed up. No wonder he hated me. I took her attention. I ended the possibilities. And when she was spending time with me, he probably missed the time they spent together.

Suddenly, I was looking at this guy in a very different light. Like he and I were actually two sides of the same coin. Both in love with a woman we couldn't move past.

"But see, here's the thing," he said, folding the label carefully in half, and then in half again. "I finally realized I couldn't call myself much of a friend if I'd rather she was still crying on my shoulder than happy with someone else."

He looked me straight in the eye, and I was speechless.

It was obvious now that Sarah was right about Marcus—their friendship *wasn't* just about his feelings for her. He might have wanted things to be different, but he was always willing to put her happiness above his own.

I began to recognize what Sarah saw in him. He *was* kind of funny, if you could get past the obnoxiousness. And he was surprisingly real once you peeled back the thin veneer of arrogance. Something about him reminded me of Jamie when he was young—too much attitude for his own good, and too little to lose to really give a shit.

I began to wonder, if Marcus and I had met under different circumstances or maybe if we'd had more time to get to know each other, would we have eventually become friends?

"What I'm trying to say is, despite the way I may have acted before, I hope it works out for you two. However you want it to, that is. And, no offense, but it doesn't look like it's working out for either one of you right now."

That hit squarely like a punch to the gut. "How is she?"

He looked me over. "Same as you, I think."

I didn't really know how to feel about that. A part of me was relieved to know she was having a hard time with all of this too—that it wasn't so easy for her to just walk away. But the bigger part of me found the thought of Sarah suffering in any way intolerable, even if both of us contributed to our present situation. Knowing that she was hurting made me feel worse. Much worse.

"Marcus, I don't know what to do."

The words left my mouth in a rush before I had time to consider them, an admission that stunned both of us. I found myself in the most absurd situation of asking advice from a guy I could barely tolerate only a short time ago—a guy who also happened to be in love with the woman I loved.

He flicked the folded label somewhere behind the bar.

"Don't ask me. I don't know shit about relationships," he said very matter-of-factly. "But it seemed like yours was pretty good."

It *was* good. Finding Sarah was like finding a needle in a haystack. Was I being too protective of myself? Too proud? Was *this* what it meant to love someone? That you just had to be willing to lay yourself wide open and hope the other person didn't trample on you when you were at your most defenseless? That they wouldn't think less of you when they were finally exposed to all your faults and weaknesses?

I closed my eyes, and pressed my fingertips to my forehead—all of this was too overwhelming for my exhausted brain.

When I looked up, he was assessing me shrewdly.

"What?"

"I was just trying to figure out what she could possibly see in you." He shook his head as if he just didn't get it. Then gesturing at my body and face, "Under all that pretty-boy bulk, you seem to have a very tiny brain. Like a T-Rex."

I just stared at him for a minute. Then I laughed. Hard. I didn't know if it was his lame joke, or if it was simply that this miserable situation had me so twisted up inside that I just needed to vent.

But pretty soon, Marcus was laughing too. We were having this bizarre bonding moment and although nothing felt resolved, it was an odd reprieve from the misery of my present state.

Once the hilarity passed, I looked at him directly.

"I can't believe I'm saying this, Marcus, but it's possible I may sort of like you."

He grinned. "I wouldn't go that far."

# Chapter 31

**Sarah**

"Hey, you have a visitor," Selene said peeking into my room.

My heart stopped for a moment with the hope that it was Danny, though I knew it wasn't. It had been several days since I last saw him, and he'd been very clear about where we stood.

Pulling myself off the bed, I headed into the living room. As I rounded the corner, I saw the next best thing.

"Jamie?" I was stunned he was here. He was carrying a large bouquet of brightly colored flowers, and looking at the photos we had arranged on a small side table.

"Hey, lovely. Good to see you."

He looked every bit the rocker in his black T-shirt and jeans, with the birdlike tattoo that covered his right forearm. It was funny, though, as star struck as I was when I first met him, now I just saw a man—a really good man, a family man.

He engulfed me in an embrace that overflowed with affection. There was nothing about Jamie that wasn't one hundred percent sincere. He just didn't have artifice in him.

"I can't believe you're here," I said, more emotionally than I meant to. I badly wanted to know if Danny knew he had come—or better, if

Danny had sent him.

"I wanted to look in on you. Make sure you were doing okay," he said with a smile.

"Can I get you something to drink?"

"I'll get it," he said firmly, waving off my attempt at basic hospitality. He brushed past me, setting the flowers on the counter, and retrieved a pitcher of filtered water from the fridge.

As I watched him move around my kitchen, a million questions swirled in my head. I was almost afraid to open my mouth for fear they might come shooting out, as though fired from a slingshot.

*How is Danny?*

*Can he ever forgive me?*

*Is it really over between us?*

Jamie made himself perfectly at home in my kitchen, though the room seemed far too small for his sizeable presence. He came up with a couple of glasses for the water, and a vase for the flowers. Then he returned to the living room and sat down on the sectional beside me, taking a long sip from his drink. His posture was relaxed, but there was a purpose for his visit and I desperately wanted to get through the pleasantries to know what it was.

"How's your mum? I heard she had an accident."

"Good. She slipped on some ice, but she's fine. Actually, she's doing very well."

My visit with my mother was good, truthfully. She seemed strong and healthy again—so much like the mom I remembered before everything in our lives went wrong.

He nodded, focused on the glass in his hand. "A lot has fallen on you, though. Hasn't it?"

I shrugged. "It was easier for me to get up to Auburn. I live closer than my brother."

"That's not what I was referring to," he said quietly, holding my gaze with kind hazel eyes. "I grew up with an alcoholic parent, as well."

His admission caught me off guard, and I just stared at him for a beat.

"Jamie, I had no idea."

He smiled a bit, I think to relieve some of the heavy awkwardness of his disclosure.

"No, probably like you, I don't talk about it much. Makes for rather nasty gossip in the tabloids, yeah?"

I knew Jamie's childhood had been difficult, but I didn't know the specifics. In a way, I was surprised that Danny never said anything about it, especially given my background. But then, he'd never betray a confidence, and it wasn't his secret to tell. He was supremely trustworthy like that. My heart ached once more with the thought.

"I'm so sorry." I knew firsthand the impact that alcoholism can have on a family. His admission affirmed the kinship I'd always felt existed between us.

But Jamie brushed away my concern. "He's gone now. Died a few years back. He was a brute and a bully, actually, but far worse to my older brothers than he was to me. I'm the second youngest of seven, you know. So he didn't pay me a lot of attention."

As I listened to Jamie talk, I remembered all the ribbing he got for his meandering stories. But this particular story wasn't like that. He wasn't making casual conversation here. He was telling me something I'd bet he didn't share outside a very small group of people.

"The thing about it, Sarah, is that I know what it's like to feel alone in the world. My home life growing up was abysmal. I was so ashamed of that and so afraid that if anyone knew, things would be even worse for me and my little sister, Cara. So I hid it as best I could. And in order to do that, I had to keep people away. You know what I mean, don't you?"

Yes. All too well. Neither of us needed me to say it.

"After a while, it kind of becomes a habit," he continued. "But I was lucky. I had Cara and Danny. Later, I had my band. Then I found Mel, and that changed my life."

"And the kids," I added.

"Nah. They're arses." The corners of his mouth lifted impishly. "My point is, it's not a wide circle, but it's enough. And it's essential. Particularly in a business where everybody wants somethin' from you."

His eyes locked on mine, and they conveyed a world of experience, of survival. I nodded, unsure how to respond.

"You have a circle too," he insisted. "But you have to let yourself be a part of it. You can't allow yourself to believe that everyone will let you down or leave you sooner or later. You have to have faith that you're not alone."

The truth was, I *had* felt alone since my dad died. I loved my brother more than life itself, but he wasn't someone I could lean on. He just didn't have the capacity for that. It was a limitation of his Asperger's. As for anyone else, either through circumstance or my own self-protection, I hadn't really ever had another person I could count on. Even, to a certain extent, Selene, though I knew that one was my own fault.

I stared at Jamie while my vision began to blur. "I went to see Danny but . . ." I shook my head, unable to complete the sentence.

Jamie wrapped a gentle arm around me and kissed my hair in a gesture that reminded me so painfully of his best friend.

"He loves you. I've known him a long time and I've never seen him like this before. He just doesn't trust you not to push him away at the first sign of trouble between you. You can't blame him for that."

"No, I can't."

We sat together on the couch in silent introspection. It wasn't awkward. It felt cathartic in a way.

"Jamie, do you think you can ever really know someone?"

He shifted in his seat, taking time to consider this. "In my experience, people tell you what they will, but it doesn't necessarily mean you come to know them any better. You can probably learn more from what they do. But ultimately, we all have a secret place inside of us. I don't think anyone is completely transparent. We probably wouldn't like each other much if we were." Dimples formed again in his cheeks, punctuating the thought.

He leaned back on the couch, and draped his arm across the back. "Songwriting probably makes me more transparent in some ways because it's my method of coming to understand things. And, sometimes that's a really frightening process. It's kind of like thinking out loud.

"I remember telling a musician friend of mine once that I'd written a song about the doubts I was feeling towards the religion I was raised with. I told him it felt too raw to sing that song in concert. He said that's exactly the reason I needed to sing it. Because the rawness was *real*. It took a long time for me to finally bring it into our set list, and when I did, it was scary as hell."

I knew exactly the song Jamie was talking about. I'd probably heard it on the radio a thousand times. It was sobering to realize that behind the recording, there was a real person trying to make sense of some very personal questions.

He watched me carefully and then asked, "I'm assuming your question is really about Danny, though."

I nodded.

"He's kept a lot inside for most of his life. You have to give him a little time to change that because for him it's scary as hell too. But I look more at what he's done—and that's how I know what kind of a person he is.

"When we were kids, I'd get picked on a lot for being different—my accent, and all. It didn't help that I also had a big mouth." He laughed. "But Danny never allowed that. He was much bigger than most kids our age, and he stood up for me more times than I can remember. He got into some pretty bad fights at school on my account."

A chill ran up my spine at the memory of my conversation with Casey.

"Many times, when my da used our grocery money for whiskey, Danny would sell his things for me—bikes, skateboards, CDs, whatever he could sell—so I could give my mum a little extra cash. Danny would've given me the shirt off his back; he didn't care. His father—Richard, that was his name—well, he thought Danny was just bein' careless with his stuff, and he used to give him a hard time about it. Said it was a sign of his privilege. Danny never set him straight, and I always felt like shite for being part of the reason they didn't get along."

"Why didn't he just talk to his parents about what was going on?"

"He knew I'd be embarrassed about it—about my da, and all. He said if his father didn't know he was responsible by the way he handled other aspects of his life, then knowing this one thing wouldn't make a difference."

Hearing this broke my heart—the fighting, the irresponsibility. It was ironic that Richard raised a son he would have been very proud of had he only known him better.

"Danny was the one who pushed me to pursue a career in music. He helped me in every way he could. He hauled gear, hung flyers, anything. There wasn't a single thing I ever asked of him that he ever said no to. I'm telling you this, Sarah, but I suspect you already know, that he's one of the best, most solid people you will ever meet. He was the very first person in my life who I knew with absolute certainty would never let me down. And he never has."

Jamie hesitated, pausing to carefully choose the right words. His face was serious, and I realized that *this* was the true reason for his visit.

"Danny deserves to be happy. And I think you can make him happy, Sarah. I do. But he has to know you're in this with him. If you can't be, then I'm asking you to let him go for good. Do you understand? You have to let him move on. I'm asking you this as his friend. And as yours. I can't watch him suffer like this."

He stared unblinking into my face, and I felt my heart thrumming loudly with every passing second.

I regretted so many things when it came to Danny. But the thing I regretted most was that I lacked the clarity and the courage to break the pattern of isolation that had plagued us both. I could have, had I fought for him, for us. But, instead, I faltered.

And I was determined not to let that happen again. He was, after all, the one who helped me to open up, myself. Could I not do the same for him?

"Jamie, I don't want to lose him. But I don't know how to fix things with him. I don't know if he'll listen to me at this point." And then, realizing the progress these next words represented, I added, "I need you to help me."

His big, goofy, mock-shocked expression made me laugh out loud, and it was the first time I'd felt hopeful in a month. I leaned my head against his shoulder and just enjoyed the simple, reassuring pleasure of his presence.

"Lovely Sarah," he said, stroking my hair. "There isn't anything I'd like more."

# Chapter 32

**Danny**

Sunday afternoon, I ditched Jamie and the rest of the guys after basketball and hit a local pub called The Wild Boar. It was a dark place, and kind of a dive, but it had a huge variety of beer on tap and plenty of pool tables. After my parents died, this was where I'd come to think and just get away. I never saw anyone here I knew.

Apparently, I was back to my old habits.

It wasn't so much that I felt like drinking but quite frankly, I didn't want to go home. Alone with myself, I ordered a pint of Goose Island and sat back on my barstool to watch a game. About half an hour in, my phone buzzed with a text from Jamie.

*Where are you?*

*Nowhere. Wild Boar.*

*Brilliant. Be right there.*

So much for getting away.

Jamie showed up and settled onto the empty barstool to my left. He ordered a pint of Guinness and a shot, and toyed with the cardboard coaster. He seemed pensive, but I wasn't complaining; I didn't feel like talking either.

Ever since I'd run into Marcus the other night, I'd been preoccupied by my uncertainty over where I left things with Sarah. Was I the biggest idiot on the planet for not taking her back when she came to me? Maybe I was—but I couldn't get past the reality that her loving me wasn't enough. It was enough to stem the pain I was in right now, but ultimately, I knew it wasn't enough to build an entire future on—a future I knew, without question, I wanted. I needed more from her than just her love. I needed everything.

And that's when it *finally* dawned on me—with absolute clarity.

I'd been asking myself for a month how she could possibly have left me over one omission—one I didn't really feel compelled to share. But I realized in that moment that she had left me for the exact same reason I broke things off with her.

Sarah left me because she needed everything too.

She needed all those things I wasn't giving her. The parts of me I held back because I was ashamed to share—because I had regrets I couldn't face.

She must have needed to know that I could be the foundation for *her* future. That was no small thing to be, particularly to someone who'd had her foundation torn away once before. No one knew that better than I.

This wasn't about the money, I finally realized; it was about knowing that I was invested enough in us to tell her. No amount of words—not even *I love you*—could equal, for her, that one simple act of faith.

I drew in a deep breath and let a wave of awareness wash over me. How the hell did we manage to screw up a good thing so badly? I rubbed my eyes and took another drink of my beer.

"Have I ever told you about my dog, Foster?" Jamie said, breaking into my thoughts.

I turned to him, my brain still making the transition from my revelation to his out-of-the-blue question.

"No. What are you talking about?"

"My dog, Foster. I had him when I was seven," he said just before tossing back the shot.

"I've known you for twenty-five years, Jamie. How have I never heard of this mystery dog?"

He just shrugged and continued his story. "Foster was a mutt. He was absolute shite—the worst bloody dog of all time. Barked constantly, dug in the yard, got on the furniture. But he was big and sweet and he did some tricks. My da thought he was the stupidest dog on the planet, but I always thought he might have been really smart."

"Okay." I mentally groaned, resigning myself to another aimless Jamie Callahan story.

"So, this one day, my brothers were carrying in some groceries and left the front door open and you know what Foster did?"

I had no clue.

"He ran away," Jamie told me. "He was gone for hours before we knew he'd left. We rode our bikes all over the neighborhood looking for that bloody dog. Couldn't find him. Figured maybe he was in a ditch somewhere."

He paused, took a sip of his beer, and resumed fiddling with the coaster.

*"And?"* These stories drove me insane.

"And, finally, we got this call from someone who lived like fifteen blocks away. The dog had run all over the neighborhood, and got tired. Must have found an open garage. And the door to this bloke's kitchen was also open, so he went in the house. Then up the stairs to a bedroom, and that dog just decided to take a nap on some stranger's bed."

I stared at him, incredulously. "Jamie, what is the point of this? Is this some roundabout metaphor of Sarah and me? Are you suggesting she's wandering off to some strange guy's bedroom?"

I was suddenly *gutted* with the idea of Sarah being with someone else. *Oh Christ*, I hadn't let myself go there until this very moment.

"No, you stubborn arse," he said, leaning in to meet my gaze directly. "My point is this: What the *fuck* are you doing here when you actually have someone to go home to?"

Hazel eyes held mine unblinking for several seconds while the question sunk in for me to an almost devastating effect. And then, finally, he turned his attention back to his beer.

*Go home to.*

Not so long ago, my home was *her*. That thought was like a knife in my stomach. With *her* was where I found everything I wanted: love, joy, laughter, acceptance, forgiveness.

The truth I hadn't allowed myself to admit was that, despite everything that had happened, *with her* was still where I wanted to be.

I was staring absentmindedly at Jamie when he looked up from his glass, nodding his chin to someone. I followed his line of sight and I stopped short at what I saw.

Sarah was standing in the doorway.

A kaleidoscope of emotion erupted through my body at once. I was absolutely stunned she was here, given the way I so purposely closed down her attempt to make amends a few nights ago. That night I drank her in like it was the last time I might see her, but it wasn't enough. I didn't think I could ever get enough.

In her white jeans and white sweater, with her hair long and wavy, she looked like an angel.

"You called her?" I was almost breathless, my heart pounding against my sternum.

Without answering, he got up, patted me on the shoulder, and threw a twenty on the bar. "Time to go home."

I think he left, though I barely noticed. I was still staring at Sarah. She was like a vision. I couldn't tear my eyes away. And I couldn't remember, even for a second, why I ever thought I was better off without her.

She made her way to me, sitting down on the seat Jamie vacated. Her presence took my breath away. I wondered briefly if I was dreaming. I wanted to reach out and touch her, to know for certain that she was here.

"So do I have to pull you out of here by your collar?" Her tone was light, but her eyes screamed vulnerability.

So many things were racing through my head. Just the sight of her here beside me was reassuring beyond anything I could imagine. But I realized that, just as I was taking comfort in her, she was becoming increasingly uneasy by my silence.

"Sarah—" I started, preparing to tell her how happy I was that she'd come. But she seemed to misread my tone. I was sure, given our last conversation, she thought I was getting ready to send her away. As if I could've ever done that again.

"No," she said, shaking her head obstinately. And I recognized that stubborn look in her eyes. It was the same one that had driven me crazy a thousand times before. The one we argued over, the one I criticized her for. But right now, it was the best look on earth. It was the look that told me she was fighting for me. For us.

"I won't let you go," she barreled on. "And it's not just because I love you desperately—it's because you changed me. I can't be the person I've been since my dad died. I can't live that way anymore.

"This last month showed me we aren't meant to be alone. And I think you know that too. *That's* why you reached out to me six years ago by telling me about your parents, and that's why I reached back in understanding. Our connection isn't that we're both solitary people, it's that we understand better than most that life is precious and fragile, and love, where you can find it, isn't something to ever be taken for granted. We may have stumbled over our own shortcomings, but our connection is still there. It's still strong. You're the other half of me, Danny. I need you. I always will."

I just looked at her, speechless, her earnest words apparently turning me mute. For all the times she'd told me she loved me, for all the ways she demonstrated it through her actions and her thoughtfulness, she had never once said she needed me. And that one thing had been the missing piece for me in our relationship. I didn't even know it.

But sitting here today, I could see in her face how much she wanted me to know that what she was telling me was true.

Every relationship required a leap of faith. And I knew if I wanted to be with Sarah, I had to be prepared to take one. After all, I was asking for no less from her.

Love is messy and perilous at times, but it's also profoundly life changing. This I could now say from experience.

"So that's how I feel," she said defiantly, confounded by my continued silence.

We'd definitely put each other through the ringer these last weeks. I couldn't remember the last time I'd seen her smile.

And maybe because I needed to see that smile again to know that we could, indeed, find our way back, I broke the silence by saying the very first stupid thing that came into my befuddled, lovesick brain.

"So a pirate walks into a bar with a ship's steering wheel attached to the front of his pants. And the bartender says, 'You know, you got a steering wheel stuck to the front of your pants.' To which the pirate answers, 'Arrr, it's drivin' me nuts.'"

I guarantee this was not what she was expecting me to say. Hell, *I* didn't even know where that came from. I watched her shift uncomfortably in her seat. She just stared at me for a moment, her mouth hanging open a little, and her eyebrows pulling together.

But then I saw it—a tiny bit of mirth in her eyes. That's when I knew for sure we were going to be okay.

"That is the worst joke I've ever heard," she said with a straight face, but with a little glint in her expression.

"But you want to laugh, anyway," I told her, feeling irrationally cocky all of the sudden.

"You are such an ass." She was biting the inside of her mouth to keep from cracking up, and her eyes were now full of humor.

"You're an old soul, and I'm hopelessly childish. That's what makes us perfect for each other."

I smiled at her—a huge, relieved, happy-to-the-depths-of-my-soul kind of smile.

"*That's* what makes us perfect for each other?" she said, now smiling too. That smile took my breath away. "And you know this from your experience as a teacher? Or a doctoral candidate, perhaps?"

I threw my head back and laughed whole-heartedly. God, I'd missed her.

"No, smart ass," I replied, carefully setting the humor aside. In its place came the honesty I'd long owed her. "I know this because never in my life have I loved anyone like I love you. And never in my life has that love felt so necessary I couldn't breathe without it. So I guess, whatever risk I have to take, whatever protected part of myself I have to expose, whatever I need to do to make sure you know without question that you are the most precious thing in my life, that's what I'll do. And however scary it is, I'll trust that there's enough between us that you'll stay, and that you'll let me play more than a superficial role in your life. I'll trust that you'll always fight for us like you fought for us today."

I reached out and took her hand, running my thumb across her fingers. I relished the warmth that seemed to begin with that simple touch, and quickly spread to every corner of my body and soul.

"I haven't been fair to you, Sarah. I realize that now. When it came to my feelings for you, I just assumed you understood instinctively all the things I wasn't able to say. And you're right that by not opening up, I was taking no risk, and yet reaping all of the reward of what we had. I never meant for you to have to question the most basic truths about my commitment to us. I'm so sorry for that."

I lifted her hand to my lips, and placed a soft kiss on her fingertips.

"I promise you this: I will never let it happen again. You and I live every day *knowing* that life can be taken without warning. But that's actually a gift because it makes us realize that every day is too important to waste. I don't ever want to lose you. I can't imagine a life you're not in."

I met her eyes again, and tears were streaming down her pink cheeks. I wiped one away.

"You're always how I know," I told her.

"How you know what?" she asked with a little sniffle.

"That I'm staying true to the man I want to be for you. When there's conflict between us, I know I've drifted from that ideal."

"Danny, you're the best man I know. You've always been that man for me."

I took in her sweet face with a gratefulness I cannot describe. And not caring where we were or who might object, I leaned forward and kissed her, tasting the tears on her lips. I was overwhelmed by how good it felt to touch her again—her warm skin, the softness of her mouth. My kiss was gentle at first, but I couldn't contain the reaction of my body to her taste, her touch.

I quickly deepened it, savoring her breath and her tiny sounds. She melted into me, raising her hand up behind my neck and into my hair, sending a flood of chills down my spine. She was soft and yielding, and I poured every bit of love and lust and adoration into that kiss.

"Come home with me." With only a look, I implored her to feel the certitude of my words. "Stay with me and never leave."

She studied my face carefully, touching my lips for just a moment with her fingertips. Then she smiled the most heart-stopping smile that seemed to light her body from within. I felt the world shift on its axis, and joy began to pour back into my life.

I was alive again.

And when I pulled her to me with a grin that felt irrepressible, she offered me the one solitary word that truly needed no other.

"Yes."

# Epilogue

## Danny

The physics of wave theory are both simple and complex. A drop of water falling into a larger body creates a ripple, a wave of energy that travels outwardly from the source. And this wave propagates through the medium of water, changing the substance of the medium indefinitely. Newton's First Law of Motion suggests that a wave in motion will stay in motion, unless a restoring force acts upon it.

In my life, the drop of water was more like a boulder, flung upon me by my parents' deaths. The ripple effect from that event was lasting and profound. It changed the way I viewed every relationship, and limited what I was willing to give—what I was willing to risk.

And that effect would have probably gone on indefinitely had it not been for *my* restoring force.

My Sarah.

She was the one who finally calmed the waters. She was the one who brought me back to equilibrium. She was my reformation. And in truth, I was probably hers.

When we left the bar that night, I couldn't stop touching her. As much as I wanted her physically, it was much more than that. I just couldn't stop reassuring myself that she was here. Mine again.

We didn't say a lot on the ride back to my place—we just touched, held hands, drank in every priceless moment. It was a peaceful quiet—not an awkward one. There was so much to say, but the urgency was gone, replaced by the silent mutual commitment to spend a lifetime saying everything that mattered.

When we got back to my place, she looked towards my house like she hadn't seen it in years, or maybe like she didn't think she would ever see it again. The expression on her beautiful face wrecked me, so I took her up in my arms and held her tight, feeling her tremble with emotion.

Every protective instinct I had kicked in in that instant, and I had this weird urge to feed her excessively and care for her in every possible basic way.

We went inside and I sat her down on a barstool in my kitchen and cooked enough food to feed about forty people. She laughed at me for that, suggesting that once again we were trying to eat our way out of trouble. In truth, neither of us ate much of anything. We just sat together on my living room floor in front of the fire and talked about the time we'd spent apart.

She told me the one positive to come out of all of this was that she had begun to reconcile with her mom. I could see in her eyes that a burden had lifted.

I told her I no longer wanted to punch Marcus in the face, and we both laughed about how much progress *that* truly was.

Finally, she laid her head on my shoulder and the world felt right again, as though everything missing had been restored. The body's memory is different from the mind's in that way. The body forgets nothing.

I did make love to her that night, and it was an experience of unparalleled joy. Paradoxical as it was, I wanted to both worship and defile her. I wanted to push myself hard into her and mark her as mine in every way possible. At the same time, I wanted to gently touch every single beautiful curve and hollow of her body. I wanted to memorize any changes I could see, and make it all familiar again. She had a tiny new scar forming on her right index finger, and there were a few scrapes on her knee from a recent hike. These were the only outward evidence of the time I'd missed, and they would heal completely and in short order.

As for us, our scars and stories might last a bit longer, but they would always serve as a reminder of everything that is more precious than pride, more precious than fear or self-doubt. Our scars would tell the story of love—the kind of love that leaves ripples that go on forever.

§§§

# Acknowledgements

Okay, so, I first want to say to all of the writers out there, holy crap! Well done, you! This book was such a labor of love for me, but I never appreciated just how difficult it would be at times to actually write the damn thing. I certainly had plenty of days (and nights) when I wanted to throw my manuscript on the ground, stomp on it with feeling, and then light it on fire in a brilliant blaze of glory. Thankfully, I never wanted to do that precisely at the time I had ready access to a match. The process has given me a renewed respect for writers in every genre who struggle to create works that move, and entertain, and teach us something about ourselves. It's not an easy thing to do.

Second, and this is a big one, I need to say a huge thank you to my husband, who was my cheerleader, my sounding board and my harshest critic. I thank you most for the last one. Asking for honesty is the writer's equivalent of "Does my butt look big?" And I admit without reservation that your sometimes-painful observations made my story infinitely better. While I did, in fact, discover some very real differences in our opinions of what "chicks love," I truly respected and valued every hard-to-hear comment.

Romance, in general, is an underappreciated genre and one that deserves far more respect than it generally receives. We, both readers and writers, are not who they say we are. So I want to extend special thanks to the romance blogs for the critical role that you play in giving opportunity to people like me. By your efforts, we can reach an audience that is far more accepting of indie authors than the publishing industry at large. It is because of your passion that voices like mine can be added to the mix. I thank you, sincerely, for everything you do.

I would be completely remiss if I didn't credit Joshua Jaden for his masterful cover art—who nailed "sexy, but not cheesy," and didn't even blink when I asked for a bigger Adam's apple. To Ashley at TCB editing, and this is a big one, you gutted me for about 24 hours, and then you made both my book and me so very much better for your involvement. Thank you for caring enough to stick your neck out . . . and of course for catching all of the little things that a thousand read-throughs on my part could never catch. And finally to Polgarus Studio for its expertise in making my book look like a real book. How cool is that??

And finally, my most humble and enormous thanks to every single romance reader who has or will open her home to my story, who takes these characters to heart, and who generously gives purpose and meaning to something I absolutely love to do. You'll never know how grateful I am to you; your positive comments and support mean more than I could possibly express. These words are wholly inadequate, but I'll say them anyway for want of something better . . . thank you. Truly.

# Sound EFFECTS

A *RIPPLE EFFECTS* NOVEL

## L.J. GREENE

**What is *your* passion?**

When an uncharacteristically rash decision lands law school graduate Melody Grayson in San Francisco's dicey Tenderloin District, she comes face to face with a dangerously tempting man who embodies every mistake she swore she would never repeat. Passionate, sexy, and far more insightful than she'd care to admit, he causes her to question everything she thought she knew about her future. Now she'll have to decide where the bigger risk lies: in the prudent path she's been working tirelessly to pursue, or in the intriguing but uncertain one he's offering.

Up-and-coming, Irish-born musician Jamie Callahan is no stranger to chaos; he's lived a lifetime of it. But in the fall of 2004, when the music industry is on the verge of massive upheaval, the life he aspires to could come at a heavier price than he's prepared to pay. And while Melody may be the ideal person to help him navigate the gambles he must take, a relationship with her might be his biggest gamble yet.

SOUND EFFECTS is a standalone dual POV adult contemporary romance that captures the gloriously unpredictable nature of life, in which the path from who you are to who you're meant to become may not be a straight one. It may also have a few bumps. Sexy, humor-filled, and relatable, *Sound Effects* is a story about living passionately, staying true to yourself, and finding that one magic person who makes the journey of self-discovery an adventure worth taking.

# Chapter 1

**Saturday, August 14, 2004**
**Melody (Mel)**

I discovered I was not above enlisting the help of a leek to improve my love life. This realization offered a rather humbling perspective on my present state. Still, I rang the buzzer on the battered front door and, not for the first time, asked myself what in the *hell* I was doing here. My host, Dan Moore, was one of the most beautiful men I'd ever seen in person—that was the obvious answer. But it was an admittedly dubious explanation for meeting him for the first time today in the grocery store and blindly accepting his invitation to a barbecue. A barbecue in the *Tenderloin* District, no less.

Striking good looks aside, the only thing I knew for sure about him was that he was astonishingly well informed on the difference between scallions and leeks, which had actually been quite helpful, if I were being honest. Apparently to my sex-deprived, overworked brain, that was sufficient. Again, some perspective.

Dan answered the door with a look of pleasure and surprise that lit his stunning face like a flame. In that initial moment, I said a silent prayer of thanks to leeks.

In the next, as he leaned in to offer a kiss on the cheek, I debated whether his overpowering cologne could actually *melt* his stunning face. Or mine, for that matter.

"Any trouble finding the place?" he asked.

"Nope, your directions were meticulous."

He smiled widely with those perfect white teeth and intense green eyes, gesturing me inside the small bachelor pad with an elegant flourish of his hand.

The entryway of the apartment was tight and made tighter by the presence of a bicycle leaning just inside the doorway. I pitied the person whose mode of transportation in San Francisco was that bicycle. Cars in the city were no picnic, but you'd take your life in your hands on that thing.

At first glance, the place was tidy, not well appointed, but respectfully cared for. On second glance, a musician lived here—or several of them, judging by the array of equipment I could see.

Dominating the space was a keyboard and three guitars on their stands. A small couch was pressed against the wall alongside a beat-up brown leather recliner. The coffee table, which serviced the two, was stacked high with music composition paper, and off in the corner was a little TV that looked as if it got sparing use.

"Are you in a band?" I didn't think he was. He'd mentioned in the market that he played Division I basketball, which would leave little time for the kind of serious composing that seemed to be going on in this living room.

"No," he said, looking back over his shoulder as we headed down the hallway. "I'm finishing up at University of Virginia—just home from school for a week or so. This place belongs to some friends."

Musician friends. The irony of that just had to be appreciated. I'd spent much of my adult life intentionally avoiding entanglements with musicians, and for a very good reason—three very good reasons, actually: drugs, women, and irresponsibility. The musicians I'd dated could fit neatly into those categories, and one overachiever spanned all three. Finding myself in a musician's apartment felt a little like cosmic payback for the rash decision-making that had landed me here.

As I followed Dan through the kitchen to a small back patio crowded with guests, I cursed myself again for coming.

But I'd spent my high school years focusing on college, my college years focusing on law school, and law school focusing on starting a career. I'm not complaining; I liked the law just fine—it was a good, practical career, and my parents were generous to a fault in footing the bill for my education. But my chosen path had left little time for much of a life, and now that school was finally behind me, I was eager to have something more to my existence than briefs and research. I was only twenty-four, but I felt as though I was on the fast track to cat ownership.

"What can I get you to drink? Beer, soft drink, water?" he asked.

I took in Dan's flawless face with a mixture of awe and wistful regret.

On top of it all—coming to the Tenderloin alone, not knowing anyone here, favoring spontaneity over good sense—this guy was just too good-looking to be anything but trouble. He was uncomfortably handsome. The kind of handsome that is, quite frankly, excessive. He had me with the strawberry-blond hair and the athletic body but throwing in the eyes and that smile; it was just too much.

"Water is fine. I can't stay long."

"What? Why? You just got here." Reading my thoughts correctly, his face changed. "These are all good people. Please stay. I really want you to."

What could I say? He was sweet.

I nodded faintly in uncertain concession, which he seemed to take as a resounding yes. Out came that smile again. Full-on, megawatt.

"Don't leave while I'm gone," he said emphatically. "I'll be right back with your water, and I'm going to throw some leeks on the grill like I promised."

I watched him move about the small, crowded yard with confidence and ease. He was especially attentive to the women present, respectful and polite in the manner of someone who genuinely *liked* women—and was probably not going to limit himself to just one.

He disappeared into the kitchen and came out holding two leeks to his head like horns. I couldn't help but laugh. He *was* sweet. But he wasn't for me.

It was a relief, really—gaining my bearings and realizing that, while I did need to get a life, I didn't need a one-night stand, even as tempting as this particular one-night stand might be. I began to feel pleasantly detached from any expectation of what this night could offer and I suppose that's what allowed my attention to casually drift towards the most remarkable voice I'd ever heard.

It was coming from the kitchen, or from somewhere just inside the apartment, but it cut through the space effortlessly. It was a rich, colorful voice—the kind that had warmth and hominess. Genial, with an elusive quality I couldn't quite identify. It took me a minute to realize the voice was Irish.

The lilt was so subtle I might have missed it completely if it weren't for the fact that, against the backdrop of distinctly American English speakers, it had a charming prominence. And it was laughing, a deep buttery sound that oozed vitality and vigor. I loved that voice, before I ever saw the man to which it was attached.

I was watching the door to the yard when he first appeared, emerging as though stepping onto a stage. He was looking down, the dimples on his cheeks still lingering from whatever conversation he'd been having. Just then, he looked up and met my gaze, as though finding me had been his intent all along.

I shifted in my stance and glanced away, feeling an unmistakable blush rise over my cheeks. I'd never been much of a blusher, but I could no more control my reaction than stop my heart from beating. When I looked up again, he was standing in front of me.

"How's the craic?"

Pronounced like 'crack,' I had no idea what he was asking. Dumbly, I just blinked.

"I'm sorry?"

"Are you enjoying yourself?"

He was a physically imposing figure—tall, broad chested, and powerful under his white T-shirt. The intensity in his light hazel eyes sent a hum of electricity right through my body as he stared at me like I could have been his very last meal on earth. I swear to God, every single hair on my arms stood erect.

"Oh . . . yes, but I can't stay long."

One silent beat passed between us and then he was laughing. Not with me, bear in mind—*at* me, dimples deeply cratering both cheeks. His laugh was sexy. Jesus, *he* was sexy.

"Completely fallen to shit already, have we?" In his voice was a hint of flirtation I thought he probably couldn't help.

"No," I said smiling, and no match for his charm. "I just—have a thing."

That sounded *incredibly* lame and we both knew it. He didn't respond immediately. Instead, he just stood there, eyes glistening with humor, drinking me in in a bold, curious way.

It wasn't just one thing about him—his beautiful eyes fringed with thick lashes, the richness of his dark, auburn hair, the curved mouth, or the solid frame—it was how it all came together so devastatingly. This man had a magnetism that was absolutely undeniable, like a secret so big it just oozed out of him, despite any effort he may take to keep it in check. And I knew right then and there, if he ever turned it loose on me for real, I'd be finished.

Because to top it all off, like catnip to a kitten, he was carrying a guitar.

It was beautiful Gibson dreadnought, slung behind his back and positioned in such an organic way that it looked a part of him. The way he cradled it gently with his elbow told me it *was* a part of him. And everything I loved and hated about musicians came rushing back in a surfeit of hormones and horror stories. He was my siren song.

"I'm Jamie Callahan." The siren had a name. *Jamie*, I said in my head. I think I may have sniffed him a little too. Subtly, of course.

Beer, soap, maybe. And something earthy. It was decidedly masculine and tempting.

"Mel Grayson."

He allowed the silence to linger between us, but never dropped that cheeky grin. His smile looked as though it hadn't had the advantage of orthodontics, but it had the good fortune of not requiring it. Any imperfections just added to his charm. God, he was something.

"How can I convince you to stay a bit, lovely Mel?"

I'd just opened my mouth to say something, not actually knowing what sort of something might come out, when Dan returned with a bottle of water and two leeks for the grill. Despite the onslaught of his cologne, it was an enormous relief. How was it that *he* was now the safer of the two options?

"What's with the guitar?" he asked Jamie before loosening the cap on the water and handing me the bottle.

"What's with the leeks?" Jamie fired back, undaunted.

"She likes leeks."

"Goats like leeks." Jamie's smile moved to his eyes, lighting them with humor. "Women want *meat*. Don't they, Mel?"

My heart did a painful *kerchunk* in my chest. How does one even respond to something like that?

His loaded gaze was fixed on mine, and I swallowed hard as something heavy and potent stirred between us. It was a very physical thing.

I wasn't the only one to notice it. When I finally broke away from that look, I realized Dan was glancing between Jamie and me, clearly reevaluating his prospects for the afternoon.

"Can I offer you a burger, instead?" he said with unconcealed mirth. I cringed.

"You're grand for asking," Jamie answered with a smirk. "I'll take two with sides, as well."

Dan gave no direct response, but the silent conversation that followed was loud enough. It reminded me of every National Geographic documentary I'd ever watched—two alpha males facing off over a female. There really was very little difference between lions, walruses, and men.

Dan tilted his head in gracious concession and left Jamie and I standing together under an entirely new set of circumstances.

"So then," Jamie said.

"So then," I echoed.

The full-dimpled grin that burst across his face lit his hazel eyes with the promise of mischief. I suddenly felt a little off-balance.

I blamed the leek.

§

"Is he going to be upset with you?" I asked Jamie after Dan returned with the burgers but stayed only long enough to deliver them.

"Danny? Nah." His eyes narrowed as he watched his friend navigate back through the crowd. "He'll be all right. He's a gem, that one."

There was an access of pure love in his voice, and I strongly suspected from his tone that the friendship between them ran deep. It left me with a warm feeling in my belly, and maybe a twinge of guilt too.

Jamie ushered me to sit in an elderly lawn chair, and then set his plate down on an adjacent one as he removed his guitar to lean it against a wall.

"Were you going to play?"

"Oh. No, I just had something in my head I was working out. I just . . . well, sometimes it's inconvenient." He waved his hand like it could wait.

But it was a curious thing for me. Not being a particularly creative person myself, I often wondered how it worked for artists. Did ideas come like sunlight bursting through the clouds? Or was it more like wrestling a cat into a bathtub?

"Does that happen a lot? Like when you're in the middle of doing something else?"

He laughed dryly. "All the time. It's a bit of a problem, actually."

I nodded in agreement, taking a small bite of my burger, but in truth, that seemed like a problem of riches to me. The musicians I'd known welcomed any and all inspiration—whenever it came. Good ideas were hard to come by.

"Well, don't let me keep you. I'd hate for the next 'Stairway to Heaven' to be thwarted on my account."

He laughed again, but warmly this time—his dimples underscoring the heartiness of the sound.

"I'd more think you'd be the one to inspire it."

What would come off sounding like a cheesy pick-up line from anyone else seemed completely authentic coming from Jamie. I marveled at this as I watched him proceed to dispose of his burgers in a very businesslike manner. This guy could eat. Though no wonder, he was a wall of a man. A few inches shorter than Danny—I'd put him at about six feet—but with slightly more mass. Where Danny was elegantly built, Jamie was dense. Not bulky, per se, but he had an air of impenetrability, like Superman, and it likely took a lot of fuel to keep him going. He hunched over his plate to catch any escaping juice and made quick work of anything there that was edible.

I did a decent job with mine too. Danny had talent on the grill.

"So, the instruments I noticed coming in are yours?"

He leaned down and picked up his beer from the ground, taking a deep pull and swallowing.

"Two of the guitars are. The bass and keyboard belong to my roommate, Greg." He gestured with his bottle to a nice-looking guy of slight build and blue eyes. "That bloke over there."

Greg had a chain hanging from the belt loop of his black jeans and with his dark goatee, I could almost imagine him a pirate. He seemed to feel the weight of our attention and turned, nodding his chin by way of acknowledgement.

"D'you play an instrument?"

"No." I shook my head in firm negation. "I took lessons once but . . . let's just leave it that I'm a great appreciator of music and musicians."

That didn't exactly come out the way I'd intended. Jamie's eyes sparkled, but he had the grace to let it pass.

The fact was, I had taken up guitar a few years back, full of determination to get myself to the point where I could just pick up the instrument and play something. How hard could it be, right? I took lessons and practiced religiously every single day. As was my nature, I felt hard work could triumph over any deficiency in natural ability. I was wrong. Hard work is essential for sure, but music is a gift—sadly, it wasn't mine.

"Come," he said, standing up with purpose. "Let's play."

For the record, I had no intention of doing so myself, but I was curious to know what he could do. I followed him back through the crowded kitchen to the living room, where he restored the Gibson to its stand. To my surprise, rather than picking up one of the remaining electric guitars, he sat down on a small bench in front of the keyboard and waved me over to join him.

"See if you recognize this."

With no music in front of him, sitting shoulder to shoulder with me, he began to play "Just Like Heaven" by The Cure. That made me laugh—I was wearing a vintage Cure T-shirt.

"Here, follow along with me. I'll show you how to play it."

He placed the fingers of my left hand on the keys, covering them gently with his own. They were much larger than mine and rough to the touch, but they were warm and sure.

I was suddenly hyper-aware of every point of contact between us—his hand, his strong thigh sheathed in denim, his corded, muscular arm. I could feel my fingers tremble slightly beneath his and fought hard to mask my body's reaction to our closeness.

"A . . . G-sharp . . . E . . . D . . . C-sharp . . . D . . . E. Now, again."

We repeated the unmistakable chord progression together many times—his hand over mine—until I could remember the pattern on my own. Then he drew back and I was playing The Cure. *All by myself!* It sounds ridiculous, but I'd always wanted to be able to play an instrument and this small exercise was thrilling.

I burst out in a face-splitting grin, which, of course, threw me off my game completely, and he had to return his hand to mine for further repetition. A . . . G-sharp . . . E . . . D . . . C-sharp . . . D . . . E.

"There you have it, then," he said proudly. "Well done."

That soft lilt did unfair things to my libido. I was mortified by the thought that he might be able to see it. But even as I told myself that, I felt an inexplicable urge to kiss him.

I didn't follow it.

"Show me another," I said instead.

"How about this one?"

He positioned his hands and launched into a flawless rendition of "Friday I'm in Love." The song was far too complex for me to have much of a roll, but I loved watching him play it, feeling his shoulders flex and give beside me as he effortlessly delivered the piece from memory. He was talented.

"I can't do that, Jamie."

"We'll do it together."

We both knew this was just another excuse to touch, but I did not complain. He laid the fingers of my right hand on a specific set of keys and essentially played over them. With his left hand, he shouldered the bulk of the melody. I was no more than a passive participant but, still, it was amazing to watch. I craved the feel of his hand on the back of mine. I noticed that he often left it there longer than was strictly required. The closeness gave me a rush of excitement every single time.

When we finished, he removed his hands from the keys and rested them on his thighs.

"I think you're a natural."

"I think I'll hold onto my day job."

"What is that, your day job?" He had the most adorable crooked tooth that gave a hint of boyishness to his ruggedly masculine face.

"I'll be a lawyer soon."

I debated with myself as to whether that was an accurate description. The truth was, I had recently taken the bar exam, but wouldn't get the results back for another three months. If I passed—and god, I could not even *think* about the alternative—I'd take my oath and be admitted to the Bar. I was, however, now working full time on a provisional basis for a boutique firm in the city. It was true enough, then, I decided.

"A lawyer?" Jamie seemed surprised. "That's brilliant."

I did my best to wave off the compliment. More than anything, I was growing increasingly aware that even in the small space, we'd somehow managed to draw closer. He was watching me intently, taking in every detail of my face, and at close range, there was no escape from the pull of his magnetism.

"Well, if I get into badness, I'll know just who to call," he said, and out came the dimples in a flash of charm.

I laughed. "Unless your *badness* involves an intellectual property dispute, I'm afraid you'll be shit out of luck, my friend."

Sitting shoulder to shoulder, I could smell the faint scent of his aftershave and feel his warm breath on my cheek. Slowly, his gaze drifted downward to my mouth and my heart stuttered in my chest. He wasn't shy—he intended no discretion in his appraisal of me—and I realized in that moment *how much* I wanted to kiss him. I was breathless with it. Just an inch, maybe two, and I could taste him. I felt a little dizzy—that's the effect he had on me.

He licked his lower lip, but he made no move to kiss me. He just continued to tease me with a look that pulsed like fire through my body.

I stared at his soft lips, his tongue just barely visible.

There was no sound between us. Just the heat of proximity, leaning in too close to be accidental. Longing turned to outright hunger and my composure broke under the weight of his gaze.

I looked away, shifting in my seat. My throat felt parched, and I swallowed sharply. "But if you get into badness by writing something that sounds too similar to this—" and I played A . . . G-sharp . . . E . . . D . . . C-sharp . . . D . . . E— "then I'm definitely your girl."

I glanced back at him, unable not to; he was so *there.*

"Hmm." He pursed his lips, emitting a sexy growl, low and deep in his throat. "I very much like the sound of that."

§

In the same manner, we made our way through a couple songs by The Squeeze and few by U2, and I was beginning to get a feel for his musical influences. It was electrifying sitting with him, watching his powerful hands move over the instrument with supreme delicacy and precision.

"Do you know this?" he asked, and launched into a beautiful descending arpeggio for a song I'd never heard. Unlike the others we'd played, it was slow and soulful, more R&B than rock.

"That doesn't sound like your genre."

"All music is my genre, really." He continued to play the intervals. "I suppose I found my voice in alternative rock, but I listen to everything. This is a song for you. Donny Hathaway's version."

"For me?" I didn't know what he was saying. He glanced at me briefly before turning back to the keys.

"No," he smiled faintly, not wanting to insult my ignorance. "It's called, 'A Song for You.'"

To my surprise, he began to sing softly as he played.

He had a beautiful singing voice that did absolutely nothing to bolster my self-control. It was rich and low, and perfectly pitched. The kind of voice with character. He didn't need any false affectations; his voice had resonance and emotion.

As I watched him play, it hit me like a ton of bricks. He was a lead singer—a frontman. Of course he was.

How could I not have seen it? He had that air of confidence, arrogance almost. Almost. But not . . . quite.

Suddenly, I was seeing him through a different lens, though. I don't know why it changed something for me that he was a frontman. But I'd had enough experience around musicians to know the general type. I'm not saying it was necessarily fair to draw those conclusions, but I didn't think my own experience was an anomaly. Jamie would be like fly paper to a swarm of women who were likewise captivated by his soulful vulnerability on stage. I'd seen it enough times to know better. I did know better. I'd been through it already and knew how this would likely play out. I could see all the images in my head as he sang—the furtive glances, the unexplained absences, the looks of pity from those who knew something I didn't.

It was time for me to go.

I rose from the bench without warning. "Thank you. This was . . ."

Jamie shot up beside me and suddenly, we were standing so close together. There was a moment I could have pulled away. I could have, and I didn't. And then his mouth was on mine.

He kissed me with no preamble. There was nothing tentative about that kiss. His lips and tongue were soft, but commanding. His firm hand caressed the back of my neck in a way that made me feel tingly and weak—as if I'd gone to putty. Without consideration, both of my hands went to his chest, where I could anchor myself against the dizzying effects of that kiss.

Whatever resolve I had was lost. I folded into his body in willing submission. I wanted him—wanted beyond any sense of logic or self-preservation. I *wanted*.

It was so solid, his chest, so formidable, and I let my fingers spread wide over the expanse of muscle and vital flesh, thinly covered by his shirt.

The pad of my ring finger brushed over his nipple and he let out a faint groan as his tongue skillfully worked its way around mine. His kiss was like a drug, warm and disorienting. I moved my hands back and forth over the defined ridges of his torso. And loving the feel of him, I carelessly drifted down his stomach, where I found no give in the slab of muscle that led to his waist.

He seemed to shudder under my touch, gripping my hip tightly with his free hand. He was wearing jeans, and I caressed the soft fabric of the belt loops and felt the sharp edge of a rivet. His mouth was intoxicating, as were the sounds of pleasure sliding from his lips into mine. I ran my fingertips over every ridge and seam I found, drinking in the taste of him—mindless of anything else. The kissing stopped, but with my eyes closed, I continued to touch his body, sliding my hands across the hard, shapely surfaces. Shapely was not the right word. He was beautifully formed—flawless even—every denim-covered rigid curve fitting perfectly in my palm. I pressed and stroked, ran the heel of my hand over his . . . his . . . wait . . .?

OH. MY. GOD!

My eyes flew open in a panic.

It was his . . . I was stroking his . . !

# About the Author

LJ Greene is a self-professed obsessive multi-tasker who writes boring stuff by day and lets her inner romantic fly by night. This California native is married to the most amazing man and has two incredible children who feed her soul every day. She's an avid reader of all genres with an embarrassingly large ebook collection, and a weird penchant for reading the acknowledgements at the end of a novel. She's also a music lover with no apparent musical talent, a travel enthusiast, and a cheese connoisseur.

Website: www.ljgreenebooks.com
Twitter: @authorljgreene